EVIL IS *Forever*

OTHER TITLES BY TRILINA PUCCI

To Die For

One Killer Night

Romantic Comedies

The More the Merrier Series

Tangled in Tinsel

Knot so Lucky

Three Ways to Mend a Broken Heart

Prep School Romance

The Scandalous Series

Filthy Little Pretties

Vicious Little Snakes

Dirty Little Secrets

Forbidden Love Dark Romance

🌶🌶🌶

The Star-Crossed Series

Just like Heaven

Sinning like Hell

Dark Mafia Books

🌶🌶🌶🌶

The King Brothers Series

Truth

Worship

Depraved

EVIL IS *Forever*

TRILINA PUCCI

Montlake

Published by Montlake, Seattle
www.apub.com

EU product safety contact:
Amazon Media EU S. à r.l.
38, avenue John F. Kennedy, L-1855 Luxembourg
amazonpublishing-gpsr@amazon.com

ISBN-13: 9781662531798 (paperback)
ISBN-13: 9781662531804 (digital)

Cover design by Caroline Teagle Johnson
Cover image: © greyj, © phototechno, © Dimitris66, © LineCraft / Getty; © Paper Wings, © Hindia creative, © Anna_leni / Shutterstock

Printed in the United States of America

To falling in love with the guy who earns you.

Dear reader,

The location for this book is heavily fictionalized. So, if you're looking for correct GPS directions in your romance or an accurate representation of LA traffic, you will be sorely disappointed. You'll also be disappointed if you think there's a calendar where all these dates align. It's fiction, we're leaning in. Now, let the fun begin.

Playlist

I Would Die 4 U—Holly Humberstone

Sorry I'm Here for Someone Else—Benson Boone

Come as You Are—Nirvana

California Love—2Pac ft. Dr. Dre

You Give Love a Bad Name—Bon Jovi

I Was Made for Lovin' You—KISS

Anxiety—Doechii

(I Just) Died in Your Arms—Cutting Crew

Psychosocial—Slipknot

Mad About You—Belinda Carlisle

Somebody's Watching Me—Rockwell

Work Bitch—Britney Spears

PROLOGUE

Him

"Hurry, someone's gonna see us. In here," she whispers.

"Let them look." He's kissing her again before pulling back to stare at her with stars in his eyes. "I'll need a witness to prove to myself this ever happened."

She shakes her head while grinning. "Shut up before your stupidity makes me less drunk and I see the error of my ways."

They're fumbling through kisses and wandering hands down the dark hallway. His back hits the wall in her attempt to take control, but then he grips her waist, growling against her lips as he guides her backward, closer to the bathroom.

This is them in the throes of passion. Mixed with a bit of liquor, laughter, and mischief. The kind of abandon two lovers show when they finally submit to their urges.

It's a moment for the two of them . . .

I lift my hands, pretending to hold a camera and take a picture.

Because I'm watching.

And they're completely oblivious to me.

They always are. I've become so intricately woven into the fabric of their lives that I'm only a thread in the tapestry of the background.

"Oh my god . . ." He laughs against her neck as she snarks. "Open the door. If we get caught, I'll have to claim some kind of deep psychosis."

"I'll show you deep."

"Eww, why am I—"

He cuts her off, feverishly kissing her again. But she reaches behind herself, turning the door handle. The creak creates an urgency because she gasps, slipping inside quickly, only letting streams of light escape from inside.

They filter out, threatening to expose the things that hide in the dark.

So I don't move.

Not even as she grabs the front of his shirt, pulling him inside, urging him slowly.

"Get in here already."

With a cocky smirk, he glances over his shoulder.

Always the protector. Even in the face of danger.

Because I'm staring directly into his eyes, but his face is relaxed and unafraid. He's looking straight through me.

With a click, the door shuts behind him, cutting me off from the rest of their fun. Leaving me alone in this small dark hall as I stare. Focused only on that door.

. . . *The lovers.* Slowly, as if I'm to savor what's taking over, I close my eyes, mind bathed in the visions of their blood. It drips down the walls, pooling onto the floor, filling the room until I'm drowning in their death.

And when I open them, there's only one thought.

Soon.

Chapter One

Evie

Six months later, end of April

"Where the hell did my sister go?" I say under my breath, looking around.

Her movie's over. Well, technically *our movie* since I was there, too, that Halloween. Something I truly wish I could forget. Jesus, leave it to Goldie to be all inspired by art imitating life and make the memory live on in film forever.

I wonder if Stephen King does this shit to his family members? Gives *Pet Sematary* a whole new spin.

Either way, the credits are rolling in the background as everyone stands and talks, but she's disappeared.

Honestly, it's probably because she foresaw what was coming my way. My brow lifts as I glance at said issue—my mother with Chase.

For the last ten minutes, I've been unsuccessfully attempting to ignore my mother because she's droning on and on about what a hero Chase is *to* Chase, who's enjoying the attention like a pig in shit.

Goldie's going to get it.

The fact that we were sat near him is an act of treason and war alone, so disappearing while I'm forced to listen to this garbage is unforgivable.

I crane my neck, looking over the small crowd for my hateful sister as my mother really lays it on thick.

"Chase, it's because of *you* that our babies are safe and sound. Seriously. You're a real-life Prince Charming for our Evie. We can never thank you enough."

Somehow I remember that night so differently. Like how I had to help him walk back to the camp because he had a witty-bitty boo-boo.

I roll my eyes. "Oh my god, Mother. Stop inflating his ego. You know the movie is an overly dramatic rendition of what happened. Between everyone, he actually tapped out first. Noah was the hero."

A deep and offended chuckle rises from beside me. *Here we go.*

"Uhhh, excuse you, Princess Diaries." *Did he just call me an ugly duckling?* "I was stabbed inches away from my femoral artery." He scoffs twice, then pauses for dramatic effect, his eyes burning a hole into my profile. "And let's not forget I was also hit by a car—"

He is never going to forget that accident, *or* let us either.

"—I'm still answering questions about my failed marriage at my checkups."

I scoff. "I promise to never pretend to be your wife just to help you again. I'll only do it if they let me pull the plug."

"Evie," my mother huffs laughingly.

But Chase smirks. "This is how you treat your Prince Charming? Last time I checked, all you did was bite an ear to protect us. So ease up, Mike Tyson. Stow your haterade and let mommy love me."

My head whips to his, our eyes connecting as I pull my fist back like I'm going to punch him before lowering it.

He winks as my mother gasps and hugs her, engulfing her with his size and turning up the boyish charm.

"Protégeme, Camilla."

He's such a kiss-ass saying it in Spanish. *Disgusting.* "Protect me? Really?"

Way to flex that Duolingo era, nerd. It works, though, because she laughs, wrapping her arms around him, and pats his face.

One day, I'm going to punch him directly in the throat. It'll be glorious.

"I thought you two called a trauma truce?" my mom teases, setting him free again.

He is trauma.

"That was a year and a half ago. It's expired." I narrow my eyes at him.

His forehead wrinkles, a wry look on his face. I hate it.

"Was it that long since we enjoyed a truce?" Something about the way he said that makes me narrow them even more. "Hmm . . . how long ago was the wedding?"

Shit. My teeth grit with the disdain of *shut your dirty damn mouth* as I glare at him, noticing people begin to file out of the seat aisles.

But my mother doesn't even notice my reaction as she counts on her fingers, then blurts out, "Six months. He's right. You two seemed to have loads of fun at the wedding, so play nice now."

I'm going to be sick, metaphorically . . . maybe literally.

She smiles at both of us. "I swear if you'd just stop hating each other, you'd see you're a perfect match."

I blanch. "Eww. Mom. Inappropriate. If I want a lifetime of regret, I'll join a reality dating show like any other respectable member of my generation."

My head shifts around again, hoping to catch a glimpse of Goldie, but all I see is Noah speaking to some of his old friends.

As I look back, Chase cocks his head. "Which island are we going to?"

"Shut it, STD."

"Evie," my mother chastises, this time swatting my arm.

But he smirks. Still hate it.

Regardless, it still holds my attention. And for too long.

It's because he mentioned the wedding. *That damn wedding.*

His tongue darts out before he draws his bottom lip between his teeth then lets it glide out slowly. I can't help but watch, because I've been suddenly transported outside to a cobblestone street. Sitting at a supremely long table on a closed-off road in Beacon Hill. Where I'm irresponsibly sipping my fifth extra-dirty martini and watching him lick a piece of lime off that same bottom lip.

All from across pristine table linens while music wafts in the air for all Boston to hear. I'm right back at Goldie and Noah's wedding, where the best man and the maid of honor became the oldest wedding cliché known to man.

Shit.

I clear my throat, blinking a few times as he chuckles and our eyes become fixed. It's momentary, but enough time for me to see two things: I've been caught, and he's got stubble on his face.

Gross.

My lips part to say something snarky, but he beats me to the punch.

"You know, Camilla, in order for us to fall in love, your daughter would have to text me back. I've been waiting since . . . oh yeah, the wedding."

My eyes pop open. *Fucker.*

"What?" my mom gasps too excitedly. "Evie . . ."

Oh my god. He's such a son of a bitch.

My mom's staring at me for an explanation, but all I have to offer is a panicked chuckle that tries to escape before I hide it and turn away quickly.

"Speaking of texts," I begin, hurrying out of the aisle while hitching a finger over my shoulder as I look back. "Where is my favorite contact? Probably the ladies'. I'm gonna go congratulate her . . . Seriously, what kind of sister would I be?"

I don't even chance another peek over my shoulder to see their expressions because I already know my mother has begun plotting my future wedding to Boston's most prominent jackass, and Chase is delighting in making it awkward.

He's just so . . . ugh . . . like the worst . . .

This is why I begged my sister to kill him off in the movie, but she said it was too mean. I guess I see her point since we literally all survived by the skin of our teeth. Still, I stand by it. One version of me should be able to live out the dream of being rid of him.

Never will I ever save his life again.

I'm lost in about ten different thoughts between how I'm going to either explain the texting or alternatively hide his body when I push out of the theater into the hallway.

Like, just stop bringing up the wedding. God, I can't believe I . . .

A deep exhale leaves me as I glare at the ground, truly irritated he outed me in front of my mother and not wanting to finish that thought.

This is why nobody likes you . . . except Noah and Goldie and my mom . . . whatever.

I look up suddenly, wondering how crazy I appear to anyone watching, but my steps slow to a stop as I glance around.

The hallway's empty and much darker than I remember from when we first came in. But it was close enough to sunset to be dark. It's just this old theater was a lot less spooky in the daylight.

I look up and down past the vintage garnet velvet walls banked in old, out-of-date movie posters framed in tarnished gold.

A shiver hits me. I swear there were people here earlier.

The swallow in my throat feels thick because I'm surrounded by the kind of silence that makes your heart beat a little bit faster and the hairs on the back of your neck stand on end.

At least, it does ever since . . . *Un-uh, don't even think his name.*

My brows draw together. "Where'd everyone go?"

I pull the sleeves of my crewneck over my hands, shaking off my unease with a deep inhale as I start back toward the lobby because that's where I remember seeing the bathrooms.

But with each step, I can't help the growing anxiety. I hate moments like this, ones where I feel afraid. Like someone's watching me, just waiting to get me alone.

I swallow, crossing one arm over my chest to hold my other, now walking a bit faster as I gnaw at my bottom lip.

You're fine. Stop. I let out a held breath. But a loud slam makes my shoulders jump and my head whip around. I'm barely blinking, frozen in place, my lips parted by small, quiet breaths as I stare into the darkness.

My chest begins rising quicker as I search the blackness beyond the theater I just left.

"Hello?" I call out with much less of a spine than I'd like.

But only silence bounces back. It makes my skin prickle with goose bumps.

"Is anyone there?" Nobody answers, but shadows are cast in too many places, and that makes me grip my sweatshirt tighter. "This isn't funny. Who's there? Come out."

Maybe it was a door? Or someone leaving?

Rational thought's trying to make a good impression, but it's ignored as my eyes shift around the space and I wait. Almost holding my breath, warring between the fear that's growing and reality.

But that's the thing about knowing what could happen just might. I can never unsee that reality. There's no Uno Reverse for living through what we did.

The memory of the glint of a knife forces my eyes to half blink because I can almost hear myself gasp again the way I did when Billy reached up and removed his mask. Staring back at us before his voice was burned into my brain.

"Gotcha."

I shudder, breaking free from the past.

"Fuck, get a grip," I say under my breath. "The movie's over. Billy's dead, ya weirdo."

I walk backward a few steps before I turn around, still staring into the darkness. Because I just need to make sure nobody's there. Damn, being almost massacred really fucks you up. I mean that sarcastically and literally because it's left me in a headspace where I can't help but always think *what if.*

Usually, the thought's so far back in the recesses of my mind I almost don't hear it. Except when I do. Then it's inescapable.

Like now. Because the thoughts are so loud they're making my pulse thrum fast enough to warrant me running, but I'm standing still.

It's all . . . *What if Billy comes back from the dead looking for revenge . . . He did it once. What if someone wants to become Billy part deux. What if, what if, what fucking if.*

I really should've gone to therapy for more than a month.

Goldie did it right. She went and stayed, worked out the trauma by writing a movie. *Still hate/love that for me.* Still, she's definitely not where I am.

Where I am is a constant state of scared shitless while privately panicking and forcing myself to do shit like become a nepo baby for said movie about my life. All the while telling myself it's as good as exposure therapy.

It wasn't. Not by a long shot. And this is why Google doesn't always help.

You can't actually diagnose or treat yourself by taking a ten-question quiz you find on Reddit. Because if it did work, I wouldn't be a formerly bold girl who currently feels like someone's closing in on her.

The thought makes my feet hustle, all but running me toward the ladies' room before I push through the door quickly, calling out my sister's name.

"Goldie."

But as I do, I'm immediately met with a scream that makes me jump and my soul almost leave my body.

"What the hell?" and "Oh my god. What is wrong with you?" are said at the same time between us as I lift my hands, scowling at her from the entrance of the bathroom, now a little out of breath from shock.

"Sorry," we both say again at the same time, but I wave her off, trying to play it cool. "I have to pee. What are you doing?"

She tucks her hair behind her ears, clearly trying to do the same thing I am—act unaffected. But that's the Monroe way—we fake it till we make it back to pretrauma us.

"I was . . ." She falters, then shrugs. "Nothing."

She averts her eyes as she heads toward the sinks, and I walk inside and go to the first stall.

But we're too quiet, and that feels awkward, so I say, "Wait for me?" *Because I'm too scared to be alone.* "Mom's trying to make a love connection with me and Chase again. I swear she'd force an arranged marriage just because he was stabbed in the leg."

Goldie chuckles and turns to point at the stall I'm about to open. "That's out of—"

Before she can finish, the door squeaks open, and I turn my head, my eyes locking onto a red wall staring back at me. Wait . . . that's not right. The tiles are white . . . but why is it . . .

Blood. It's everywhere.

Every moment I've prayed to forget floods back, seizing all my senses. I'm paralyzed. Frozen. My entire body trembles as I process what I'm seeing.

A human heart, staked to the wall, two words smeared above.

SHE'S MINE.

It's happening again.

I distinctly hear someone screaming before I realize it's me. That's when my knees buckle, and I faint right into Goldie's arms.

Chapter Two

Evie

One of LA's finest, who looks a lot like an older, balder version of Channing Tatum in *21 Jump Street*, holds up a red-smeared evidence bag with the mangled heart inside it.

"Who wants this?"

I shoot my hand into the air, irritation all over my face. "Me. I do."

Noah, Goldie, Chase, and I have been waiting around in the lobby of the theater since the cops arrived. And since we discovered that the heart was fake, just like the blood.

It was still way too close for comfort.

Doppelgänger Jenko hands me the bag with a smile on his face. "I've never given a girl her own heart before, only mine."

Eww. I scowl, curling my fingers around the bag.

Chase huffs an unamused laugh, stepping in front of me and the cop, forcing me back another step unless I want to eat the shirt he's wearing.

"Yeah, okay, Brooklyn Nine-Nine. Let's dial back the charm and leave some for the rest of us. Plus, shouldn't you keep that as evidence?"

I'm nodding, as is Goldie, who is firmly tucked under Noah's protective arm instead of hidden like me. He hasn't let her go since he and Chase came busting into the restroom. Jesus. I drop my eyes momentarily, still trying to shake off the lingering fear.

We're okay, *but what if . . .*

Jenko's partner joins us. I guess that makes him his Schmidt.

Cop number two shakes his head at his partner.

"Hey, what did I say earlier?" Jenko looks at Schmidt, but Schmidt holds up a hand and continues. "You're not a real cop. You can't do real cop business."

Wait, what?

We all look at each other in confusion until the real cop addresses us.

"I apologize. This is Rio—he's an actor. He's doing a ride-along, researching a role. *I* am Officer Lewis, a real police officer."

Rio smiles widely and makes finger guns at Chase. "Sorry, guys, but the Brooklyn Nine-Nine reference was such a compliment. Thanks, man."

"You're not welcome," Chase says under his breath before I start to hand the evidence back but can't because I'm trapped behind Chase.

So I push him aside, possibly ensuring the pointiest part of my elbow really digs in, as I groan, "Move."

He grunts, grabbing his side, and whispers, "Ribs, Evil." But I ignore him—because that's what men deserve—and stand my ground. All five foot four of it as I extend the bag out in front of me.

"Did you already check the cameras—"

That's all I get out before Officer Lewis shakes his head and cuts me off.

"Sorry . . . Rio got that part right." He points to the bag in my hand, and my brows draw together. "There's no real crime here. The heart's fake. And I mean, you've got the vandalism, but the owner said there's no point because this theater is sold and scheduled for demolition. You guys were the last rental he allowed." He hooks his thumbs into the sides of his bulletproof vest. "Frankly, we see these kinds of pranks all the time in this business."

Rio looks pleased with himself, but all I can focus on is that he just said *no crime*. What the hell?

Noah's head draws back, drawing my attention. "You see fake hearts stabbed into walls referencing attempted massacres? Weird."

The cop narrows his eyes on him, clearly not liking his tone. "We see petty offenses committed when someone makes these types of movies. You'd be surprised how common it is."

"I bet I would," Noah adds dryly before shaking his head.

"Hold on." I breathe out, still stuck on the first part of what he said. "What did you mean 'no crime'? What about harassment?" I wiggle the bag. "Isn't that a crime?" My heartbeat picks up the pace. "It's obvious somebody re-created this from the original one I made to make a point. So there's no way this wasn't a crime or just a prank, because this was Billy's heart."

I hear Goldie's intake of breath next to me. We don't say his name. Ever.

Fake Cop exhales. "If I may . . ."

"You may not," I answer immediately before Officer Lewis looks directly at me.

"Like I said," Real Cop presses. "It's a prank by some overly enthusiastic gore nerds. Besides, taking you all down to the station to fill out six hours' worth of paperwork isn't saving any lives. I suggest you guys go home, relax, and celebrate your big night."

I shake my head quickly, my voice rising as I motion between the four of us.

"Relax? How? A psychopath that we Michael Myer'ed might be back from the dead . . . or worse, inspiring people from the grave. Do your job. We're unsafe."

I know how panicked I sound when I say the last part. How completely fragile it came out, but I can't stop the way my heart is thudding and how my mouth suddenly feels dry.

Because fear never stops being my bestie.

"Exactly," my sister echoes. "Do your job. Investigate. Look at the cameras or something."

Out of the corner of my eye, I see Noah squeeze my sister closer.

Officer Lewis looks between us, but Flaw and Order leans in toward me, making me blanch as he winks.

"Speaking of dead people . . . You know I was an extra on *The Walking Dead*? I played Finger-Eating Zombie Number 1, which was distinctive because I had a line . . . well, it was more of a grunt, but I really committed. I'd love to show you my reel over a drink."

I blink back rage. Never did I ever think I could dislike someone more than I hate Chase, and yet . . . He must know I'm thinking about him because when I open my mouth to launch a string of expletives at this wannabe actor, I can't.

Two exacting words silence the room.

"Back up."

My head turns quickly to Chase, whose jaw is tense as he stares back at Phony-Copony. *Whoa.*

I'm so stunned that it takes me a minute to catch up. *What is he doing?* Still, I roll my eyes, ready to tell both guys to shut up, until Officer Lewis frowns, looking between the two men.

"Let's keep cool heads here."

I'm about to say *Yes, let's keep cool heads and realistic expectations. Nobody likes either of you,* but Noah beats me to it.

"Chase," Noah calls from beside us like he's saying *Chill.*

Oh god, if he gets arrested for this, I'll never be able to escape him. My mother really will try to force me into an arranged marriage like we're in a modern-day version of *Bridgerton*. Except Chase would be the diamond of the season, and I'd be the grumpy, unwilling scoundrel one eye roll away from permanent damage.

If I believed in God, I'd start a prayer circle right now for his freedom because the alternative is actually more terrifying.

There are a few more beats of silence as thick tension hangs in the air, making it hard for everyone to breathe. I wish I had the over/under on who gets tased first.

But before I'm actually forced to worry, Officer Lewis slaps a hand on Rio's chest and moves him backward, then looks at the future recipient of Will Smith's slap, adding, "We don't flirt with civilians on the job."

Chase smirks, but Rio raises his brows, clearly embarrassed, before he throws out, "Flirting would be asking her to accompany me to the opening of 617 West next month."

My "Jesus Christ" comes out at the same time Chase says, "We're booked." But apparently, Rio only hears Chase because his face whips to our very own *Top Chef* kids' edition.

"Hold on. You're *the* Chase Beckett. Sorry, man, I didn't recognize you." He slaps Officer Lewis's shoulder. "This is the guy I was telling you about today. The owner of the hottest restaurant to hit LA since ever."

Chase grins. "All good."

I all but turn in a circle, throwing my arms and bagged heart in the air. Jenko and Schmidt look at each other excitedly before Real Cop says, "Oh, wow, we're both big foodies. I was actually reading about you in the *LA Times* the other day. Loved the part where you called vegans joy haters. You know the writer called you the Michelangelo of food. Said they saw a few Michelin stars in your future."

Kill me. What is happening? Did everyone suddenly forget there could be a lunatic on the loose?

Chase chuckles. "I read that. You never know what will happen, but the Michelangelo thing was clever because I actually did sketches of the food for the menu like he did for his grocery lists . . ."

Oh my god. I may die of proximity to smugness before anyone stabs me.

"Excuse me. Can we get back on track?"

I'm ignored again. Dammit, I hate being short. Tall people never pay attention to anything below their chest equator. So I put the bagged heart between my teeth and clap my hands together hard, drawing everyone's attention. And their silence.

Thank you.

I pull the bag from my mouth and smile, but it comes off the way I mean it—annoyed.

"Michelangelo was illiterate—that's why he sketched," I bite out. "So I guess you're in perfect company." I turn my attention back to the cops. "But I assume everyone *here* can read. So how about we try it on the room?"

Noah snorts a laugh, but my sister swats his chest. I continue.

"Maybe this *was* just a prank, but two things can be true. We *were* almost killed eighteen months ago. And now, someone's writing 'She's mine' in corn syrup using a replica of my heart. It doesn't take a genius to see someone wanted to scare us."

Rio raises a finger like he's going to speak again, but I level my gaze on him. "No, no . . . do not say a word. Not a damn word."

He shrugs, wincing. "Maybe just one . . . sound bath."

"That's two," I growl, but he keeps talking.

"It really works for calming and reining in thoughts that get away from you."

"Oh my god . . . the only bath I want to see is one I can hold you under . . ." I'm glaring at him as I take a slow step forward. I can feel my chest rising and falling too quickly as I grip the damn heart bag in my hand tighter. "This is not a movie, Chips—"

I'm so mad that I'm pretty sure the worried look now on his face is justified.

"—it's our fucking life. So while you've been pretending to run from bad guys, we've been doing it IRL. So quiet on the set, dick."

I raise my arm, ready to shove the heart directly into his chest, when I hear "Evie" . . . "Shit" . . . and a chuckle.

But that doesn't stop my tirade. What does is Chase grabbing me by my belt loop and forcibly jerking me backward, making me gasp as my arms fly in the air. I'm then spun around behind him, my braids covering my face.

What. The. Fuck.

His strong wrist is a tree trunk beneath my free hand while my mouth hangs open as we stand back-ish to back, with me on my tiptoes, a wedgie firmly in place between my cheeks.

No, he didn't hang me out to dry like laundry behind him.

"Sorry about her," he offers coolly. "Evie's allergic to reason. Instead of breaking out in hives, she believes she's a few inches taller than she is."

Everyone laughs, and I hear them speak, but I can't tell what's being said. I'm that gobsmacked.

I once heard someone say their flabbers were gasted, and now I think I know what they mean. Flabbergasted is an understatement. This dick just perched me behind him, holding me up by the ass of my jeans, and made a joke about me.

I'll find him in every life just to ruin it.

I start to wiggle harder, signaling him to let me go, but instead, he lifts me higher, making me suck in a breath as Officer Lewis says, "Listen, we'll look into it. Okay—"

Holy shit, for two reasons: One, did his dumbass just sweet-talk them? And two, I'm pretty sure this is the most legitimate camel toe I've ever had.

Still, my heart's beating slower. Goldie raises her brows at me before I feel the grip on the back of my jeans loosen, and I almost breathe a sigh of relief, but then Sergeant Stupid adds, "It's the least we can do for LA's favorite new chef. Plus, we don't want you in trouble with your spunky little lady . . ."

Oh. My. God. Absolutely not.

"Little lady, my a—" starts missiling out of my mouth, but I'm cut off by Chase's deep voice.

"That's awesome," he says smoothly over my outrage. "Thanks so much. The little lady and I really appreciate it. Here, take my card—"

Little lady? Bury me. Now.

My brows wrinkle as I look around for a moment until I feel him reach into his back pocket, probably to pull out his wallet. His hand brushes my ass, and the movement jostles my body. Somehow, that registers as consent for my brain to picture his bare ass.

Oh god. Someone burn my eyes. No, no, no, no, no. If he doesn't let me go, I swear to god . . .

I rock my body again, hitting my butt against his, finally making him release me. But only for his hand to audaciously grip just above my waist before I'm guided quickly back beside him.

"We really appreciate it, Officer." His deep voice—no, more like nails-on-a-chalkboard voice—stays calm as he smiles at the cops. "And we'd love to hear any info you find out. Seriously. In fact, if you find something, you can tell us about it over dinner. Anytime, on me. At LA's hottest spot."

They each smile obnoxiously wide, even though the offer is only for Lewis. "Holy shit. Absolutely, Mr. Beckett. We really appreciate it. We'll definitely turn over every rock."

Will you now? Not because it's your job, though.

I'd love to say everything I'm thinking. But that's the equivalent of cutting off my nose to spite my face. I really should get more credit for the things I don't say.

I'm also not stupid enough to look a gift horse in the mouth, so I smile tightly, saying, "Thanks," while thinking many, many other words. Most of them pearl clutchers.

The four of us stand there, watching the corrupt police officer walk away, and I want to yell *Smarter people hold out for cash when they're bribed,* but I don't.

Instead, I wait until they're far enough away they won't hear me, and then I spin and face Chase before doing my best impersonation of him.

Ensuring he sounds like the "bro" he is.

"You can tell me over dinner. Anytime, on me. At LA's hottest spot . . . here's my card." I scoff. "Did it say Michelangelo, food god?"

He crosses his arms, smirking. "I don't know. I can't read. I'm illiterate, remember?"

I scowl. "Ha. Ha. Ha. You're also annoying."

His eyes pop open wider as he speaks with his hands. "What are you mad at me for? You wanted them to do their jobs, and now they're doing it. The situation just needed a little honey, *honey*."

My eyes narrow almost by default.

"I wish I could slather you in it while you cosplay Macaulay Culkin from *My Girl* with real wasps," I bite back.

The smirk on his face grows into a smile before he rubs his stubbled jaw. Disgusting. I give him another hateful look, but he takes a step forward, making me blink and match it, backward.

"You're mad I saved the day." Another step from him matched in the opposite direction from me. "Say it."

I furrow my brows, thrown off balance by his boldness.

"You saved nothing. Except their bank account when they get free food poisoning."

He shakes his head, still walking toward me.

"Nah, you just can't stand that I solved your problem for you better than you could."

My face screws up. Men really should only speak when spoken to.

"I literally just said the opposite. Are words hard for you? Or have you always interpreted sarcasm as truth."

He keeps walking me backward, the look on his face too cocky, so an annoyed huff leaves me.

"Goldie," I bite out, looking to my sister for help until I realize she and Noah have disappeared.

Shit. When did that happen? I blink just a little too fast before bringing my eyes back to Chase. He smirks.

"Don't get meek on me now," he teases. "Where's that bite I like so much?"

Oh, I'll bite you. And not in the fun way.

His eyes are locked on mine, and suddenly, my stomach flips just before I shiver and my back hits the wall.

"Shut up" is all I manage before I lift the heart between us like a shield, hoping he can't see mine beating too fast.

One at a time, his palms press to the wall on either side of me, and goose bumps explode, littering my skin with the trash reaction.

Say something. Tell him off.

Fuck.

"What I mean, since denial isn't just a river, is that you're mad that you can't hate me. You want to, but you can't. Admit that. I saved the day. Just say you like me, Evie."

I half blink, feeling like I can't breathe. It's probably just an automatic response like fight or flight. He's the equivalent of a fucking train wreck, so that makes sense.

"I would never admit that nonsense, because I don't lie."

"Mmhmm . . ." he growls, too close to me. "Keep telling yourself that."

I'm staring directly into Chase's stupid green eyes, trying to find the words I need. But even in the dim lighting, his eyes are so . . . some people might say sexy and provocative. Mainly because of the way he stares like he's fully locked in and present. Like you're the only person in the room. As if he sees only you.

Sure, some people might say that. But not me. No way.

Frankly, I find his attention unnerving. Maybe even sociopathic? But who am I to diagnose him? One thing I do know is that he should see a doctor for the color of said eyes. That kind of green isn't normal.

It's like mold. Probably some kind of infection.

He winks. I scowl.

"I should've told those cops you have a warrant out for your arrest. I hear the jails on the West Coast look the other way in the showers."

"If you wanna see me on my knees? Just ask."

"I hate you."

"Marry me."

On the inside, I scream. On the outside, I punch him in the armpit, making him jump and step away as I let out a growl-scream before pushing him further with one hand.

He rubs under his arm, chuckling. "Stop flirting with me. I'm wholesome. At least take me to dinner first."

"So long as you choke on your food." I point at him. "And don't ever put your troll hands on or near me ever. We are never going to happen. Got it?"

I turn with gumption and start to walk away as he calls, "*Again—*"

All my breath gets sucked into my body because I'm halted, frozen in my place as butterflies erupt in my chest. Either that or his one word just gave me an arrhythmia.

"We are never going to happen *again*," he repeats a bit louder.

I turn on my heels, immediately shushing him as the wedding plays in my mind at warp speed.

"Shut up." I glance around, ensuring nobody's around. "Nothing happened. Nothing, Chase."

There are regrets in life you hate yourself for and will never do again. And then there are crimes against your humanity you'd definitely recommit. Even though *they're the worst, most drunken, you're an idiot* decision you've ever made.

But I'd never admit that. Especially to him.

"So you do lie," he whispers, but before I can lob another insult, Chase's lips hit mine, pressing into them.

I don't breathe for the longest three seconds of my life before he pulls away and grins, running a hand through his sandy-colored hair. But my chest rises and falls with a murderous energy as I peel my middle finger from my lips, where it was sandwiched between the kiss. He might be quick, but I'm always quicker.

"You really do want me to fall in love with you." He grins.

I wipe my lips like I'm using lipstick with the fully erect, strongest possible message of *fuck off*, removing any of his gross-ass spit.

"I'm not busy tonight, if that's what you're asking," he says low and gravelly.

So I lean in and whisper, "Die," before I turn around and walk the hell away.

But just as I round the corner, heading toward the entrance, I hear, "Only over you."

I take it all back. He's the kind of regret to never be repeated.

Chapter Three

Chase

Three weeks later, May

She hasn't texted. It's been all day.

My fingers tap the metal countertop in the kitchen of my restaurant before I break and pick up my phone for the three hundredth time in the last ten minutes to wait for bubbles or an answer.

Me: Heard from the cops. They found some kids breaking into the theater. Said it's them. Punks. But it was a prank for sure.

Noah: Great news.

Goldie: Thank god. You're the best Chase.

I thought she'd be happy with the news. I know I was.

It wasn't that I thought shit was hitting the fan again. Lightning never strikes twice, so they say. But you don't get chased by a fucking psychopath through a creepy old summer camp and not end up leaning into paranoia. I mean, the unbelievable happened, so now anything is literally possible.

Which means when you find a heart staked to a wall, there's a call to investigate. Duh.

Plus, she was scared. I could hear it in her voice. So, I really wasn't letting those cops go without answers. Or at the very least a promise of one.

I'm chewing the inside of my cheek, rereading the message again like that's going to change the outcome.

What the hell. I even texted the family chat so she'd be forced to answer. *Come on, throw me a bone.*

"Chef?"

I glance over my shoulder, pulled back into the present by my new sous chef, Eddie, or Prince Willy as we call him because he has a British accent.

"Where'd you come from? What's up?"

He looks at me expectantly, but I can't remember what the hell I was just doing other than obsessing over Evie Monroe.

What is wrong with me? Lock in, Beckett.

Like a toddler, I need context clues, so my eyes immediately shift between the phone in my one hand and the spoon in my other. Which is hanging suspended in the air. *Oh shit . . .* with food on it. *Got it.*

"Sorry," I breathe out before I shovel it into my mouth, immediately spitting it out. "Jesus. What the fuck is that?"

"Whoa." He blanches, jumping back and wiping the Jackson Pollock of black from across his chest.

But I mumble, trying to wipe what tastes like possible shit from inside my mouth. "What kind of nasty garbage was that?"

His brows draw together as he flicks what's smeared on his fingers to the ground, and I toss the spoon on the counter.

"It's the anchovy paste for the sauce . . ."

I blink, suddenly remembering I was making pasta for the crew dinner. *Shit. No, double shit.*

The butter.

I reach out in a rush for the saucepan that now holds very burned butter before he pushes my hand away and wraps a towel over the handle, moving it off the heat.

"Chef, are we feeling unwell?"

I shake my head, chuckling to myself as I tug my apron over my head.

Jesus, this woman has me off my game. I'm a mess. A complete fuckup, and not in the usual way because in here, in the kitchen, I'm infallible.

She's managed to conquer a god.

I've been reduced to a mere mortal who's crushing so hard on a girl that I don't know if I should wind my ass or check my watch . . . that's not right . . . check my ass or wind my watch? *Why would somebody need to check their ass?*

Jesus. I blow out a harsh breath, putting my hand on Eddie's shoulder.

"Eddie, there's this woman . . ." I grin. "And she's leaving me on read . . ."

He cuts me off. "Say no more. Women are the nectar of life, and if you're not careful, you'll drown in them. Let's go for a smoke."

I nod before he turns, and we walk out a side door that opens to the back parking lot. He's already got his pack in his hand, pulling out his fancy UK cigarettes as I jump up onto a concrete pony wall and plop my ass down before I run a hand through my hair.

"Here's the thing," I level. "She fucking hates me. But she's a goddess."

He sucks in a drag, standing far enough away that I don't smell it. "Everyone hates you until they know you."

I raise my brows, and he adds, "Not me. I fell in love months ago on day one."

My grin's ever apparent. "She does know me."

He exhales a plume of smoke and cocks his head. "Interesting twist."

I put my head in my hands, tugging my hair a little and groaning before I look back up, all askew.

"Come on," I bark, shooting my hands out in front of me. "Give me something better than 'interesting twist.' You come from the land of Shakespeare and Gordon Ramsay."

He flicks some ash on the ground, his shoulders bouncing. "What does Gordon have to do with romance?"

I shrug. "The way he cooks gives me a woody."

"That may explain why she hates you."

I growl frustratedly, turning my face up to the sky, and stare at the smog for a long beat of silence.

There aren't any stars in LA. It's weird.

A frustrated breath leaves me as I look back at Eddie. "I've known her for a year and a half, and it wasn't until six months ago that I even thought I had a real chance. But how do I convince someone who wants to hit me with a mallet to let me tenderize their meat?"

When I look back at him, he's staring at me, half-amused. "Who needs Shakespeare when you can tell her you want to tenderize her meat? Which sonnet is that from?"

"Shut up," I bellow and laugh. "You're not helping."

He takes another drag and blows out little rings, seemingly deep in thought, before he points the two fingers holding his cigarette at me.

"I hate to state the obvious in your moment of hysteria, but have you thought of just calling and telling her how you feel?"

I cross my arms and draw my head back.

"This is why you lost the war. The problem is, we're never in the same place. Evie was in LA, working on a movie, and I was in Boston . . . then I came here, and she was back there. I tried to text a few times, but I didn't know what to say, so I left it."

My phone buzzes, so I reach into my pocket far too quickly to be cool before I look at the screen, not knowing the number. I immediately decline to continue with what I'm saying, but it starts buzzing again, making me roll my eyes seeing the same spam call.

"Get fucked," I grunt before turning my attention back to Eddie. "Here's the thing—this fucking chemistry between us. A buzz. I can tell by the way she looks at me that she wants me as bad as I want her."

I drop my eyes to the asphalt as our dirty little secret comes to mind. If I'm honest, the memory is more of a constant thought, easily pulled to the front of the room anytime I want to revisit the happiest night of my life.

She grips my hand hard as I press the back of it to the wall, holding both of them above her while kissing the delicate indentation on her throat, where her clavicle meets. Fuck, she's even more beautiful this close up.

I'll never be able to stay away.

I gently make my way up her neck, kissing her skin in slow, lazy movements.

"Chase," she purrs. "We have to hurry. Someone might hear."

I palm her throat as our eyes lock.

"Evie, I've been waiting for this moment for-fucking-ever. I'm taking my time."

Eddie's chuckle pulls me back into the present, making me blink and rub a hand over my jaw, hoping my smile doesn't betray my thoughts.

"I hate to say this to you because you're just crazy enough to fire me, but telling by the look on your face, I think you're fucked and on the way to a restraining order."

I'm about to cuss him out, but my goddamn phone buzzes again. I scowl, pulling it back out from my pocket, and jump off the wall. "If you're not Evie, stop fucking calling me."

But the moment I look down, I recognize the name on the screen.

"You're right," I toss out to Eddie, obviously full of shit as I answer the call. "You are fired. Now, go back to work. My real best friend is calling."

He smirks and gives me a salute before he walks back inside, letting the metal door bang closed behind him.

"Who are you talking to?" Noah mumbles.

"I know people. What's going on? How's the Adlers' European vacation? Did you guys have a threesome yet?"

"Dude," Noah levels, making me chuckle.

"You're in France and you didn't think I'd make an Eiffel Tower joke? To be seen is to be loved, Noah. I see where I stand."

The lovebirds finally decided to take a honeymoon and left yesterday. I made them promise to be back in time for the opening, or I'd never forgive them.

"Cool the jokes. It's 4:00 a.m. here, and I've got shit news." I frown, listening more intently. "Your apartment lady called. Apparently, you weren't answering." I raise my brows, connecting the dots to the spam call. "Since I'm your emergency contact—"

"Spit it out."

"A pipe busted—correction, pipes. Your ceiling is now your floor."

"Goddammit."

Annoyance strikes me hard. It's not as if I'm losing any valuable items. The apartment came furnished. But this is not the hassle I need when I'm a month out from opening this damn restaurant.

"Yeah," he yawns. "They're estimating a month before you move back. She said it looked like someone took a sledgehammer to them. But you could go by in a few hours and see what's salvageable."

"All I had were my clothes . . . fuck." I jump through some mental hoops, trying to remember if I brought anything important. I didn't.

"Chase," Goldie's voice chimes in, and she sounds sleepy. "Just go stay at our place. You can wash your clothes, and if they're ruined, you can wear Noah's stuff. We're not back for three weeks anyway, so you can stay until after the opening. I'm sure Evie won't care. She's staying with us."

God, is that you? A smile breaks out on my face. I didn't know she was staying with them while working in LA. Noah's getting a strongly worded letter tomorrow regarding my disappointment.

"Are you sure?" I say completely disingenuously, pouncing before my ex-best friend can take Goldie's offer back. "You're my favorite Adler, G-Money. Don't tell your sister. What's the code for the door?"

Goldie softly giggles before Noah rattles off the longest sequence of numbers in history, but right now, I'm more locked in than the guys with the nuclear codes. It's never leaving my memory.

"Got it. You two go back to bed. And tomorrow, make sure you buy some croissants, but try and pronounce it like the French. They really love that."

Noah doesn't even say goodbye before he hangs up. I'm still smiling because just when I was about to count myself out, fate delivered a bright neon sign.

And it says, **Back in the game.**

I snap my fingers a couple of self-congratulatory times before I pocket my phone and head back inside. There's a definite bounce in my step as I make my way toward the door, but as I reach for the handle, a rattling sound catches my attention. It's like cans getting kicked around.

My head swings over my shoulder as I search the empty parking lot. Empty with the exception of a few cars from the crew.

I'm waiting, listening closely. The soft sound of tires beating against the pavement echoes in the distance, trailing off back into the kind of silence that only the night offers.

That kind of eerie stillness that makes nothing feel like something.

My jaw tenses as a few more seconds tick by before I inhale deeply, finally shrugging it off, and turn back.

But it's as if someone was waiting for me to stop looking because it happens again. This time, the clinking rattles louder. It's coming from the alley next to the building.

My feet are already moving because we don't have cameras installed yet, so that means we've had our fair share of people experiencing homelessness.

"Hey," I call out. "Who's back here?"

As I round the corner of the building, all I see are the dumpsters tucked back in the shadows. My head shifts, and I narrow my eyes, trying to make out if somebody's back there.

There's something about almost being killed that's made me fearless and simultaneously the biggest fan of my gut instincts.

And right now, that gut says someone's back here.

I take a tentative step further away from the lights of the parking lot and into the dark before I let my voice carry again.

"Hey, you can't be back here. It's dangerous when the trucks come, and there's locks on those dumpsters."

My shoes crunch over some loose asphalt, probably broken under the weight of the garbage trucks, as my heart begins to beat faster.

Another step, and my breath gets shallower. So I flex and relax my hands, trying to keep even while still staying on guard.

"If you're hungry, I can help you."

My voice bounces off the dirty brick walls, but there's still no answer. I blink, nearing the trash, the stench making me wince. But as I start to call out again, a can rolls out, followed by a squeak as a rat bounds from the far side of the alley between the dumpster and the wall.

"Jesus." I bristle, my hands clenched into fists, but I'm immediately silenced because a hand shoots out and catches the vermin.

What the fuck.

I instinctively take a few quick steps back, blinking too quickly as I swallow.

A man stands there, the fabric of his clothes scraping over the wall as he does because he's wedged himself into the space to hide. He doesn't face me, his profile partially shadowed by the hoodie on his head.

We're about twelve feet away from each other as the seconds tick by, and my chest feels like it's heaving. Kind of like how my pulse feels thrumming on my neck.

But I don't move.

I just clear my throat to speak. "Do you need help?"

He brings the rat closer to his chest, but it's not moving, as if it's scared.

"I could get you a spot at a shelter tonight . . ."

He shakes his head, his body hunching away from me.

"Okay," I say cautiously. "That's fine, but you can't be back here. You're gonna need to go."

He nods, and my shoulders ease. Only slightly.

Because my eyes are still glued to him, watching as he bends and grabs the edge of what looks like plastic before he steps backward, dragging it over the ground. It scrapes, like a loud hiss, as he pulls the bundled mess out inch by inch.

I blink before my eyes volley between him and the jagged construction scrap. Seconds feel like minutes as he moves slowly. My chest caves with an exhale before, out of nowhere, he hurls it into the air.

Directly toward me.

Everything happens so quickly I barely have time to react as I scramble, furiously jerking the tarp away from my face. I'm grunting and coughing, stumbling around as it lands on the ground at the same time footsteps hit hard against the pavement, running away.

I'm breathing hard, the back of my hand wiped over my mouth as I stare at his back before he's out of sight.

"Holy shit," I pant, my hands coming to my knees as I let out a whoosh of air and shake my head.

"Cameras in place tomorrow," I whisper to myself before standing and gripping the back of my neck as I head out of the alley, stopping to look around and ensure he's gone.

He is. But my fucking heart is still pounding.

I grab the door handle of the restaurant, opening it and peeking inside before locking eyes with Eddie. "Hey, I'm cutting out. But heads up, we had a visitor in the alley. A dude and a rat . . . I'm more concerned about the latter, so call pest control. But make sure everyone gets out of here tonight without problems. Okay?"

He nods but frowns, so I grin, taking the subject back where it should be. "And don't call me unless it's a real emergency. I have a date."

He looks confused. "What about the girl?"

I smirk, and he knowingly chuckles. "Interesting twist. Good luck."

What do they say? Success is when opportunity meets luck. Well, here's hoping that in four weeks, I have the restaurant of my dreams and my dream girl on my arm.

Chapter Four

Chase

"*Where are the towels?*" I whisper to myself, looking around the spacious en suite for any hint. Shit.

I walk over to the sink and open the cabinet while dripping water over the fancy Moroccan tiles. Goldie and Noah's house in LA is a definite upgrade from their last place.

I open another cabinet, finding nothing. "Seriously . . . no towels, guys. What am I supposed to do . . . air-dry?"

When I look up, I spot a standing armoire. I walk over, raking my hand through my hair and shaking off the water, but when I open it, I chuckle.

"One fucking hand towel. You've got to be kidding me?"

Beggars can't be choosers, though. Had I known my friends had nothing, I would've brought my own. Then again, all my shit is sitting in garbage bags in their laundry room. A pipe bursting was an understatement.

There was a tsunami in my apartment. When I went by before coming here, I had to make my way through at least an inch of water still on the ground.

I snatch up the towel and start at my shoulders, thinking, *God, she's gonna be so pissed when she sees me here.*

I'd hoped Evie would be home when I arrived. She wasn't. But I know moviemaking can go long into the night, and that's probably better because it gives me time to strategize.

First off, I need to rectify my misstep. I jumped the gun at the theater when I kissed her. I should've waited for a better moment. But she was just looking at me with those pretty amber eyes that make me feel like I'd be willing to do terrible things to keep her attention. And I was looking at her.

And it was a moment.

Until it wasn't.

Dammit. I have to be smarter this time. Bring out the big guns.

First thing in the morning, I'm going to start with food.

Mainly because it's my love language, my version of Shakespeare, and like Eddie said, I have to show her how I feel. Plus, everyone knows the way to a man's heart is through his stomach—I figure it might work on her since she wears the pants in this hopeful relationship.

I just want her to know that I like her. That I like when she mean-flirts and rolls her eyes. And I especially like when she turns feisty and acts like she's a foot taller than she is.

I'm mid-swipe over my junk when I pull from my Evie thoughts, realizing I should've dried off in a different order. *Whatever.* I bring the towel to the back of my neck, then over my hair, as I head out of the bathroom to change into a pair of Noah's sweats I stole.

I wonder how she reacted when they texted her. There's no way that Goldie hasn't shot off a text to her sister by now.

Shit, maybe I should sleep with one eye open.

I grin to myself as I pass through the doorway before I'm immediately assaulted by the loudest fucking shriek I've ever heard. It's like there's a pack of fucking coyotes in the room.

My hands fly up, towel sailing through the air before I'm gut-checked. My stomach caves in as I fold over with a grunt.

"What the fuck!"

I let out a winded exhale as I hear, "Chase?"

Evie.

My eyes spring open as I shoot to standing and see her holding a fancy iron lamp. It's still aimed at me like she's going to try and impale me again.

"Oh my god," she screams again. "Put it away." She dramatically covers her eyes, dropping the lamp and muttering, "My eyes. My eyes."

I cup both my hands over myself, even though she isn't looking, as I frantically look for the towel, internally cursing Noah even further for not having actual towels. Although it's not like she hasn't seen me in flagrante delicto before.

My head's swinging around before I spot my tiny towel and swipe it off the floor, holding it in front of me like a ridiculous salmon-colored loincloth.

"Are you decent yet?" she presses, peeking through her fingers. Before I can say anything, she answers for me. "Stupid question. You've never been decent."

I narrow my eyes. "Calm down, Virgin . . . ia Woolf. It's not like you haven't seen the goods."

She crosses her arms, her eyes locked to mine. "Beer goggles are a cruel bitch. I've had enough disappointment this year."

Oh, she thinks she's funny . . . I chuckle, but more like I might wring her neck as I raise my brows.

"Yeah," I toss back, "you sure you don't want to do a little comparison?"

I pretend I'm going to move the towel, so she shoots her hand out.

"Okay, okay. I take it back. That was too low. Keep it covered."

I suck my top teeth before I give her a small nod as an acceptance of her insinuated apology.

Evie blows out a breath, swinging her braids over her shoulder. "Why are you in my shower? Because what the hell, Chase? Did you actually think because my sister offered you her house that it included me?"

I frown. "What?"

She ignores my question. "This is so like you. God. We had one moment that lasted seventeen minutes and thirty-four seconds. Why would I ever want to repeat that?"

I scoff. Not once, not twice, but four times, then stab my finger toward the bed.

"Number one, I know you knew I was coming, so this is premeditated assault. Number two, I thought this was the guest room. Come on, what kind of psycho makes the bed like that?"

Her lips part to talk trash, then press together as her eyes shift to the bed. *Uh-oh, Evie's at a loss for words.* The only thing I can think about is that Oprah interview with Harry and Meghan where she said, *Were you silent or silenced?*

Ooo, silenced Evie.

It's like she can hear me celebrate in my head because her eyes meet mine before they roll again.

"You're such a cretin. Crazy people don't make beds; polite ones do. But by all means, keep living like the Peter Pan frat boy you are. I bet you wipe your ass with your hand."

"Wanna check?" She scowls as I add, "Then go on, Miss Manners. Turn around, unless you want a full shot of my ass—"

Dammit. Why is she so good at this? Sarcasm is like her superpower. Still, I keep trying to hang and do a little spin motion with my finger for her to turn around.

She does as I continue my tirade.

"Polite isn't in your wheelhouse . . . Plus, girls always have shit all over the counter. Where's your shit? Regardless, let me assure you, my choice had nothing to do with getting in your pants . . ."

I'm about to say *I've already done that* when I'm arrested by a repeat thought: I've already done that . . . In fact, I was a fucking Olympian that night.

A grin begins to grow over my face as I stare at Evie's back, her hands on her hips.

You counted the minutes and seconds . . .

Little miss mean girl said seventeen minutes and thirty-four seconds.

I stare at her, keeping all my thoughts on the inside. *How do you know the time? Why were you counting, bae?*

Did you think I didn't count too?

I'm giddy as I blink and stand there, quietly debating how to play this. Because the one thing I'm positive about is that she knows because it mattered.

She liked it. Just like I did.

If I out her, she'll say it's a reach. *But you knew down to the seconds.*

"Are you glitching?" she snarks over her shoulder, but I chuckle.

New plan. Kill her with kindness until she kills me.

"Listen, I'm sorry I used your shower." I can feel the *what the fuck* on her face. "And I'm sorry I scared you. Just give me a minute, and I'll head out to my room . . . unless you're hungry. Then I'll feed you if you'll let me."

"Pass." She says it with way less venom. And the way she twists her shoulders tells me I'm making it hard for her to be mean. It's like her body is trying to physically reject my niceties.

It reminds me of that part in *The Exorcist* when they throw holy water on the demon.

I walk to the bed, my eyes still on her. *I can't believe you counted.* I grab my boxers before I drop the towel, then tug them on, followed by the sweats I stole.

"You can turn around now."

She turns slowly, like a cat examining where to strike, her eyes narrow.

"You're still shirtless."

I scrape my teeth over my bottom lip, feeling a tad more arrogant, humming, "Mmhmm, we do live in LA."

Evie's pretty eyes are locked on mine as we stare at each other in some kind of standoff. *What are you thinking?*

God, she's the embodiment of tiny terror, but I wonder if she feels what I feel—that crackling. The fucking buzz.

In answer to my thought, her eyes dip to my chest before locking with mine again. I can't help myself. I smirk when she swallows, like in the theater when I caught her drifting, dirty thoughts written all over her face.

"Stop looking at me like that," I tease quietly, rubbing a hand over my chest.

Or keep doing it.

"I'm not looking at you like anything," she bites back.

Liar, liar, pants on fire.

I gather my things, swiping my phone off the bed and pocketing it before I genuinely smile.

"Yeah, you were." I keep my voice quiet, not giving her an inch to take a mile. "But if you're not careful, I might think dad bods are your type."

She clears her throat. *Did I hit a nerve?*

"Shut up. I'm looking at you like, 'I wonder why he hasn't left yet?'"

I point to the door as I walk toward it. She blinks a few times, her brows drawing together before she adds, "PS, I don't care what my sister said. This arrangement is temporary at best. I expect you to get a hotel tomorrow."

The way she says it with the utmost confidence, as if I'm going to cave, is remarkable. But it's never happening.

"No," I level, not turning around. "But I'm happy to set one up for you if you'd like."

I'm out the door and halfway down the hall as her voice follows me.

"I am absolutely *not* getting a hotel."

I stop in front of my door, turning my head, our eyes locking. "Then that makes two of us. Text me if you get hungry."

When people say *looks could kill*, they're describing Evie staring back at me right now. She's like facing a bear; the only way to survive is to be scarier so it'll just maim you rather than kill you.

Evie looks me up and down with one glance before she says, "Sure. Hold your breath until I do."

Yep, there's a solid chance I'm waking up to a pillow over my face.

"Or maybe I'll just count the minutes."

Her eyes grow wide before she slams the door behind her. And that makes me smile.

Round one wasn't a total success, but it wasn't a massacre either. And in battle, it's important to celebrate the small victories.

I walk inside the room meant to be mine, looking down as I notice I've been joined by Noah and Goldie's cat, Princess Peach.

"Are you scared of the mean lady? Come on, you're safe with me."

She purrs, letting out those cute crackly cat meows as I toss my shit on the bed and pull out my phone, shooting off a text to Noah.

Me: If I don't make it through the night, I want you to know that dying by the hand of the woman you could love is poetic. Just promise me I'll get the last word—make her give my eulogy.

Chapter Five

Evie

My breath catches in the back of my throat as I gasp. My body's already quivering, and I can't stop myself from curling my fingers into his shoulders.

"Chase," I breathe out, arching my back away from the wall as his hot kisses trail down my sternum, between my breasts, and even further toward my belly button.

Goose bumps explode in the wake of lips as his strong hands hold my waist, keeping me in place.

"Please," I whisper, begging for more because he's been teasing me all night.

His tongue dips inside my belly button, making my stomach contract and my body shiver before he nips my skin.

I laugh, running my fingers through his messy hair, watching him do it again before he sucks the spot, leaving a deep mark behind. Everything feels like it's coiling inside of me, ready to explode. And I want him to touch me so bad I can't concentrate on anything else.

It's as if he reads my thoughts because he stands in a flash, gripping my waist tighter and spinning us around before he picks me up, dropping my bare ass onto the bed.

I gasp, my palms landing on his chest for balance before they press into the sheets.

My legs are spread as his hands run up the inside of my thighs.

His eyes are locked to mine. "I want to taste you."

I want that too. So much. He jerks my body closer to the edge, making me squeal before his eyes drop to my exposed center.

"Tell me you want that, Evie."

I'm unable to speak, but my eyes are fixed on him as I nod and watch him kneel down in front of me. It's slow and sexy as hell as he looks up at me with reverence.

This is a man.

My hand cradles his face as he licks the pad of his thumb and brings it to the strip of hair on my pussy, parting me as he drags over my clit.

I shiver and throb in all the right places.

But my eyes never leave his. Even when he brings his finger back to his mouth, licking it clean.

Fuck.

"Baby." The way he says it makes my elbow buckle. "I'm about to make a fucking meal out of you."

I sigh, deluged by the memory of my dream. But almost as a reminder that I'm around people and not asleep, a voice slaps me directly back into present time.

"Should his tongue be longer?"

"Huh?" I look up, blinking behind my magnifying glasses, too shocked to look innocent.

Dammit. This is conservatively the four hundredth time since this morning I've thought about him. *You suck, Chase.* It's not even a reach to blame him because he's the one who's been leaving me mind-blowing bowls of pasta in the fridge. And pasta equals sex dreams. I don't make the rules.

And that also means he cooks while I sleep, which *also means* he still isn't holding his breath waiting for my text like he was told.

He's had days, specifically Tuesday through Friday, to get it right. Is it so hard for men to listen?

Worse, though, they've all had notes on them that say *Eat Me*.

I hate to admit it: I think it's clever, only because, considering who we are, that could be interpreted in a host of different ways. I can almost hear him laughing to himself as he writes them. So obnoxious.

"I said the tongue is too short," one of the Double D's offers again.

Double D's stands for Devin and Derek, my two very young (nineteen and twenty respectively), adorable, dipshit shadows, who are also the sons of my boss's boss. And since they're attending film school, I've been made a mentor of sorts.

I honestly don't mind having them around. First off, they revere my talent, as they should, which means I'm treated like a special-effects celebrity. Secondly, more men should benefit from the opportunity of having a woman in charge; that way, they'll stop being so sassy and emotional.

It's a win for feminism.

Derek crosses his arms with a sly grin. "All I'm saying is that vampires are like the Girthmaster of the paranormal. The tongue should be a statement. You know?"

Devin cuts in. "Exactly. Like a fallacy symbol."

I scrunch my nose, pushing my glasses onto my head.

"You mean phallic . . ." Derek starts to rebut, but I shake my head.

"Nope, that was a statement, not a question, little buddy. And we're not shooting porn, ya weirdos. It's already at a realistic and respectable length. PS, what kind of porn are you two watching . . . Girthmaster? Really?"

"We're in film school?" they say at the same time with brazen sincerity, and it makes me laugh.

I start to make a joke, but my phone dings from across the room, making them look at me expectantly, so I jut my chin toward it.

"Well, what are you waiting for?"

My two little golden retrievers run to my phone, Devin speaking before Derek can.

"It's your sister."

"Seven, six, five, two, one, one," I call out because neither of them can seem to remember the code for my phone.

I'm waiting for them to read as I lower my glasses back in place, making my eyes huge again, and get back to work. After all, I am working on a B-rate version of *Buffy the Vampire Slayer*, poignantly named *Muffy the Vampire Hater*, so clearly, ensuring realism for my vampire dummy should be top priority.

Good god, everyone in the meeting that day should've been fired and banned from the film industry. Who thought that title was a good idea? It had to be a room full of straight men.

Absolutely no girls, gays, or theys would've ever let that happen.

I'm grinning to myself when I realize nothing's being read, so I glance before doing a double take as my brows rise. *You've got to be kidding.*

They're silently bickering, each with a hand on my phone, tugging about an inch back and forth as they stand locked in a battle of the glares. I almost laugh because they're trying to intimidate each other by opening their eyes wider and wider while mouthing words through tight lips.

"Guys," I bark, forcing them to look at me. "Just take turns, toddlers. Sheesh, read me what she said." I shake my head as they clear their throats before I add, "Your mother deserves the Medal of Valor. Call her later."

As I look back down, I hear a smack before Devin says, "Oww," and Derek reads, "I haven't heard a peep from either of you. Did you kill him?"

No, I've avoided him. She's unbelievable. I've been in LA for three weeks and seen some wild shit. There was a Spider-Man charging a hundred fifty for a pic down at the Hollywood Walk, all while wearing a costume that looked like he stole it from a child and smelled like stale beer and hepatitis. But her text letting me know I was getting a roommate was the wildest shit ever.

"Just type: Wouldn't you prefer plausible deniability?"

Her question begets the answer. Why would she think I'd ever actually be nice to him? He's basically the *See All* on the Wiki page for the word "Ick."

Devin laughs, swiping my phone back from his brother and whispering, "Give it. I'll do it. You can't fucking spell."

I hear the clicks of his fingers flying over the keys before there's an immediate ding in response to my response.

Here we go.

Derek voices the text. "Don't be unreasonable and mean. He saved your life."

His voice trails off at the end, maybe because of what he read or maybe because I've just smacked my tools down onto Count Phony's chest.

I stare up at the guys as irritation washes over me, making me blink too fast.

Devin starts to chuckle, but Derek shoves him, so Devin points to his eyes, making fun of how big mine look, so Derek smacks him again. If I weren't so annoyed, I'd laugh.

But I am annoyed. *God, why do she and my mom always do this?*

"I'm so tired of everyone always reminding me that he saved my life. I know. I was there. I'm well aware, so just shut up already. Stop bringing it up every ten seconds—"

I tug my stupid glasses off and set them down, letting out a huff.

"You know what? She's a real piece of work. She's forcing me to live with the one person she knows I would rather eat glass than talk to. He's like a giant toddler, running around and throwing his shit on the walls. But oh well, right? I'm just supposed to suck it up and take the high road, no matter what kind of asinine stuff he does. And trust me," I scoff, "there's a lot."

I scowl, wagging my finger at the Double D's. "You know where taking the high road gets you?"

They look at each other as if they're unsure whether to answer me before Devin shrugs and Derek shakes his head.

"It gets you hurtling off a damn cliff. That's where. Proximity to stupidity is the real number-one killer in this world."

Derek looks at Devin, who lifts his own phone to his face like he's going to google what I've said.

Another ding.

Both boys glance down, then perk up, turning my phone my way. "Ooo, the Eiffel Tower."

I scowl. "Who cares, Derek? This is so like my sister. She just sweeps in and barks directions because she's always the one in charge, and I'm supposed to obey. No . . . not this time. I am a grown-ass—"

Another ding.

"Just call a truce," he reads flatly.

"A truce," I snap, making a tiny growl. "You know what that got me the last time?"

More dumbfounded silence, accompanied by witless looks.

"A lifetime of regret," I bark.

"Genital lice," Derek whispers to a nodding Devin.

I dig my heels into the ground, rolling my chair away from my vamp and forcing the boys to take a step back before I stand and close the distance between us, snatching my phone from Derek's hands.

"No. I didn't get fucking crabs, Derek."

Another ding.

My eyes narrow on the message.

> **Golds:** Just try and be friends. Do it for me? Pleeaasssse.

The moment I read it, another text comes in.

> **Golds:** I feel better knowing there's an extra person out there who has your back.

I faintly hear *What did she say?* before one of the boys shushes the other, and I feel them sidle up behind me, looking over my shoulder.

My eyes narrow. Oh, I'm so mad at her.

I should've been an only child, because this is a prime example of sibling manipulation. The FBI should study Goldie's techniques.

Ding.

Golds: I swear it's not a guilt trip. It's just being this far away makes me worry. We haven't been apart until now. I love you. We're soulmates remember.

A deep exhale leaves me as my body recognizes defeat.

I don't want to type what I type. But I do anyway because I don't want to ruin her damn honeymoon. Especially since I know I'm being difficult, but what am I supposed to do?

Me: Okay. Fine. I'll try and find something redeemable about him.

It's not like I can tell my sister that part of why I hate him so much is because I can't get rid of how horny I am over him. It's disgusting. Truly.

Although I should, because if she'd eloped like a regular human instead of forcing people to celebrate her, I wouldn't be in this mess. *It was a nice wedding, though.*

But what if what happened at the wedding happens again? Because it's clear to me, and not because I looked it up on the damn internet (I did), that this "attraction" is solely a trauma response. It's the only explanation for why I'm sexually attracted to the human equivalent of a hot dog.

Chase is all lips and assholes smushed into something that resembles a dick.

We just went through some weird shit, and now, in the recesses of my brain, I sometimes see him in the narrative my mom and sister keep trying to push on me.

I'm nodding to myself, remembering a Reddit I read by Immareal1. They had a similar experience happen to them. According to their post, this is a thing. And they are a *real one*, as stated in their name, so the advice seems solid.

I mean . . . without that theory, I may start to believe the lie. That he's actually *something*. And he's not.

"He's like a real-life Happy Gilmore. Except worse," I breathe out, my fingers hovering to text her, but she beats me to the punch.

> **Golds:** I know
> you're thinking this
> will be hell. But
> hear me out. I've
> got three reasons
> I think you two
> would make great
> friends

—and delete.

There aren't any reasons other than head trauma that could make me like him.

I mean, I had sex with him . . . and not just sex. I literally remember every minute. If only his personality matched his skill level. He'd be unstoppable in this world, like Pedro Pascal winking at any camera.

Instead, he's more like accidentally buying milk after the expiration date—it looks fine until it makes you sick.

There's no way I don't regret being the nice sister. No way. I type one last text before I commit myself to trying to forget how my new life in LA is now tainted by a taint.

Me: Go do some more French shit. I'm adulting.

Golds: 😂 It's almost midnight. I'm just spamming you with photos from earlier. But thank you for agreeing. He's actually pretty great when you give him a chance.

Then you date him.

Oh my god. Wait a minute. Back it up. That is not what she said or asked. Why did I just think that? What is wrong with me?

My shoulders pull to my ears as I physically cringe.

This is going to be the longest month of my life. It'll literally take years off.

"Shit. How am I realistically going to do this?" I say aloud, hearing them both answer with an *Mmhmm* before I continue. "How can I be nice to the guy who, when we first met, gave an entire soliloquy about how the pinnacle of women's beauty began in 1967 and how it's all been downhill ever since? He literally insulted every woman in the room and did it all while stuffing his dumb face with his own homemade tzatziki."

The image of him shoveling a piece of pita into his mouth before licking his fingers is suddenly summoned into my mind. And unfortunately for me, it's zoomed in to where his mouth met his thumb . . . Also, sadly, it's running in slow motion.

Fuck.

The moment I think it, my phone dings, and I swear I almost toss it across the room.

Golds: Please take in the beauty of this countryside, and also remember (just in case you're starting to regret your decision) fighting in front of the baby is unhealthy.

"You have kids together?" Derek blurts, but I shake my head and glance back, watching them try to pretend they weren't reading over my shoulder.

Me: Your baby licks her own ass. I think we're past unhealthy environments.

Golds: Evie! You dare speak ill of my child?

"What the fuck? Babies do that?" Devin whispers.

Me: Frankly, your child is a traitor, because the minute he moved in, she slept in his room.

Golds: Cats are a good judge of character.

"Oh shit, it's a cat, dude," Derek whispers back.

Me: Perhaps she was dropped at birth?

Golds: No, mom said you were tho.

Look at her making a funny joke. I'll let her have it since it's so rare.

Me: You know you're going to owe me a suitcase full of Hermes as payment for this atrocity.

When I turn around, the boys jump back, guilty-as-charged smiles all over their faces like two little snooping Sallys. They really are like puppies.

Devin grins, not even pretending. "Why do you hate him so much? What did he do? It can't just be because he loves women from the sixties?"

That question makes my eye twitch. "I already said he's a man-child. He says and does everything wrong. That's not enough?"

"Yeah, but what did he save you from?" Derek throws in, stealing my chair and sitting on it backward as they both stare at me. "Because that's kind of hot, right? Girls like protectors."

What, are they taking a poll? Geez, people say women like to gossip. These two are salivating.

But joke's on them, because as public as the attack was, our identities were kept private, so I do the one thing I was afforded—I lie. There's no way I'm telling them the truth about any part of my life.

"Fine," I rush out like I'm giving in. "He actually saved me from a cult."

Their eyes spring open, much to my amusement, and I swear they move a smidge closer, saying "No way" simultaneously.

I nod, leaning my bottom back against my worktable. "Yeah way, it's true."

"What was it called?" Devin presses.

"MYODB." I add a shrug as if they should recognize the name.

They repeat it, looking at each other like they're trying to figure out if they've heard of it before.

"Was that the one with the sneakers?" Derek whispers to his brother before he answers, "No, I think it was that one from the Bay Area."

I have to stare down at the ground to hide my burgeoning smile.

"Is it an acronym?" one of them asks.

"Yeah," I manage with a heavy tone before I level, "It stands for mind your own damn business."

They instantly groan, and I toss a paint-stained rag at them. "I'm not telling you my whole life story. This is not us living out our girlhoods. Go back to work. We have a lot to do." I chuckle, but my throat suddenly feels tighter. "Now, raise your hand if you wanna get me a soda."

Neither of them raises a hand, unless I count the ones they aim at each other as they fight to be first to walk out the door. So I yell, "And a cookie from craft services. The good chocolate chip ones."

The door hangs wide open, making me roll my eyes, but there's something about the instantaneous silence that makes me roll my shoulders back.

Or maybe it's that I got just a little too close to the truth in front of them.

I take a deep breath, feeling the familiarity of a panic attack building.

"Not now," I whisper. "Please, not now."

Chapter Six

Him

I watch her stand, my gaze funneled through the steel frame of the lighting gear I'm holding as she takes a deep breath and wipes her brow.

But it's the shiver that gives her fear away.

Uh-oh. It's happening again, isn't it? The panic's coming.

First, soft, shaky breaths will flitter out from between your lips. Then you'll stand in place for a second and wait, trying to decipher if what you're feeling is real, until there's a pit in your stomach that begins to grow.

That's when you know it's too late.

"Shit," she breathes out.

The side of my lips tick in satisfaction.

I could make that go away, just not before it kills you.

Her throat bobs, and I stare at her neck. I'd like to feel it under my palm. To press and restrict her breath as she tries to swallow.

"I don't need this right now," she whispers again, but I bet her vision's getting blotted.

She turns around, her palms landing on the table as she drops her head, eyes closed. My gaze is focused on her lips, so plush, repeating instructions over and over. She's trying to picture a beautiful field . . . or a sunset.

But it's not working, is it?

My hands tighten around the steel I'm holding as I watch her chest rise and fall faster. Fuck, I'm almost aroused, enjoying her falling apart. Because there's nothing more intimate than watching her crumble.

It's as if she knows what I desire most—her end.

My heart beats faster and faster, following the pace of her chest before her head springs up, eyes popping open. She's desperate for anything to help stop what's coming.

I feel like I'm drowning in her fear. I can almost taste it.

Until she locks on an anchor. She's staring at her fish tank. At that fucking goldfish she named Ruth Bader. Her face softens.

My eyes narrow. *Dammit. You were so close.*

I know what you're thinking. It's about the day. The one when he got you that fish. Guess what, Evie? You're not the only one who remembers the story. I close my eyes, letting it wash over me.

Chase holds out a bag with a bright orange goldfish. The way he acts is boyish and charming, which shouldn't be his brand, and still, he tries it on effortlessly.

"His name is Knievie. Like Evel Knievel, but Evie—"

"Yeah," Evie snarks, "I got it."

"Who the hell gives someone a fish?" She chuckles and licks her lips, the panic subsiding. "You're lucky I am an excellent fish mom. God only knows what would've happened if I gave you to your father."

My blood cools as I stand in place with my eyes locked on her.

You don't deserve that comfort. It's boring. You're better than that.

Steps click down the hall directly past me before a person peeks her head into Evie's office.

"Hey, Evie. He wants you now."

"Gotcha," Evie says back, grabbing her walkie-talkie.

By *he* the woman means the director. I still don't move. Not even when she looks away from Evie and speaks directly to me.

"I told Raul that if we had extra lights, they should be on set."

I nod as Evie joins her in the doorway, still adding stuff in her pockets.

"Erin, please tell me he doesn't want to try and blow something up on last-minute notice or have me make yet another prosthetic that has nothing to do with vampires."

"It's worse—he's rewritten the script. We now have werewolves. Let me ask you: Can you make a crossbow that also shoots silver bullets?"

"And to think there was a time when I really wanted to live out my dreams. Now I'm thinking between home and work, I should just make a time machine and go back to the beginning, because clearly all the wrong choices have been made."

They laugh, finally walking by, but I can't help myself. I extend my pinkie, letting it brush her hand. I want to savor the feel of her flesh before I rip it off her bones.

"Sorry," she offers, half turning her head over her shoulder, never really laying eyes on me.

I say nothing because all I can think is *You will be* before I count her steps, knowing how many it takes before she's gone.

. . . three, four, five, six, seven . . . gone.

I brush my hoodie off with a measured breath as I prop the light stand up, abandoning what I'd stolen as I take steps toward her door. I touch the handle slowly, as if it might burn me.

The whine of the joints makes me pause, but only for a moment before I walk inside her workshop and shut myself in. My gaze lands on her fish.

All things truly wicked start from something innocent.

Time to murder your innocence.

Chapter Seven

Evie

"Dammit," I groan. I'm so annoyed as I try and multitask, shooting off a text to the set designer while putting in the fifty-thousand-digit-long numerical sequence that Noah coded for the door.

I hope nobody ever has to pee when they get home because that's a disaster waiting to happen. But truthfully, I'm less annoyed with the door than I am with the conversation I'm having with this set designer.

Even though it's not her fault the director is eccentric or that someone moved my damn fish.

I hold my phone to my mouth as I leave a voice note.

"Listen, I'm super excited he's had a werewolf epiphany, but creating a spring-loaded system for a car takes more time than a day . . . especially when it's for a moon doggie to drive through a human bat. He's going to have to wait, or his stunt double will be collecting workers' comp. As well as whoever took my fish, when I find them."

I know she's fine. It's just annoying. I need my baby.

I finally get the door open while pocketing my phone before I stop inside and look down at the tile.

"Goodbye, day," I exhale, letting all the shit in my hands slide down my arms to the floor, falling into a messy pile before I just leave it there and walk toward the modern Spanish-style great room.

But the further in I walk, the more I realize something's different. My eyebrows draw together.

Music's playing faintly in the background. Not just any music—Fleetwood Mac. And the gas fireplace is on. Only in California can you run that at night in the middle of what already feels like summer and have it feel appropriate.

I swear I look like a shifty-eyed villain in a cartoon as I look around, because this vibe is different. A lot like I've walked in on someone's date.

Does Chase have a girl here?

The thought makes me stand straighter until I'm suddenly enveloped by the most delicious aroma, making the thought fade away and my shoulders sag. Like an animal, my head lifts as I take a deep breath, enjoying whatever is cooking.

I turn my head just as the kitchen comes into view.

If I was worried that being nice would put rose-tinted glasses on me, then I was stupid. Because I should've been more worried that Chase, under the amber glow of dimly lit lamps and cooking in a kitchen, would make my toes tingle.

Good god.

Or maybe my nervous system is shutting down, like fully tapping out because it's done with me too. I mean, there's always room to hope.

Fuck. He's standing behind the island, chopping something . . . onion, maybe, before he adds it to a pan behind him. I walk closer, feeling like I shouldn't, as it sizzles in the butter. He wraps a cloth around the pan's handle, lifting it from the fire to swirl the contents.

Oh god, not a veiny forearm.

Why, God? Do you hate me just because I have questions about your validity? Because this seems petty. Even for someone who invented periods.

Although, no more petty than the fact that Chase is wearing a white T-shirt that says *Tip Your Waiter* and a loose pair of jeans.

And he's barefoot . . . actually . . . that's a con. I take the drool back. Men shouldn't have feet. They're either gross, smelly, or hairy—usually all three.

I nod to myself as I think, *This is good.* I just need to remind myself that what I'm seeing is smoke and mirrors . . . a sexy illusion. He's just smelly athlete's foot and an endless string of jackassery.

Yeah, that'll break the spell.

Chase puts the pan back on the stove, turning down the heat before running his hand through his damp hair. I swear he's practiced that move, because it was smooth. Too smooth. What kind of whack job has practiced moves other than Elle Woods?

The bend and snap is the exception, not the rule.

Wait, did he just get out of the shower?

Oh god, I do not want to think about him right out of the shower . . . again.

My tongue darts out over my bottom lip the moment he turns around, so I cough.

Not on purpose, but that's what happens when the person who's getting sexualized without their knowledge locks their moldy eyes on you. My body literally rebuked the thought.

"Honey, you're home," he says, surprised to see me.

I scowl.

He chuckles and adds, "Too soon? My bad. I thought we were gonna be friends."

My sister . . . She's quickly becoming insufferable, kind of like my PTS over his D. I'd like to say something snarky, but the lingering sound of sizzling reminds me to be nice so I stay out of hell.

"Mmm" is all I can manage, making him grin as he scratches the scruff on his face.

Facial hair is for men who live off the grid. I've never loved it . . . always hated it . . . so much. And I will live in that truth until it actually *becomes* the truth.

I let out an empty laugh, trying again. "I guess it's good to see we've both been in contact with the parentals and know the rules."

That was still meaner than I meant it. *Shit.*

I don't know how to play this. I promised to try and be friends but gave zero thought as to what that looked like when I got home. I am way too unprepared for this. I need to, like, meditate (I've never done that), do a shot (I've absolutely done that), and maybe even pay someone on Cameo for a motivational video.

There's nothing like D-list celebrities telling you to hang in there for fifty bucks.

Alas, there is no time, so I just dive into deep waters with Chase and hope I don't drown in annoyance from this decision.

But what else am I supposed to do?

I made a promise.

He gives me a smirk like he can hear my internal battle before sliding an empty wineglass toward the edge of the counter, all the way until it can't go any further.

"This might make me more tolerable," he offers teasingly.

Something tells me I may need the bottle. On second thought . . .

I'm waiting for him to interject a comment about the wedding because that's where my head just went, but much to my surprise, he doesn't say anything.

Instead, he picks up a bottle of red and pours me a glass, never looking at me once before he turns back to stir what's in the pan.

I hesitate, staring at the wineglass, chewing my bottom lip.

This is a peace offering.

But then why does it feel like I'm losing the battle? Like he has the upper hand? It's because he clearly prepared for his ethics and morality test, and I just showed up with my heart as black as those truffles.

Ooo, truffles.

Jesus, focus.

I squeeze my eyes closed the way I would if I were jumping out of an airplane, before I open them and step forward, taking the glass and immediately sipping.

I can do hard things.

"Did Goldie tell you they're country hopping the day after tomorrow?" he says over his shoulder.

How bad could it be? I'm being dramatic. It's not like I'm going to jump back into bed with him . . . though, technically, we were against a wall the first time.

I hold the rim of the glass to my lips as I fix my eyes on his back. I mean to give it a dirty look for good measure, but instead, I think, *Has it always been that broad?*

"They're headed to Italy. It's what inspired our meal," he adds over my thought, but I'm still lost in it.

Why . . . why can't I stop doing that? Sexualizing him has become my sickness.

He does not deserve this kind of attention. My body is acting like Jason Momoa is cooking for me. No . . . the meal is a Momoa, the man is an Adam Sandler. Well, maybe he's a little hotter.

Chase kind of looks like that one actor from that movie remade into a television show—the one that accomplished multigenerational trauma: *One Day*, I think to myself. He's a Leo Wood-whatever-his-last-name-is look-alike.

Chase motions to the long strip of rolled-out pasta on the counter. "Funny story—I was gonna text you and invite you to a *peace talk*, but that felt too presumptuous. Even after you talked to your sister—"

Presumptuous must be your word of the day.

Good job, me. Way to use my inside voice.

"—and telling by the look on your face, tonight may be more of a last supper."

Shit, note to self: Fix my face.

I grin, hoping it bleeds into my words, before taking another sip of my wine, then say, "Don't worry, Chase. I may contemplate stabbing you in the hand, but I doubt I'll nail you to a cross."

"Phew," he breathes out dramatically, making the smallest dimple in his cheek expose itself as he holds my gaze. "But look on the bright side. There's always time to work on your upper-body strength."

Dammit. I laugh. He got me.

He motions with his head to the woven natural-seagrass barstool in front of the island, and for some unknown reason, I walk there and sit.

I'm not even going to analyze that.

Although I think he does because he smirks, but to his credit, it's aimed at the marble counter. He scoops out some filling from a bowl and places it on the rolled-out sheet of pasta before he starts speaking like he's hosting a cooking show.

It's cute . . .

No, no, it's a little attention-whorey, but sacrifices must be made, so I should just pretend. His deep voice holds my attention.

"On today's menu, we are having ravioli. But not just any kind." His eyes tick up, locking to mine for a quick second. "Truffle and burrata . . . which I think makes the regular four cheese look like the amateur hour it is."

My stomach growls as if on command. In my defense, all I had today was two craft services cookies and a bag of stale BBQ chips.

He raises his brows. "Glad you approve."

I take another sip of wine, watching as he works the filling into perfect mounds, over and over. It's kind of mesmerizing. Neither of us speaks as he smooths and rounds the savory dollops.

They're so messy, but he's still so precise as he runs his fingertip around the pasta, cleaning it off and leaving none of the good stuff behind.

Whoo, I think I'm getting wine flush—it feels hot in here. But I still bring the glass to my lips again, only contemplating getting water before I take a bigger sip.

He smiles at me as he picks up another long sheet of malleable pasta. "I'm glad you like the wine."

My eyes dart to my glass. How is that almost gone? Jesus.

What is wrong with me? But the thought barely gets out before my eyes are right back, picking up where I left off.

"Pasta requires a gentle touch," he says, and I swear his voice is more gravelly. "You can't get it too wet. It's about finding that perfect balance."

Wet?

He lays the new sheet over top before dipping his fingers into a bowl of egg wash. My lips part. He submerges his thick fingers into the liquid and draws them out once, then twice, before the liquid carries up with him like a long tether before it breaks.

I swear I gasp. Just not loud enough for him to hear.

I'm blinking too fast, glass lifted to sip but suspended in the air because I am locked in, completely hypnotized by the way he's slowly tracing a circle around the little mounds of goodness.

It's slow, circling around and around gently . . . torturously . . . just like . . . My eyes close as I remember something I shouldn't.

"I know how much you love to talk shit—"

I nod, watching him dip his thumb into his drink before he puts it in my mouth, his other hand traveling further south.

"—so let's keep your mouth busy while I work . . . Suck."

I've never been accused of being a good listener until today.

"Mmm," he hums, pulling up my dress and tucking his strong fingers inside my panties.

He's rough but not aggressive. Kind of like his personality. I bet he's crude in bed too.

I don't have to wait around for the answer because two fingers push inside me, dredging my lust back out and over my clit as he slowly, teasingly circles it.

"You like that?"

I nod, but he tsks, correcting me. "Yes, Chef."

I faintly hear the sound of the pasta cutter clicking before I shiver, pulled from the delicious memory, and an exhale escapes. I've completely forgotten where I am because I bite my bottom lip, slowly opening my eyes.

That is until I realize the sound's stopped. Full fucking stopped.

Oh god. He's looking at me. *Is he looking at me?*

He is. My eyes grow wide.

What is wrong with me?

First off, I'm thirst-trapping a live person. I've turned him into those guys I watch for countless hours who slap bread dough like it's your ass or indecently finger a grapefruit. And second, I have to figure out how to cancel the subscription to the area of my brain that keeps tuning in to the damn wedding.

He clears his throat quietly before the clicking starts again, but now that's just the representation of the bars closing at the jail I should be thrown in. I'm depraved. Unfit for society. A flagrant debaucherous lech.

The verdict is in: I am not, and frankly may have never been, fit for human consumption.

The heat on my neck rises, heading directly for my cheeks. But I try and ignore it while also ignoring the fact that I can *feel* Chase still staring at me.

I lift my glass to take another swig of wine, but it's empty. Jesus, how did I get through it so fast?

"Have another."

Two words. They just hang there, surrounded by quiet. Not really a question, not really a demand. But I don't know what to say because I am living my humiliation.

I admit it. I am attracted to him. I also admit that if I stay here for three more minutes, he will probably say something that will make me wonder if the census can even count him as a human.

He is not the one. Will never be the one. Because I say so.

I push from my stool and place the glass on the counter, trying and failing to avoid eye contact.

"Have anything. Just stay," he offers, looking directly into my eyes before they drop to my lips, then back up.

Stop looking at me like that, dammit. He can't know what I was thinking . . . but why does it feel as if he did?

It's because I know that look on his face. It's the same one he had on that night. And if it's not, then that's all the more reason for me to leave.

"Check, please," I whisper. "I think the wine's bad. I'm gonna go lay down for a minute."

I can't even look at him to try and sell it, but it doesn't matter because he steals my glass and fills it before taking a drink, calling my bluff.

I can't handle this. My flesh is weak.

"It's delicious."

Shut up.

"Just call me when dinner's done. I've had my fill of you."

Oh no . . . that came out flirty.

"Really?" He tilts his head as I stand there, silent. "I'd hoped you never get enough."

"Shut up," I snark, but it doesn't have the same bite as usual.

He licks his bottom lip before he rests a palm on the marble, locking out his arm. It makes the muscles more defined. And him even more fine.

Goddammit.

"Come on, Evilicious." He smirks. "How are we supposed to be friends if you take off every time I make you shiver?"

This motherfucker.

If my jaw was open, it would've snapped shut. He's really calling me out. Without apology. Ooo, the smile on his face is so tempting to slap.

I scoff, rolling my eyes. "Listen, I'm as surprised as you that I got cold, considering the room seems to be full of hot air. Have fun making your SpaghettiOs . . . Sorry, is that insensitive? Since your spaghetti never gave me any O's?"

Lies. But desperate times and all.

He wipes his hand over his jaw, smiling widely as I walk away to my bedroom, only hearing him chuckle when I close the door.

Sicko.

I frown-smile because I'm not sure which one of us I'm talking about.

Well, that settles it. I cannot ever leave this room again.

A laugh hits me because I really hope the rosebush outside my window isn't the thorny kind.

Fuck my life.

Chase

She ate in her room, and I ate at the table. But I'm still counting it as a win. Technically, it was a victory when she shivered.

There isn't another sound on this planet I would recognize faster.

Because I've heard it twice.

And she knows I know she's a fucking liar, over here pretending my spaghetti wasn't getting it done.

It was once on my fingers and once—*god, she was so hot.* Her lips were parted, her eyes on mine as she trembled and came undone. But the after was my favorite part because she shivered and then bit her damn lip.

I swear when I saw it again in the kitchen, I almost busted a nut because there was only one thing she could've been thinking about.

Truth be told, I was, too, while sealing the fucking ravs. Who knew food could be erotic? I mean, I did, mainly because I'm a pervert and everything reminds me of sex, but the fun discovery is that she is too.

That's the thing, though. Bed chemistry isn't our issue.

It's convincing her—the most stubborn woman on the planet—that I'm not who she thinks I am. Even though on more than one occasion—scratch that, more than seven or eight occasions—I've given her every reason to believe I am.

The thing is, I know where I land in life. I'm an acquired taste.

I'm well aware a girl like Evie is out of my league, but I firmly believe I just need to cook, and I don't mean in the kitchen.

See, there are guys like Noah with universal appeal and a personality to match. Then there are guys like me. I need to grow on you.

Because I get it—I say the outrageous shit most people only think. I always call it like I see it. Which, on occasion—well, more often than not—offends people.

I'm only six feet tall in sneakers, I cuss like a sailor, spit on the street, act like an arrogant ass. I'm possessive, opinionated, crude, loud, and I'm blond—that was her insult the first night we met, not my low self-esteem.

But at the end of the day . . . I'm for her.

I knew that shit the day we met. She hated me, but I didn't care because nobody else in the goddamn room could keep up with her. And they tried.

But I did.

She'd reminded me of my dream girl, Lisa Bonet, who blessed my eyes in 2006 when I watched her sing "Baby I Love Your Way" in *High Fidelity*. I was middle school toast, completely cooked over that woman.

And that was Evie the first time I laid eyes on her. Feisty and stunningly beautiful. I tried to lay the foundation for my point, but she didn't get it because I wasn't in her orbit, even if I already knew I needed to be in hers.

Winning her over might be impossible, but nothing worth having comes easy. *Although it didn't seem that hard to get her there the last time she gave me the chance.*

I smile, lying on my bed, my arm behind my head as I tap my fingers. I've been turning over idea after idea, trying to figure out what to text her.

"The night can't end with a silent dinner, us back in our respective corners. You feel me, Peach?" I whisper to the cat, who's purring next to me.

"But what do I say? Advice is needed. What time is it?"

The words barely resonate before I swipe open my favorite group text, aptly named the Hookers—dealer's choice, not mine. I was just added. It's basically me and four sassy senior women in their seventies.

I met them when my head was in a messed-up place right after we'd all lived through our live-action slasher film. And not because our friendship needs a stranger twist, but we met skydiving.

It was kismet. These Golden Girls are all too often the highlight of my day. I tell them everything. It's like having four grandmas who want to give you a quarter and tell you how great you are.

Best part is they're night owls. It's a whole "I'll sleep when I'm dead" thing for them.

Me: Ladies. You know where we left off tonight . . . but I wanna text her. Not leave the night on a quiet note. Give me some good opening lines. Don't disappoint.

Joyce: I was hoping for this. I spoke to that psychic. She says you two are a match.
Birdie: You need to be clever. And don't listen to Joyce—the psychic is a ninety year old woman who does Ayahuasca and binges her husband's dopamine meds.
Gail: He knows to be clever. When

is he not. Don't tell him what he already knows.

Mimi: Turn your phone down Gail. I can hear the gosh darn clicking all the way in the living room.

I laugh. The fact that they live together makes these texts all the better. God, they're the best.

Me: I need to ease in, be clever but not too in her face. Right?

There's a dirty joke in there somewhere . . .

Gail: That's what she said! 😂

There it is.

Gail is the comedian. All her jokes come from her fourteen-year-old grandson.

Joyce: Will you stop that nonsense. We told you it wasn't funny.

Mimi: Oh shut up. Don't be an old fuddy duddy.

Birdie: Maybe you should tell her a joke! You're a funny guy, Chasey. We all think so.

That's not a bad idea.

Me: Dirty or clean?

Mimi: No, be romantic. I was reading this book where the man told the woman he was convinced she was at the same place as him because he could smell her.
Gail: That book is about werewolves, so unless Chase has sniffed her ass we're out of luck.

I can't stop laughing as I scratch the scruff on my chin before I type back.

Me: This is hard. The problem is everything that

comes out of my
mouth happens
to be the dumbest
thing she's ever
heard.

Joyce: Oh honey,
you can't listen to
a girl when she
calls you dumb.
It's unreliable.
Sometimes she
means it . . . but
Evie doesn't.
She wouldn't
have kissed you
at the wedding
otherwise. I vote to
say the dumb shit.

I may have spilled the tiniest bit of tea to my gals. But it's the Hookers. They're my hall pass . . . in the most nonsexual of ways.

I'm typing back when Birdie's message pops up.

Birdie: I second
that. It doesn't
matter what you
open with, baby.
Just get your foot
in the door. If she
lets her guard
down for even a

second she'll fall
in love with you.
Because what's
not to love? You're
generous and kind,
thoughtful and
irreverent.
Mimi: That's
right! And if she
doesn't we'll hold a
grudge.
Joyce: And slander
her name in all our
Facebook groups.

I'm smiling like a goofball, all hopped up on my faux granny pep talk, as I let out a deep breath. I got this.

Just get my foot in the door.

I flip my phone over in my hand one last time before I swipe it open to our messages—mine and Evie's.

The very last one I sent her, the day after the wedding, still makes me wince. But I scroll up anyway, looking over the smattering of them, all beginning and ending in twelve hours.

Me: Where'd you
go?
Me: Breakfast?
Me: or come here
and I'll cook and
eat it off you.
Me: Why am I on
read?

Me: Are you ghosting me? Answer with a ghost.

Me: Joke's on you. You can't hurt my feelings. I grew up with two sisters who told me if I spoke too much my tongue would fall out of my mouth. I was basically mute for three years. You're gonna have to try harder, Evil.

Evil 😈: 🤐 I'm a fan of repeating some history. Let's start with yours.

I audibly exhale, closing my eyes. It's like a knife to the heart. Fuck it, I've been here before . . . on the verge and then over the humiliation cliff. I just have to rip the bandage.

Let me cook, girl.

I stop thinking and just type.

Me: Do you have any towels?

I hit Send before my brain catches up, but the second it does, I stare down at my phone, just blinking.

Aw, fuck, why did I send that? *Do you have any towels . . .* Of all the things I could've said, this is what I chose. I am a loser. That's maybe the one wrong choice I could've made. Dammit.

But the moment the bubbles appear, I hold my phone above me.

I'm immediately strategizing out loud to the cat.

"It's gonna be a yes or no, so I have to figure out where to take it. Maybe I ask to have one? Then I could see her in the hallway for a minute. Or maybe I talk about how there was none in her room the other day, and we can laugh about what happened?"

Peach meows, and I nod. "Yeah, I agree. That's perfect."

I'm deep in thought when my phone finally dings, and I drop it on my face.

"Fuck," I groan, scrambling for it as I blink past the pain and fuzzy eyesight before I frown.

A thumbs-down.

She left me a fucking emoji. Come on. And it's not even on its own. It's as a reaction. Oh . . . that's diabolical.

Still, I need to answer quickly, try and coax a response while I have her attention. But I'm at a loss for words, just looking around the room, dumbfounded, because I feel like I've been checkmated.

"Just thug it out, thug it out, thug it out," I breathe out, rolling onto my side, and type.

Me: Do you know where I could find extras?

It felt embarrassing the first time, and yet the second might be worse. But she has to use words this time, so I'm doing okay.

Bubbles, then no bubbles before bam, a fucking shrug.

Is she kidding? Just say you hate love already. Jesus.

No. I don't accept this. We're speaking tonight. I will not throw in a white flag.

Me: Where did you get yours? Because when I took a shower in your room, there were none. Are you just air drying?

An eye roll. I mimic it in real life.

She'd be an outstanding villain. My foot's bouncing a mile a minute under my covers as I shake my head, staring at the phone.

I don't need this. If she doesn't want to talk to me, fine. Whatever. I toss my phone on the bed before swiping it right back up and texting quickly.

Me: Are you really just gonna answer all my questions with , or ?

A ding.

My brows draw together as I stare down. Is that the fucking flag of Denmark?

I literally have to swipe out and look it up, only to confirm it is, in fact, the flag of Denmark.

So you want to be a smart-ass, huh? You think I can't figure out how to make the best of this emoji shit? Baby, you better stop underestimating me.

Me: Funny story
about Denmark,
I spent a month
there with my
family when I was
sixteen and became
a local hero because
I saved an old
woman and kitten
from a burning
house. It's also the
first time I thought
I might want to be
a chef.

The one thing I'm certain of is she immediately called bullshit, then texted her sister to see if that's true.

"Every word," I whisper, petting Peach.

I'm smiling as I wait for the next emoji to pop through. Because it will. She's not shying away from this fun.

Come on . . . take the bait. You know you want it.

Ding.

Yes! She never disappoints.

It's a roach.

Me: Once I ate a
chocolate covered
one on dare from
my sister, Poppy.
She didn't tell
me it was a roach
tho. She lied and
said it was black

licorice which I hate. Crimson, my oldest sister had bought them from some specialty chocolatier and neither of them wanted to try it so I was dared. I ate one, puked when I realized the truth. Then stole the box, cleaned the chocolate off all the rest and hid them in their shoes and clothes. They hated me for months.

My head swings over my shoulder to the wall behind me because I swear I heard her giggle through the wall.

So I do a little celebratory dance before the ding owns all my attention again.

I chew the inside of my cheek because this time it's not a reaction. It's a message with *two* emojis—a parrot and Santa Claus.

"Hmm," I hum, looking up at the ceiling and trying to recall a memory to match, not that I'm opposed to lying to keep this game going, but it's more fun if it's the truth.

A chuckle pops from my chest as I remember my trip to Costa Rica three years ago.

Me: I'm glad you brought this up. I was just thinking about that Christmas in Costa Rica. I've never had a better time in my life. It may have been because of all those chiliguaro shots on the last night. But I highly recommend dancing 'til you drop at bonfires on a beach with a parrot on your shoulder like a fucking pirate.

Like Pavlov's dog, I grin as another ding comes through, and before I know it, we're four more deep. She's sending, and I'm answering. It's heaven. This might be the best nonconversation conversation I've ever had.

But I want more. I want to know her. So I try and flip the script.

Me: My turn . . . tell me something now. It's only fair.

I choose an easy one for her to start with.

Me: 🎬

Damn, the bubbles stay up forever, but all I get back are Z's, the ones that mean sleep. A tough nut to crack.

"Sweet dreams, Evie," I whisper to myself before sending back a half-moon and placing my phone on the nightstand.

"Man," I breathe out. "I almost had ya."

Just as I close my eyes, my phone dings.

Evil 😈: Extra towels are in the closet at the end of the hall.

The smile on my face is fucking obnoxious, because you know what? Hell yeah.

Chapter Eight

Chase

It's been thirty-six hours since Evie and I texted. I'm not even embarrassed I'm counting. We're already to June 1, so every second matters in the battle of wills. Plus, I think I had more of an impact than I anticipated. She didn't even insult me yesterday morning . . . and she made me coffee today.

Which I'm drinking, sitting on the couch, an uncomfortable leather one, as I listen to Eddie tell me about some girl he hooked up with last night.

"Hear me out . . . last night was spectacular. I think I'm in love. So what I'm saying is, I can meet you in about an hour and a half *after* I make a proper cup of tea and say our goodbyes." I hear the whistle of his kettle go off in the background.

"Goodbyes? I didn't know your dick could speak."

He laughs, but just to fuck with him, I add, "And are you using a kettle? Just microwave the water."

I stifle my laughter as he starts on a tirade about fucking Americans and how uncouth we are. Fucking British people and their tea.

"Calm down, Earl Grey," I laugh. "I'm fucking with you. And an hour and a half works fine. Let's hit the Hollywood Market. Not the

Santa Monica one—that's too far. I'll jump in the shower real quick and make a list."

"Sounds good. I'm looking forward to this master class. However, not so much to training everyone else."

"That's fair."

He may hate the teaching part of cooking, but outside of creating a menu, my favorite part is passing down how to make the dishes. It's incredibly rewarding to invite someone inside your head and let them see what you see. To witness the creation.

Kind of like if the universe gave someone a sneak peek while it created the stars.

And this is why chefs have the reputation for being assholes. We have god complexes. Just like Evie accused, I think I'm a food god.

But I don't apologize for caring about my craft and doing the fucking work it takes to be the best. Or being arrogant about it—I've earned that shit.

"Hello, earth to Chase Beckett."

I laugh in response. "Sorry. Zoned out."

"Giving another acceptance speech about your greatness?"

"Shut up," I shoot out, turning my head to see Evie coming down the hall, her voice getting louder with each step. She looks pissed.

"What do you mean shut down?"

Evie stops in her place, a hand on her hip as she stares at the ground, frowning. Damn, the grip she has on her phone is turning her knuckles white. She *is* pissed.

"What does that mean, Erin?" Her voice is louder.

Whatever is being said on the other end is not something she likes, because she blows out a harsh breath.

Eddie's in my ear. "Is that the woman who hates you? Why is she yelling?"

I shush him.

Evie throws up her hands. "You're fucking joking. This is a joke. I hate to keep repeating myself, but what do you mean she needs a closed set to commune with the werewolf?"

I'm watching her with rapt fascination because irate Evie is not someone I would want to make an enemy of. She's a force of nature, all five foot three of her.

She shrugs, dripping in sarcasm. "Oh, well, that makes the difference. Needing to bond with the fur suit and not the man totally makes sense now. Of course . . ." She's silent, and I'm pretty sure the person on the other end took her seriously because she adds, "No. I'm being sarcastic. What the fuck is wrong with this girl?"

I almost laugh, but that would most definitely put me in the line of fire.

Eddie's in my ear again. "Your girl is sharp as a knife. She cuts to the bone."

I shush him again, not wanting to miss a moment of the show.

She drops her head back, eyes on the ceiling, before she rubs her forehead.

"What I'm hearing is that although my list for effects keeps growing, production is shut down for the day so that our actress . . . who has only been in hemorrhoid ads prior to this breakout role . . . can get spiritually in touch . . . not with the man but the costume in which the werewolf lover will be playing. I just want to make sure I have it right."

More silence, and then she says, "My whole team gets the full-day rate. I'm not kidding. And for the love of god, find my goddamn fish."

"Oh shit . . ." Eddie whispers as I try not to even blink. "Looks like someone's got a paid day off."

Fish? She kept Evie Knievie?

My mind starts churning. *This is a sign.*

I search the space in front, thinking. When I was young, my mother used to say that I was good on the fly, and my sisters used to hate me for it because it meant I could come up with a lie at a moment's notice to avoid getting in trouble.

But it's like fate was training me for this very moment. *She kept our fish.*

I quickly look away and frown, raising my voice. "What the fuck, Eddie?"

There's silence on the other end before he says, "Huh? Me, Eddie? Or . . . who are you talking to?"

The laugh stays deep inside because I have to commit. Fuck.

"This is really inconvenient," I level. "You can't just cancel at the last minute. I rely on you."

"What the fuck are you talking about?" he shoots back. "I told you I was meeting you in an hour and a half."

"Eddie, you're my sous. My right hand."

"I know, but please slap me with the left one because what are you talking about? Are you going mad?"

I turn my profile away from Evie because there's no way I can hide my smile now. He's going to kill me for this.

"Leaving me high and dry for this farmers' market defeats the purpose of your position. I thought you understood this."

I hear his kettle slam onto the stove.

"Chase. What are you saying? I do understand the importance of my position." His voice moves further away as if he's looking at the screen. "Hold on, am I muted? Can you hear me?"

Fuck. I cover the laugh that starts by coughing and forcing my words out stronger.

"I'm really disappointed. This restaurant isn't just my dream. I'd hoped that what you learn would help build your own one day."

"Are you fucking high right now? Were you caught eavesdropping and hit in the head?"

I let the silence stretch out before I say, "Listen, I don't want to use words like 'unprofessional,' but that's what this is. I'll just have to find someone else to help me today. We can talk about this tomorrow. Got it?"

More silence. Then he erupts.

"You son of a bitch. This is about the girl. Hey, hey, hey . . . don't oversell it. Be cool. And good luck, sir. You owe me for the slander."

"Absolutely."

I hang up and dramatically toss my phone across the couch, cracking out "Fuck" before letting out a hoarse exhale.

Please have bought it. Please . . .

A thought strikes. *What if she walked away and this is all for nothing?* So I roll my neck like I'm stressed before I glance her way, not even having to feign surprise when I see she's staring at me.

"Oh damn," I rush out. "Sorry, I didn't know you were standing there."

She stares me down like she's trying to see through my bullshit before she shrugs.

"You didn't hear me?"

Hear that I have a baby mama? I shake my head.

"No, were you talking to me?"

"No. But it sounds like we're both having a rough day."

I raise my brows. "I hope yours isn't as bad as mine. Because I'm fucked."

Am I being devious? Yes.

Do I feel guilty? No.

What's a man to do when he yearns for a woman? Play dirty, of course.

She crosses her arms. "My production got canceled for the day because of an overly dramatic actress. I'm not fucked, but I'm irritated."

I make a face like *Ah* before stretching my arms across the back of the couch. "My sous bailed on me for the farmers' market. So now I have to push training my crew."

She returns the *Ah* face.

"But I still have to go pick up the ingredients," I toss out, laying the groundwork. "I need two of me, ya know?"

I chuckle, but internally, I'm patting myself on the back because I'm masterful right now. I've got her right where I want her.

"Yeah, well, good luck with that," she says, turning around. "I'm going back to bed."

Fuck. No.

I shoot to my feet. "Maybe you could help me?"

You're a dumb prick, Chase Beckett. She turns back around, the look on her face like she's smelled shit.

"Why . . . ? Nooo."

"You're off work, though," I blurt out. She narrows her eyes, so I add, "I just need an extra set of hands."

Her lips part, but she doesn't say no, so I keep going. "I'll buy you a smoothie while we're there. It's legitimately for like an hour."

"Still no."

I walk around the couch toward where she's standing. "I know it's a lot to ask, but it would be really decent of you . . . you know, in the spirit of a new friendship?"

It's a reach, but I really hope I scored some points the other night, or, at the very least, I make her feel guilty enough for leaving me to eat alone.

She groans, scrunching her nose before rolling her eyes. "Fine. Okay."

"Yeah?" I clap my hands together.

She begrudgingly nods. "Yes. Just let me change. Give me ten minutes."

I smile, trying not to look too enthusiastic. "I need a shower, so I'll meet ya back here in ten. It's a date."

Shit. I hear it the moment it comes out of my mouth.

Evie points at me, her forehead wrinkling. "Oh my god. Nice try. Forget it. No. I should've known better."

"It's a figure of speech," I rush out as she turns and walks toward her room with me on her heels. "I swear. I just need the help. And for the record, I'm gonna try and not be offended that you think I'm undatable, as well as thinking I'd plan the farmers' market as a first date."

She spins back around, forcing me to almost skid to a stop as I say the last part.

"—I'm a lot of things, but unromantic is not one of them."

Oh man, I'm floundering and digging myself deeper in this hole.

"Gimme a break," she snarks. "I've never even given you *that* much credit. You strike me as a guy who brings a girl to his restaurant and cooks while you drone on and on about your own genius and how you're so creative. It's all blah blah broody . . . blah blah misunderstood . . . blah blah rich. Then she has sex with you."

I'll never admit that I've actually done that and had that exact result. Jesus, she could start her own psychic network with skills like that.

"Oh yeah?" I level, already feeling how weak my comeback is about to be. "Well, if you're so good at planning first dates, then brag about what you do."

She laughs, but only once. It's more like a nonarticulated *Moron.* And that's fair. I am.

"I would never plan my own first date. This is why you're single and girls don't like you."

No, I'm single because I'm holding out for a hottie who's turned me into a kink-freak for degradation. *Keep saying mean shit, because at least you're talking to me.*

Dammit, there's no time to play these games. I need her to commit.

I throw out some reverse psychology seasoned with a smidge of sad-sack, crossing my fingers it works.

"Whatever, fine. Don't come. I was asking a friend, but I get it . . . I'm not that to you. It's cool."

I walk past her toward my room, reaching for my door handle before I hear her take a deep breath, so I freeze.

"I'll help. But this is not a date," she says resolutely.

"Yeah, duh. Never was," I lie, staring at the door.

I mean, I guess it's not a total lie. This isn't a date until she suddenly likes spending time with me; then I'm happy to revisit the definition. It's more like a flexible hangout.

Just get to know me already, soulmate.

"Okay. We rally in ten."

I smile down at my hand, opening my bedroom door. "Roger that."

The moment I'm inside my room, I book it to the shower, uncaring if the water is hot or cold so I can get my ass back out and in the car with her.

By the time I'm done and pulling on my jeans, it's been nine minutes, twenty-seven seconds. There's still time for my socks and shoes.

I hear her in the hallway, so I move quicker, hopping around to get my sneakers on before I take one look in the mirror.

Game time. I walk out nonchalant as hell.

"Hey," I greet, walking into the kitchen to swipe my wallet off the counter, along with my keys.

"I'm driving," she says, drawing my attention, but when our eyes lock, she adds, "because this is not a date."

I act as if I don't care, extending a hand and motioning for her to lead the way. Truthfully, I like the view from back here anyway.

She walks past the couch, and I follow before I lock the front door behind me. But the moment we get to the driveway, she stops in front of our cars, looking between them.

"Are we admiring our cars?" I joke, but she crosses her arms.

"Have you always had this car?"

I shake my head. "No, bought it here in LA."

"I rented mine."

Look who gets to drive after all . . . I almost chuckle because same, Evie. I got a chubby when I saw my baby too.

I don't even try and hide how full of shit I am. "A Kia Soul's a good car."

"Hmm . . ." she answers.

I don't bother to hide my smile because, damn, I'd like her to look at me the way she's staring at my car.

"It's a 1969 Ford Mustang Boss 429 . . ." I shove my hands in my pockets and lean sideways, getting in her space. "7-liter, 375-horsepower V-8 . . . 0 to 60 mph in 5.3 seconds."

Evie's smile blooms bigger and brighter with every word I say before she turns her face up to mine.

Your eyes are so pretty.

She blinks. "It's John Wick's car."

I nod, then shake my head, motioning to the custom license plate that says **CHEF*KSS**. "No. It's Chase Beckett's car."

Damn, I could stare at her all day.

She holds out her hand. "Give me your keys."

I stand tall again, immediately shaking my head. "No fucking way."

This girl is wild. She doesn't want me to drive—she wants to drive my car.

She raises her brows. "Give me . . . your keys."

"No fucking . . . way," I spit back in the same cadence.

But it's in this moment that the most delightful thing happens. This beautifully mean-spirited little sprite asks me nicely.

It's a miracle on Magnolia Street.

"No, but seriously, please, Chase? I love this car so much. I'll be your best friend."

Gah, she said the last part all singsongy. I'm toast. If she only knew what that sentence just did to me. Or how the way she's looking at me with those amber-brown eyes and her perfectly blush lips could get me to commit crimes.

My whole body feels like that dude's hand in that *Pride & Prejudice* movie my sisters made me sit through for the entirety of their puberty. I want every part of me to touch her, but I can't.

"Okay," I relinquish, handing her my keys, our fingers brushing. "But I drive on the way back."

She snags the keys with a squeal before all but bouncing the whole way to the driver's side. I follow her. Because when she unlocks the door and reaches for the handle, I gently guide her hand away, opening it for her.

Evie's face meets mine, but I smirk. "It's not a date. I'm just a gentleman. And a feminist. You can open mine next time."

She rolls her eyes for the hundredth time since I've known her before she slides inside and I close the door, walking around to the passenger side and getting in.

"Where are we headed?" she breathes out, stroking the steering wheel.

Stop making it sexual, you asshole.

"Hollywood Farmers' Market."

I buckle in and narrow my eyes because I'm feeling like she may want to try and go a little fast. No sooner do I think it than this girl has the engine revving and we peel out of the driveway making a hard right, tearing ass down the street.

Men love fast cars. We love growling engines and danger. But I'm in touch with my feminine side. So I clutch my hand over my chest and scream.

"Fuck. What the fuck, Evie!"

She's laughing, not a care in her F1 world.

"Slow down," I shriek again as she takes another hard turn, and my hand slaps the window for support.

She laughs harder, looking over at me for a split second and wagging her brows.

"Eyes on the road, Hamilton. Jesus Christ, how fast is the speed of light? I think I'm gonna pass out."

"Oh, grow a pair, ya big baby." She shimmies her shoulders. "This car's fucking sexy."

We pull to a whiplash stop at the light, and she lets out a *Woo*.

But I'm not feeling *woo* unless the rest of her sentence is *zy*. Because I think I'm having a heart attack and maybe about to puke.

"What is wrong with you?" I say, half-breathless, realizing just how much of an old woman I sound like. "You're too small to act this big. Jesus Christ, let a guy call a few people to say his goodbyes before you make his life flash before his eyes."

She laughs again, and despite the fact I may have shit my pants, it's becoming my favorite sound.

The light turns green, so I make the sign of the cross and grab the oh-shit bar, holding on for dear life. If I hadn't been convinced before that we should date, I'd be cemented now, because if I survive, then I simply deserve her as the reward for the trial by fire.

Evie

"Stop staring at me," I gripe.

"I'm not staring at you," he chuckles back.

Bullshit. He's been doing it since we arrived. I drop the white peonies from my face and turn toward him, motioning around to the busy farmers' market.

"I thought you needed help? Like, another set of hands . . . but all we've been doing since we got here is browsing vintage T-shirts and looking at flowers."

He shrugs, grinning that grin that makes his dimple show. I'm glad it's still there. A part of me worried I'd permanently scared the smile off his face driving here.

"Sor-reee," he dramatizes and side-eyes me playfully. "Forgive me for trying to enjoy a peaceful moment between us. Especially after the car ride."

I have to bite my bottom lip to not laugh because his scream was surprisingly high pitched for somebody with such a deep voice.

"You know, I always wanted to be an astronaut when I was little," he continues. "But after that car ride, I'm positive I'd never have made it through reentry."

"Stop it," I whisper, then smile.

I'll never tell him that I may have driven even faster just to torture him.

Chase walks over to a stack of records, thumbing through them as he speaks. "But seriously, would it be so terrible if we used some of today to actually get to know each other?" He glances over at me, and it's . . . I don't know . . . almost nervous. "Like maybe fix why you hate me *while* you save my ass."

Oh. *Hate him?* I almost say *Don't overexaggerate your importance*, but I don't because damn, he's being sincere.

He softly taps the tops of the records, waiting for me to answer as I blink, and a pit grows in my stomach.

I feel like such a jerk.

Because I *am* a jerk.

Yes, Chase is annoying. And yes, I'm annoyed at how attracted I am to someone who is *so annoying*, but I don't hate him. Not for real. I mean, I say that, but that's just what we do.

He tells me I'm pretty, I say die. But I don't actually want him to get hit by a bus. It's just that he seems to push all my buttons at once.

"I'll make you a deal," I level, stepping in closer. "You try not to say something that embarrasses me in front of conservatively two hundred people, and I will do my very best to *stop* treating you like human sewage . . . because I don't hate you, Chase."

"No?" he says in question.

I shake my head. "No. I'm just intolerant of you. You're like cheese."

"They have pills for that."

My eyes are locked on his mouth as he draws in his bottom lip between his teeth before it slides out slowly. I grin and pop a shoulder.

"Roofies are illegal."

He laughs, looking around. "Jesus Christ, Evie."

I grin, satisfied to have been the one who embarrassed him for once. "Just behave, and we'll work towards cool."

"Maybe even the coolest?" he fires back. "I mean, you never know. We might be besties by the end of the day."

"You're gonna ruin it."

I chuckle as he pretends to zip his lips and put them in his pocket before he holds up his hands.

If this doesn't get me into heaven, nothing will. I nudge him over so I can look through the records, too, not looking up at him as he keeps talking.

"You know what, though . . ." His voice is full of humor, and I can tell he's about to say something bullshitty. "If we're gonna be friends . . ."

I cut my eyes at him.

He corrects himself, "Or like friend adjacent—"

I smile as he continues.

"—then we need to start off on the right foot."

He holds up two Britney Spears records.

"Britney circa 2001, where not only was she a slave for you but also poignantly not a girl and not yet a woman. Or . . . the 2003 version of Britney Jean Spears, where we all learned it was not just her against the music and that we all loved her a little bit toxic?"

My jaw is almost on the ground. I want to ask why he knows so much about Britney Spears, but to be honest, this might be one of the hottest conversations a man has ever had with me. He's so weird.

But that dimple.

He raises his brows. "Come on . . . Which era reigns supreme? And there is a correct answer."

I give him a deadpan look. "Yeah, there is . . . and it's 2000 'Oops! . . . I Did It Again' when she had vocal fry, a red jumpsuit, and a headset mic." I raise my hand, looking away. "Fight with yourself."

He drops one of the records back into its slot, grabbing my attention again, revealing the album I just named secretly held in his hand, and says, "Correct."

I laugh.

All right. Maybe friends.

We meander to some trinkets, looking at them quietly, only glancing at each other before he points to the pathway, so I nod and follow him.

This is so strange because it's not uncomfortable. Chase is kind of easy to be around as long as he's on his best behavior. Actually, that's not true . . . he was easy at the wedding too. And he was definitely on his worst.

I'm fidgeting with my fingers before looking up at him. "I have a question."

"Shoot," he says, reading a sign for some food truck.

"When we were texting . . ."

He cuts in. "When I was texting, and you were just reacting."

I giggle, stopping at some sunglasses and pulling a pair out to try on. "Semantics. Come clean—were those stories true?"

He grins and puts on a pair of blue glasses with hearts over the lenses before flicking the lever on the side of them, making the hearts flap open and closed quickly.

I shove his immovable arm. "You're ridiculous. Answer my question."

He grins. "Yeah, they were all true."

I draw my head back, surprised, as I look over the top of my aviators. "So you knew you wanted to be a chef at sixteen?"

His brows rise. "You're just gonna pass over that I saved an old woman and her kitten. Cool."

Chase puts his heart eyes back before he starts walking again, making me rush to do the same and keep up.

"Wait . . ." I rush out. "No . . . How did that happen?"

A group of people laughing and talking walk by, so he touches my waist, guiding me out of their way as he speaks.

"Well, my grandmother lived in a small village in Denmark. I used to go there every summer and stay with her. That year, she made it my mission to learn how to cook. Really cook. She showed me everything. I remember being awed by edible flowers—"

The way he's talking about his grandma keeps making me smile. It's sweet. And unexpected. I mean, it's Chase . . . I know he has a family, but I'd also believe he was spawned and found in a cave like a troll.

He lets out a breath, looking down at the ground momentarily, and it makes me frown until he starts back up.

"It was the best summer of my life. Until I accidentally set a grease fire in her kitchen and the house went up."

I freeze, shocked. "What?"

He stops walking, too, turning to look back at me.

"Hold on . . ." I say, my eyes wide. "Are you telling me the old woman you saved was your grandma . . . and the fire was arson?"

"Yeah," he chuckles and wags his brows before rubbing his always-stubbled jaw.

"So you're not so much a hero as you are a felon."

"I mean, it wasn't on purpose, Judge Judy. But since she was well respected, she made a big deal about what a hero I was, so they put my face in the paper, and I became a local legend."

We're standing there staring at each other before I shake my head. "This is so on brand for you."

He shrugs, continuing our walk, but I smile, looking ahead at the crowd.

"I bet she's really proud of how you turned out. At least it paid off, right?"

He doesn't say anything, so I look up at him. For the first time ever, there's no bullshit on Chase's face. His smile is so gentle, wistful, even.

He tips his head in a single nod before he says, "I hope so. She passed the next year, but I think she'd be really happy that I'm not starting any more grease fires, for sure."

My words catch in the back of my throat because I feel embarrassed I didn't know. But before I can say anything, he changes the subject, pointing toward some other food carts. "Hungry?"

I follow his lead and nod, even though I'm not.

We're quiet for a bit as we make our way to a food truck, but then all my unsaid thoughts begin gnawing at me.

"I'm sorry," I awkwardly blurt out. "I didn't know . . . I . . . I wouldn't have brought it up if I had."

"It's all good." He lifts his hand to the back of my neck, gently squeezing once before letting go. But goose bumps explode over my skin. "I like talking about her."

I swallow, trying to ignore the feel of his hand still imprinted on my skin.

"Were you close?"

I can't believe I'm even thinking this, but I want to know more about him. Goldie was right—I almost bristle at the thought—he is different than what I expected.

"Yeah, we were really close. I always looked forward to seeing her. My sisters never wanted to go for more than a week, so it was just me the rest of the time." We fall in line for food, but I'm not paying attention to anyone but him. "My family's cool, don't get me wrong. I am loved. But growing up was always boarding schools, galas, holidays, trips. We didn't do, like, family dinners on a Sunday or binge-watch television together. That was summer with my grandma. We laughed for hours on end, gossiped about all her friends, and played countless hands of poker. She taught me so much of what I know about food and life."

I stare at his face, and for the first time, I have nothing snarky to say. In fact, I have nothing to say at all. I'm just happy listening.

He smiles down to me. "She kind of reminds me of your family. It's probably why I like your mom and Goldie so much."

I beam. "That's a really great compliment, because Grandma sounds pretty awesome."

We move up in line, and I'm still staring at his profile when he flips the script. "Your turn. You know enough about me for now . . . Tell me something I don't know about you."

"Oof," I breathe out, dropping my face to my hands.

"How about when you fell in love with horror?"

I narrow my eyes and say something more honest than I expect from myself. "Since I can remember . . . I was a weird kid. I literally hid in my room and watched *The Exorcist* at, like, ten, and then tried for months to re-create the pea soup—"

He laughs, but I roll my eyes, amused too.

"—but now, my lifelong romance feels more like it's heading toward an impending divorce. I'm just not . . ."

He cuts in. "It's too real."

Not a question. A statement. As if what I feel is the obvious correct conclusion. He's not trying to pry or fix me; he just gets it.

"Yeah." I nod. "I mean, I knew that art imitated life, but I never thought like this . . . and it sucks because I loved what I do."

"Is that why you asked G to get you the spot on the FX team on our movie? It was like your version of exposure therapy."

I giggle. "Yeah, kind of. I thought I could, I don't know, put it back in its right compartment or something?"

It's so surreal talking about this shit out loud because I haven't said this to anyone else. Not even my sister. But I guess if I think about it, it makes sense. I don't want my sister to worry about me, and I don't have that fear with Chase.

"How'd that work for ya?"

The people in front of us leave with their food, making us next up.

"Well, I'm scared of the dark, and I sleep like shit still, soo . . ." I level but smile as he motions for me to look ahead.

I lift my eyes, seeing a menu, and the first thing on it says: *Gamja Hot Dog.*

He remembered our shared love of them.

A sweet Korean woman speaks in Korean to a teenage boy behind her before facing us at the counter.

"How can I help you?"

Before I can order, Chase rattles off an order . . . in Korean. My head snaps to his profile, shocked.

"What! Who are you?"

He laughs. "What are you talking about? Did you want one with cheese? I assumed because of your allergy . . ."

Smart-ass. I push his chest. He doesn't budge.

"You know what I'm talking about. Since when do you speak Korean?"

"His accent is pretty good," the lady offers before turning to make our order. "You've been studying hard."

"Thank you," he says to her before grinning at me. "I speak three languages, actually."

Three? Do I even really know this guy?

"This is a bit." I smile with my mouth wide open. "This isn't real. You're pulling my leg. You don't speak three languages."

"I do."

I cross my arms as I turn my whole body to face him. "Prove it."

He runs his hand through his hair, amused by me. "Well, there's English. I'm speaking to you in it."

"But you said three," I press.

"What is the big deal?" He grins, grabbing some napkins. "You don't speak anything else?"

I shake my head. "No, I'm one of those Americans who feels dumb in Europe because our mother was a terrible teacher and never taught me or Goldie Spanish."

"You don't even know a few lines or curse words?"

His phone dings in his back pocket, making him pull it out as my eyes pop open.

"Oh my god. Wait, I remember. It's Spanish . . . that's three. You spoke it to my mom."

He laughs and shakes his head as he checks the message. "No, I just know a few things here and there."

"Then tell me what the third language is."

His phone dings again, and this time, he smirks, reading the text.

Who's texting you this early in the day? That's dumb.

"Read your text," I blurt out, immediately wishing I could put the words back inside my mouth. But I can't, so I add, "In the language . . ."

His eyes lock with mine as he stares at me for the longest minute, and then the side of his lip quirks up.

"Tes yeux sont couleur champagne et étoiles. Et je veux m'y noyer en te regardant sous moi." *(Your eyes are the color of champagne and stars. And I want to drown in them while I look at you beneath me.)*

Jesus Christ.

Our hot dogs are ready, so he turns to get them, letting me grab the drinks. But I feel as if *I've* been dipped in that hot batter because Chase speaks French . . . like really sexy French. Not that there's any other version.

I swallow, quietly watching him before I try and squeak out "What did you say?" nonchalantly.

He shrugs, teasing me. "I can't tell you because it's none of your business."

My brows draw together as I blow on my hot dog, following him over to a bench, and we trade a beverage for a dog. "Oh, come on. Make it my business. I just need to know."

"Why?"

I'm caught. There's no answer for that question that doesn't out me as thinking he sounded sexy. And to make matters worse, he's looking at me like he wants me to take that bait.

I can't stop smiling out of embarrassment. I'm positive my cheeks are red.

"Fine. Don't tell me," I toss back, needing to stop looking at him. I take a bite of my food but immediately *hashahasha* as I chew.

He chuckles. "Want me to say something else?"

I'm not answering that because the only thing I'll say is *Yes, please.*

He relaxes back onto the bench, his leg crossed and his arm extended across the back as he eats, still staring at my profile. *I will not look at you.*

But I can't help but glance over. He smiles. I take another bite of my food.

Chase leans in close to my ear, stopping my chewing.

"Voglio essere il tuo ragazzo, quindi la prossima volta che sarò così vicino, mi lascerai baciarti." *(I want to be your boyfriend, so next time I'm this close, you'll let me kiss you.)*

My eyes grow wide before I turn my face to his, blinking too close to him.

"You said three languages," I whisper.

He doesn't move. "I just started learning Korean. Those Netflix dramas really got me in a chokehold."

I can feel a light breeze glide over my arm as our eyes stay locked. Oh, we are way too close, but I don't move away either. Heartbeats count as seconds before my thoughts begin to bleed through.

Are we having a moment? Oh yeah, this is a moment . . . Wait, no. We can't have any moments. Shit.

I quickly look away, hearing him exhale softly before he goes back to his figurative corner.

"Are you going to tell me what that meant?"

He huffs a laugh. "It was my answer to Noah's text earlier."

It feels safer to look at him, so I chance it, seeing he's enjoying whatever's about to come out of his mouth next.

"I told him to bring back the good olive oil. Said he'll know it because it's slicker than lube."

And ladies and gentlemen, he's back. Foreign-language crush, crushed.

"If you ever wondered why you're single . . ." I hand him the stick from my food before I take the last sip of my drink, holding that out, too, so he can throw it away with his. "What you just said is why."

He stands, and so do I as he throws away our stuff before we start walking again.

"Yeah," he breathes out. "Girls do have a hard time with exceptional humor. You know, 'cause they're not funny." He laughs and jumps away from me, wincing because I instantly shoot daggers from my eyes. "Kidding." His voice is boisterous and filled with humor. "I swear . . . but since you're a love expert, when's the last time you were in something other than a situationship?"

He motions his head toward a row of tents with stacks and stacks of fruit as I answer, "Don't you know? I'm in a permanent relationship with my independence."

"You don't think you'd live out a poly relationship with your independence and a dude? I hear you can have both nowadays. Shit, you're even allowed to vote, in case you haven't heard."

I laugh. Like truly unguarded. Every once in a while, he's actually kind of funny.

But still, it's not a question I want to answer, because the only answer is that I'm a little fucked up. There's too much baggage coming along with this ride.

I not so slyly change the subject.

"So almost four languages, huh? Was that the consequence of boarding school?"

He shakes his head, so onto me, and raises his voice. "Hell has frozen over. She wants to talk about me, everyone."

"Shut up," I rush out, reaching up to cover his mouth, but he grabs my wrist, lowering my arm gently. "Sue me. I'm fascinated. I kind of always thought you were a rich-boy douchebag whose only saving grace was that he wasn't an elitist. But it turns out you're a nonelitist rich-boy douchebag who speaks three, almost four languages and saved your grandma from a fire . . . that you started."

The way he laughs is like an explosion. It's loud and intrusive, but if he was a wine, he'd be a really expensive bottle with a bold flavor.

And I can't help myself—I pull out my phone and take his picture. When he looks at me, I shrug and say, "Proof of life . . . for our guardians."

But really, it's proof that I don't completely despise hanging out with Chase Beckett. No matter how problematic that feels.

Chapter Nine

Chase

It's been two days since our outing, and I've only seen her at breakfast. And although they've been successfully sans insults, I need to make more headway. But I can't just ask her to watch a movie or hang out—she'll say no.

Thus the birth of tonight's harebrained genius: get her to the restaurant to spend time with me in my element.

It was actually Felix, my sommelier's, idea. He even chose the wine for me to pretend to forget.

"We're sure this is gonna work?" I say, looking up at the table full of kitchen staff, aka twenty cupids.

They're all nodding as Felix points to my phone, his heavy French accent eating up his words.

"Yes. It's like a rom-com. She'll eat, drink, and then sometime during the night, she'll look up, and you'll be talking and looking distinguished . . . and bam, that's when she'll think to herself, *Wow, he's special. My heart needs him.*"

I narrow my eyes. This sounds so much dumber the second time around.

A deep laugh from the table precedes, "Is her heart under or below her belly button?"

Napkins fly at one of the younger line cooks, accompanied by insults and curses.

"I will fire you," I bark, shaking my head and pointing at him.

He lifts his hands, looking apologetic. "Joking . . . joking . . . on my best behavior, I swear it, Chef."

A heavy breath leaves me. Damn, I'm nervous.

"This is a terrible idea," I breathe out, dropping my phone to the table. "I can't bring her here with you swine."

They laugh, but Felix shakes his head and hands my phone back to me.

"Let her see you. A woman will never fall for a man unless he invites her into his life. Tonight is about you. She should be here. And if what you say about her is true, she can more than handle Gage over there."

I groan before I nod and let my fingers fly over the keys.

Me: Hey, what are
the chances you're
home?

Immediate bubbles. *Yes.*

Evil 😈: If you were
a betting man,
you'd be a winner.
Why?

I'll never admit that I already know she is because I may have peeked at her schedule yesterday. But a man has to do what he has to do to facilitate love. It's not like she makes it easy.

How am I supposed to show her how diverse my personality portfolio is if I'm only relegated to watching her eat crepes?

Me: Amazing. I need a favor.

Evil 😈: Sorry . . . who is this? I don't have this number saved.

I chuckle.

Me: Don't be a hater. You're home and you're my friend, remember?

Evil 😈: You lost me at friend 😑

A smile breaks out on my face. She's so mean. Fuck, it's such a turn-on.

Me: Come on, Evil . . . I thought we were past all the hate. I'm desperate.

Evil 😈: I mean I've known this for quite some time.

Me: Glad you're gaining some self-awareness.

I don't care what it takes, I will get her to bring those bottles.

But even as I think in confident bravado, my face scrunches up, thinking about what I'm going to do if this planned attack doesn't work.

Me: Will you stop it. There are four bottles of Cabernet on the counter. Grab and bring to me.

Evil 😈: Are you lying about owning a restaurant? Is this a Talented Mr. Ripley thing you're doing because how don't you have wine?

Me: You think I look like Matt Damon?

Evil 😈: Please say AI is texting me.

Me: You're staring at the picture you took of me. Stop being so obsessed . . . but it makes sense since we're both jacked blondes with undeniable appeal.

Someone calls my name in the background, but I don't pay any attention. I'm too immersed in this delicious little conversation.

Evil 😈: I'd say you're more a Gwyneth Paltrow.

Me: All I'm hearing is that I'd fuck me.

Evil 😈: Great! You finally found someone who will.

A genuine laugh bursts from my chest. This is the most fun failure I've endured. Dammit. Come on, Evie, just give.

Me: Fella, bring me the wine. I'll pay you for your time if that's what you want.

Evil 😈: Ooo, I'm only looking for stock in peace and quiet . . . are you selling that?

For fuck's sake. She's impossible.

Me: EVIE!!!!!

Evil 😈: I know how to spell my own name. You're the illiterate one. Remember?

That's it. I'm pulling out the big guns.

Me: Never mind. It's cool. Noah's calling. I'll figure out something else.

The most valuable lesson I learned from having sisters is if begging didn't work, go straight to fear of exposure. *Noah's calling* is my adult version of *I'll tell Mom and Dad.*

Evil **:** Calm
down loser. I'll
be there in ten
minutes to three
hours depending
on traffic. PS. You're
on kitty litter duty
until you move out.

Hell yeah. I turn to the room and raise my arms. "Got her." The crew breaks out into applause, and I stand in victory, laughing. "Now, let's make me irresistible."

♥♥♥

Evie

It took me twenty-three minutes to deliver Chase his four bottles of Caymus to the restaurant, so he's already barreling out the front.

"Hey," he says, opening my car door literally as I put the car in park.

My keys are still jingling in the ignition as I whip my face to his eyes that are as bright as his smile. I can't help it, because it feels contagious, so I grin too.

"Hi," I breathe out, sounding a bit winded.

There's a pause as we stare at each other before my brain catches up, and I lean over the center console, pulling the bag of wine from the passenger seat into my lap, careful to not let the bottles clink.

"Delivered straight to your door. I expect a large tip. Something in the eighty- to ninety-percent category will suffice."

He reaches inside and takes the bag right off my lap.

"You're a lifesaver. Seriously, the guys were about to riot."

Guys? Oh, duh, yeah, his staff must be here.

I look through the front windows of the restaurant, because it's designed to be one of those dining experiences where you can see the chefs cooking, so there's a giant cutout that gives everyone a view.

A bunch of guys are sitting inside, in the kitchen area. Some lifting a glass in cheers, others laughing or speaking animatedly with their hands. All backlit by an amber glow. It's like a scene out of a movie.

"Sorry it took so long," I say, looking back at him before biting my bottom lip. "I thought you were using it for cooking, not a party. I really shouldn't have gone just under the speed limit on every single street."

He tilts his head, tensing his jaw like he's trying to hide a smirk, before he props a hand on the top of my door and bends down, bringing his face too close to mine.

"Would you have driven faster if you knew it was for other people?"

I raise my brows. "Duh. Yeah."

He laughs, and my eyes drop to the steering wheel. Why does this suddenly feel like high school when you're in the parking lot after school and a boy's talking to you?

We never would've dated in high school . . . We'll never date now.

"Okay," I announce, wanting to drive away from my thoughts. "Have a good time . . ." I try and gently urge my car door closed, but he doesn't take his hand off the frame, so I press, "I'll see ya later." I look up at him, frowning. "Hello? Let go of my door. I'm leaving."

But Chase doesn't seem to care about what I'm saying because he motions with his head toward the restaurant. "Nah, come inside. We're just getting ready to eat. Let me feed you."

Only he makes *Let me feed you* sound dirty. Or maybe it's because his food is fucking orgasmic. Either way, I'm not joining tonight.

I shake my head, trying to pull my door closed again, but he still doesn't budge.

"Let go," I draw out.

"Get out," he says, mimicking my tone.

It makes me involuntarily chuckle before I catch myself.

"No. I look like trash. I'm not going in front of people."

His eyes do a once-over on me, and I squirm, momentarily looking away.

"You look good."

Why is he saying it like that? And why is his voice so deep?

I scowl. "I'm literally wearing a pair of hospital scrubs I stole from a guy who made everybody call him doctor when he was a dentist—"

He grins. Damn that stupid dimple.

"—and this sweatshirt is not just a Boston University flex, it's the home to these oil stains." I point them out as if he couldn't already see them. "I murdered a Philly cheesesteak in a very unladylike manner once."

"You're always the most impressive girl," he levels, reaching in and removing my keys from the ignition before pocketing them.

My eyes spring open as my pulse picks up pace. "Chase. I'm wearing mismatched flip-flops on my feet. Pink and orange are not the same."

The grip I have on the door handle tightens before I try and win a battle of tug-of-war. That is until he covers both my hands with one of his, removing them from the door as if my grip strength is undetectable.

"Chase," I hiss, but I'm hauled out of my car, the door kicked closed.

He tugs me forward, our bodies too close as he holds the bag of bottles like a football and stares down at me.

"Nobody gives a fuck what you look like. All my friends are in there, and you're a friend. Plus, you couldn't look like trash if you tried."

I groan as he turns around, still holding one of my hands hostage as I'm dragged behind him like some kind of errant child onto the sidewalk.

"Plus," he says over his shoulder, "I'd fire anyone who says otherwise."

The commitment I show to keeping my head on straight should be rewarded, because I have to dig my teeth into my bottom lip to make the smile trying to bloom stop and wilt.

"Can we be done being friends now?" I gripe.

He chuckles, letting go of my hand to open the door, his eyes meeting mine.

"No."

Fuck. I stand there for a second, staring at him with my arms crossed, before I finally give in. I mean, how bad could it be? I look like shit, but they're all probably food stained and perfumed with garlic.

"Fine. But if the food sucks, I'm writing like ten Yelp reviews."

He lifts his leg, kicking me in the butt, and herds me inside. "Get inside, loser."

I can't help but squeal, bouncing inside the grandiose glass doors before I'm immediately hit with boisterous laughter and what sounds like a passionate conversation about duck fat wafting from the kitchen.

The smile on my face is immediate as Chase moves in behind me, whispering down to my ear.

"Welcome to my home," he whispers.

Home?

I blink. Taking it all in at once.

While he may have said his "friends" were here, I think he meant family, because it reminds me of mine—loud, boisterous, and full of joy.

Home is that kind of perfect place that makes you feel cozy and the most yourself you'll ever be. I grin, realizing this is a place where he's himself.

Someone yells from the back in French, and I see white napkins fly, so I turn and look at Chase over my shoulder with a smile still on my face.

But he just grins. "Don't worry, you'll fit right in. They'll love you. Just bring your A game. The sarcasm is top tier here."

I blink too quickly as he takes the lead, walking quickly, so I follow. And while I'm less worried about my appearance, I'm somehow more nervous.

Wait, why am I nervous? If they're anything like him, I'll deserve severance for the good acting job I'll be forced to do before I quit this dinner and run.

We weave through the front room, filled with unsullied tables topped with expensive linens and tiny gold lamps. He glances back at me as the noise from the kitchen grows louder.

"It's beautiful," I say, because pride is written all over his face.

He should be proud. Even the gold-leaf wallpaper-banked walls are gorgeous and elegant. And yet, it feels cozy like his restaurant in Boston. There's a distinct comfort while still feeling elevated.

He's good at this . . . Nothing else, just this.

"Yeah." He winks. "You should come back when it's open . . . say, two and a half weeks?"

Goldie told me about the opening, but I'd planned to have other plans.

I shrug. "Put me at Goldie and Noah's table." I reach out, touching a sage green menu with gold lettering that's stacked on a table. "This place looks expensive. They can pay."

He laughs, opening one side of a set of black double doors with his back, letting me walk in first.

But as I do, the kitchen goes silent. Only the sound of the doors swinging closed can be heard as I come to stand next to Chase.

Well, this is awkward. There are too many sets of eyes on us and quiet swallows of wine happening along the family-style table.

I tug the sleeves of my sweatshirt over my hands while lifting my face to Chase's.

Without any form or formality, he says, "Fellas—Evie. Evie—fellas."

I give him an empty laugh before I turn my face back to theirs, raising a hand and waving hi. But I immediately start laughing because, like an explosion, cheers erupt, along with whistles, before suddenly everyone's up on their feet, coming to greet me.

What is happening?

Chase steps away, throwing me to the adorable wolves as I'm pulled into handshakes and hugs. So many people are introducing themselves and kissing me on both cheeks. And although I'm good with names, it's a little overwhelming . . . but in the best way.

I find his eyes, watching him watch me before he walks to the other side of the table smirking. Maybe because I'm asked a slew of questions that sound more like statements.

"Have the lamb . . . Do you love lamb? Have the lamb." . . . "Red wine . . . not white. Yes?" . . . "Why it take you so long to finally come here? It was too long."

The last question is said with an accent. Chase's voice interjects casually, "Lasciatela stare. È qui ora." *(Leave her alone. She's here now.)*

Hot. *Wait, was that Italian?*

Because his friends are what I imagine a bunch of Italian grandmas would be like. The man who spoke last laughs, waving his hands in the air before giving me a wink.

This is wild. Oh my god.

Out of nowhere, a chair is produced, and a plate of food appears. One of the guys, who introduces himself as Felix, whips a napkin in his hand, dusting off the seat, before another someone takes my hand and I'm seated, the aforementioned napkin placed in my lap.

I laugh and say thank you, but I barely get it out before a glass of wine is poured and placed in front of me, with too many voices saying, "Eat, eat."

Chase stands at the other end of the table, handing the wine bottles off one by one while staring at me. I smile as a cork pops and his glass is filled.

He lifts it, quieting the table. "This has been a helluva journey. It's been blood, sweat, and tears—"

"Most of them from Gage," someone jokes, and they all laugh.

Who's Gage? I have no idea, but I laugh too.

But Chase just smiles. "Here's to our first supper . . . and to all the people who understand that food is more than restaurants and money—"

"But we like that too," another guy bellows to more hoots and hollers.

Chase raises his glass higher. "It's about old friends"—he looks at me—"and new ones. But most importantly, it's about family."

Everyone raises their glasses high, cheering, but I'm silent because Chase Beckett is really starting to get under my skin. And not in the way I'm used to.

Maybe real friends aren't the worst idea after all.

The night moves slowly, but it's still over too fast.

God, I wish I had two stomachs. We dined on the whole menu.

It was a final tasting, and damn, was it tasty.

Between the caviar-topped scallops and the poached cod in the most insane orange sauce that felt like I was eating a creamsicle, I was in heaven. But the pièce de résistance was slices of wagyu with potatoes that are three hundred dollars a pound called la bonnotte.

I'm ruined for life. He's literally made it impossible for me to put anything in my mouth other than him . . .

What the hell did I just think? Other than his food. Jesus.

I slide a hand over my tummy because it's so full it almost hurts. Or maybe it's that I've laughed so hard tonight between Felix the Frenchman and Leo the Italian Stallion, as he calls himself, that I decreased my capacity for food.

But they had so many stories to tell me about Chase. And it's weird because it was like they were talking about someone I'd never met.

Who he is here, in this place, is so different from the dumbass Noah Adler sidekick in the outside world.

Or maybe that's just the box I put him in.

As I think it, I hear a familiar conversation coming from his side of the table, but it's hard to make out because dishes are clanking as everyone begins to clear.

"Leo, Leo, get in on this. Chase is defending his love of women born in the sixties."

Leo hums like it's vibrating his chest, but I roll my eyes, remembering back to the first time I heard this nonsense. I could've done with missing out on this for the second time.

"No," Chase bellows, his dimple flirting with me as he holds up a finger, staring directly at me as if he knows I'm judging him. I am. "Put that look away. Let me make my point. I am not saying women in the sixties. All women are beautiful, from every era. I just happen to think that the bar was set by one . . . and she was born in 1967."

He leans back in his seat as I lift a brow, waiting for the reveal. Because he's so full of shit with whatever buxom playmate he self-cared to because he found a dirty magazine somewhere.

I'm folding my napkin on to the table, about to go off about how men have no place in a conversation about women's looks. How their standard isn't about beauty but sex, when his voice cracks my feminist rage.

"Lisa Bonet," he levels.

Oh. I mean . . .

My eyes narrow the way they always do when I feel like he's one-upped me. And he smirks the way he always does when he knows he has.

There's respectful agreement from around the room as I stare at him. But I'd be a liar if I said my stomach wasn't doing that weird flutter thing. Because while we're locked on each other from over the table, noise happening all around, I'm in a bubble, remembering that night at the wedding when he leaned in and said, "Has anyone ever told you that you look like Lisa Bonet?"

Our gaze breaks because I'm too chicken to let it be held. Because while I don't like him . . . I did like that.

I glance at my wineglass, hoping I can blame the Cab for my thoughts, but I only had a sip since I have to drive home.

"You look like her," Felix offers, like some kind of op trying to kill my resolve.

I laugh and hold up my glass, determined to change the subject. "To the best dinner I've ever had. And to whoever's doing the dishes. Because, not it."

Laughter abounds as they all jump on board, saying *Not it*, until it reaches Chase, who says "Fuck you, guys," making us all laugh harder.

I take another sip of my red wine and place the glass down, looking between my new European besties.

"Maybe we should help clear, too, so he has all the dishes in one spot when he pulls his weight?"

They laugh and agree. So I make my way around, gathering plates and glasses, sometimes handing them off to others and other times walking back to the sinks to place them myself.

And while I don't avoid Chase's eyes on purpose as I chat with everyone else, I don't search for them either. Conveniently, he's deep in conversation with someone I haven't met yet.

"My angel," Leo seduces with that damn accent as he points to where Chase is standing. "The plates there . . ."

I make my way over, trying not to think about the Lisa Bonet of it all as I reach for his friend's plate, saying, "Let me just grab—"

But Chase is doing the same, and our fingers brush. I gasp because you'd think we'd been hit by lightning the way both of our hands jump back, and we immediately lock eyes.

"Sorry," I rush out, but he's already shaking his head.

"No, it was all me. I . . ."

His voice trails off as his friend laughs and picks up his own plate. I turn and greet him, trying to ignore the moment. But before I can say anything, he beats me to the punch.

"Wow. Evie Monroe, in the flesh."

He's staring down at me, his gaze intense as I hear someone start talking to Chase, pulling him from *this* conversation. It makes me frown before I fix my face and smile.

"Yes. The one and only . . . but I'm at a disadvantage. I don't know your name. I guess we were seated too far away tonight."

Or you didn't want to meet me. Which is a real possibility from his body language.

He crosses his arms, smirking like he wants to keep his name a secret before he adds, "And that's a shame . . . because I feel like I've known you my whole life."

What a weird thing to say.

Whoever this stranger is lets that statement hang out there for a second as I give an empty laugh, suddenly feeling awkward behind my smile. But then he winks.

"I mean, because I've heard so much about you from Chase. He never stops talking about you. I'm Eddie, by the way, the wayward sous chef."

He doesn't hold out his hand for me to shake like everyone else. Still, I smile, remembering where I've heard that name, deciding not to pull out any digs because I can't tell if Eddie's unfriendly or just British. So I play it safe and go with "Nice to meet you," before Chase's hand lands on his shoulder.

"What'd I miss?"

Eddie shakes his head. "Nothing. I was just about to tell her the story about you threatening to chop off your old sous's hands if he so much as touched her plate . . ." He leans in like he's letting me in on a secret, but my head draws back. "Figured it's a solid excuse for avoiding you tonight."

He smiles. I don't. Because while I'm positive that's a true story, since it's too on brand for Chase's dramatics, it's the way he's saying it. Eddie doesn't like me.

The smirk on Chase's face doesn't hide how much he enjoys that memory, as he shrugs nonchalantly. "She came to be fed the best. *I'm* the best."

There's so many barbs I could throw, but I'm only focused on Eddie as he says, "You'd maim for her. Interesting."

I manage a barely there smile as I step away. Weird British humor or just weird? Who's to say, but what I do know is Eddie feels like a hard pass for me.

Chase motions to the door with his head.

"I'm going to walk him out before I have to get started on all those dishes. Wait around for me?"

I scrunch my nose. "Only if I don't have to help. You didn't purchase that subscription for this friendship."

He laughs, nodding, and counters, "I'll have to email for an upgrade," as he guides Eddie to the side door.

"Sorry. Sold out," I toss back, but I notice Eddie doesn't laugh.

Well, then, no sense of humor means you are just weird. *How are they friends?*

With a sigh, I look around the table, noticing that for the most part it's clean, before all the noise that's quieted restarts as I'm hugged and goodbyes are said.

One by one, the guys leave out the side door, some patting Chase on the shoulder, others shaking his hand, but all of them congratulating him.

And then just like that, we're alone, the slam of the metal door closing highlighting that fact.

"What an incredible night," he rushes out, wiping his hands down his face. "Did you have fun?"

I smile. "I'm glad I was bullied into staying. But aren't you going to ask me if I liked the food?"

He lifts a brow. "No. You all but licked your plate, and anything is an upgrade from the food you're always complaining about eating on set. Plus, I know exactly what you like."

I swallow, because the way he glances at me when he says that is bathed in insinuation. But he doesn't elaborate, just grins while heading toward the double doors, motioning with his head for me to follow.

So I do. *Dammit.* I really need to start saying no to that little motion.

The moment I breeze through the doorway, he points to a few lights by the front windows. "Turn those off? The switch is by the front door."

I nod, heading that way, still marveling over how beautiful this restaurant is. The click of a switch from one of the dim table lights catches my attention as he leans over to turn it off.

"Does it ever just knock you on your ass that you're really doing this?" I let my voice carry so he can hear me. "I mean, you've really made it, Chase. You have two highly rated restaurants before the age of thirty-five, in arguably two of the biggest cities . . . It's impressive."

He laughs, placing his palm down on the table, leaning onto it as I click the switch, leaving us in the dark—well, as much as the streetlights outside allow.

Yet it's still the dark. And the reality that I am not scared doesn't get past me. Because if I'm honest, I'd admit I haven't been afraid since he showed up.

"I don't know if it's set in yet," he answers, kind of beautifully bathed in the moonlight. "But what's with the compliment? You don't like me enough to say all these nice things. What are you, working undercover for *Food & Wine* magazine?"

I shrug, feeling unburdened by my niceness.

"If I was doing that, I'd have already run my exposé. You say dumb shit on a daily basis."

"I do not," he scoffs.

We're walking toward each other, closing the distance as we banter back and forth.

"You do too."

"Name one time tonight where I said something stupid . . ." When I don't speak fast enough, he says, "See, you can't."

"Bullshit, I can name like ten. How about we start with all that Lisa Bonet nonsense? I felt set up."

He stops in front of me, and I can see his grin more clearly.

"Okay, I admit that."

"Ha." I clap my hands together once. "I knew it. Why do you always say stuff like that when you know it won't get you anywhere with me?"

He takes an inch of a step closer to me.

"I'm not making shit up, Evie. You always think I'm so full of it—"

I cut in. "You are."

He chuckles. "Fair. But maybe if you let me finish a sentence, I'd surprise you . . . like I did tonight."

The silence wraps around as he stares down at me, and the way he looks at me . . . I don't know how to describe it. He always looks at me the same way—gentle and intimate.

I start to take a step backward because I'm suddenly feeling warm, like we're standing too close, but he nabs the fabric of my sweatshirt right above my belly button to stop me.

His voice is low and gravelly as he whispers, "Is it so bad that I think you're pretty?"

Goose bumps explode under my sweatshirt as I half blink, unable to tear my eyes from his.

Is it so bad? I blink before the answer populates in my head and tumbles out of my mouth.

"I don't want to give you the wrong idea."

His lips tilt up like they're going to form a smile before they stay neutral.

"How does me saying you're pretty give me the wrong idea—"

Jesus. I can hear my heart beating. Or maybe that's my pulse whooshing in my ears. Either way, the blood is flowing through my body quickly, especially when he finishes his thought.

"The real question is, does it make you reconsider me? Especially since you've been wrong for a year and a half."

My lips part as if there's an answer prepared, but there isn't. Because the truth is, Chase is not my ideal boyfriend-partner-soulmate. His personality ruins that for him.

But I have to admit that he has his moments . . . and this is one of them.

I drop my eyes to my chest, seeing my sweatshirt moving too quickly because I'm breathing too fast. Shit. My mind warring between reason and lust.

We're standing too close, and his voice is too deep, and his thick-ass fingers are still pinched on my sweatshirt.

Oh god.

I look up just as he's leaning in. Holy shit, he's going to kiss me. Right here in the middle of this restaurant. And I feel almost powerless to stop it.

Almost being the keyword.

My palms land on his sturdy chest and with a gentle press, I say, "We shouldn't."

But he presses back. "We already have."

I shake my head, my voice quiet because I feel like we're so close my breath could tickle his skin.

"Chase, that's exactly why we shouldn't. You asked me to be your friend. I think we leave it there."

His eyes close for a second, but it feels like an hour before he nods and takes a step back. "Okay."

A silent exhale of breath leaves my body, because if he only knew the kind of restraint I'm using to keep us in the safe zone, then he would know all he'd have to do is grab me and kiss me, and then I'd make every bad decision there was to make.

Thankfully, as much as I can count on Chase being a complete idiot, I can also rely on him to be a gentleman. Even if sometimes it's an unorthodox version.

He crosses his arms, smiling back at me. It's the kind of smile that's shared embarrassment because I'm wearing the same one.

"Welp," he says loudly. "I never thought being friend zoned could be a positive. But considering where we started, I'm counting it as a win."

I wince, then say, "You're welcome?"

We stand for a second, smiling at each other, and it's not awkward, but it is all at the same time. He must feel it too because he pretend punches my shoulder.

"Friends it is. But then again, I'll take you any way that I can get you, Evie."

His words sound sincere enough. Still, there's no part of me that believes Chase will suddenly stop liking me. And I have to admit there is a very quiet part that wishes we had some more moments.

But that part is clearly toxic and trying to sabotage my life.

RIP me.

Chapter Ten

Him

They weren't always the plan. They were just the cherry on top.

But watching them through the window, silently intruding on this intimate moment as they stare up into each other's eyes, is proof of life.

They're the heart of this beautiful destruction.

Evie and Chase, Chase and Evie, I think as if it were a song.

They've been so connected, even since I first saw them running for their lives. It was Chase who calmed her. Him she felt safe with.

Now, they're all but wrapped in each other.

The fearless, independent little sister with the tie that binds.

Look at you . . . Their future anguish is writing itself—laid out first in how he wants to kiss her so badly he can taste it.

He's wanted it all night.

My eyes fix to where he's grabbed her sweatshirt, stopping her retreat. *Don't be a pussy, just kiss her.*

God, the way they stare at each other, always waiting for someone to call chicken, is transcendent.

It's amusing how it seems everyone around them sees their compatibility, except for them.

She pushes him away, but he holds his spot, hope written all over his face.

Do you want him to kiss you, Evie? Or do you wish he'd fuck you again?

I wonder how you'll cry when I slit his throat . . .

My lips quirk as she pushes him away. But it doesn't matter, because she is a forgone conclusion. Her eyes searched for him all night too. Discreet glances that went unseen.

Except I see you.

I never take my eyes off you. A good predator never does.

He takes a step back, nodding, retreating, but this isn't the end. That's what I know about him—he's determined.

I can count on that.

The steadfast hero always there for scared little Evie, just waiting for her to see him for who he is. But a woman like her needs to feel safe enough to expose her vulnerability. And that takes time and maybe a reminder . . .

Because they will fall.

And when they do, I'll rip his heart straight from his chest so that Evie will feel like I killed her too.

Two birds. One stone.

And the cherry? She'll never see it coming.

Chapter Eleven

Evie

I hate the dark, and I hate this set.

Because I'm standing in the middle of Frazier Park, which is a cold-ass forest, in the middle of the night, inspecting fake rocks that are hiding the fog machines—machines that keep malfunctioning and creating too thick of a haze over the Styrofoam headstones in this man-made graveyard.

Yeah. This sucks.

My radio goes off, so I reach down to silence it. Fuck, I'm in the worst mood, no matter if it's Friday. Maybe it's because after the dinner at Chase's restaurant, I went home and drank a bottle of wine while revisiting every single moment before and after the *almost* kiss.

Then repeated the overthinking over the next few days.

Shit. Why did I do that?

I mean, I know why—him and his moment . . . I just need to make it another few weeks, and then I'm home free and safe from any more regrettable decisions.

Plus, since I'm on location for the next few nights, avoiding him should be easy.

My thoughts are interrupted by the Double D's.

"Night shoots," Devin says like he's a rapper saying *West Side* as he and his brother join me.

I turn and try to smile . . . I don't have it.

"Oh. Our buddy's salty today," he says to his brother, who responds, "Brine it up."

"There truly isn't enough sarcasm in the world to bring me even the slightest bit of joy in this moment."

Devin puts his arm over my shoulder. "We have some good news that might cheer you up . . ."

I look up at their faces, lit up with the kind of golden retriever enthusiasm I've come to find endearing. I'm still frowning, though.

"Okay . . . out with it."

Derek looks at Devin, who nods before Derek says, "We found your fish."

My eyes spring open as my lips part. Yep, that turned me right around.

"No way. Where was she? Who took her? Did you bring her?"

I look around, not seeing her bowl until I notice they're looking at each other in that silent-communication way that always ends with me being annoyed.

The pit in my stomach hollows me out, dousing my happiness so I narrow my eyes.

"Why are you looking at each other like that? Explain *found* . . ."

Derek shrugs. "Well, not found-found . . ."

Devin jumps in. "We sweet-talked the lot security guy, and he let us see the surveillance. Some extra took her—"

Derek cuts back in. "But we figured we could track them down, because the other day, when you told us the story about how you got her, we felt so, so—"

I cut him off, feeling like this might be the straw that makes me break his back.

"So you thought you'd Scooby Doo it? You're gonna unmask evil Count Von Peterson, who's been hiding among us in his prosthetic mask, and save my fish?" I snark as Devin starts to nod, but Derek slaps his shoulder.

I snap my fingers and stare them down. "I barely have the patience to live today, and you two might push me over the edge. Speak only when spoken to. Got it."

They nod as I drop my bag to the ground and look around for what I came to do.

"Okay," I breathe out, returning my attention to the Double D's. "Go find someone to turn on the fog machines. Let's see what's happening."

My puppies take off out of the graveyard just as my name is called by the guy from the FX team who works primarily on mechanical aspects, aka these stupid machines. So I point the boys in the right direction and wait.

But I still feel antsy and so on edge. Because it's not just the almost kiss with Chase. It's this set, the dark, and being out here without . . . Absolutely not.

If I complete that thought, I'll need to check directly into a facility that deals with psychosis.

Joe waves at me again, standing with the Double D's, letting me know he's ready.

"Let it rip," I call out, hearing the hiss of the machines as they kick on. It sounds a lot like a big cat hissing as the liquid spits and flows through the hoses.

I wait to see how big the problem is, but I don't have to wait long because in two seconds flat, it looks like an LA sky.

"Holy shit," I blurt out. "You made smog, not haze."

"My sentiments exactly," Joe calls over to me. "And it doesn't lessen with fewer machines. It's all coming out this thick."

I close my eyes for a moment because I have to remind myself that I am the boss for a reason, but stupid never gets easier. Especially when I'm in the trenches with this Chase hangover.

"Have you tried watering it down?" I say as nonchalantly as possible, hoping my face isn't giving away how truly stupid Joe is.

"Look, I just poured in the stuff labeled 'fog juice' and got smog."

The heat traveling up my neck reaches my chin as I suck in a breath, ready to blow, but the Double D's save Joe's life.

"We're on it . . . More water, boss, less glycerin."

I nod, turning around and staring at the gathering fog as my phone buzzes, so I pull it out of my pocket while raising my brows because I can't even see my feet.

> **Golds:** Missing you. Just checking in to say hello and inform you that hangovers aren't a thing with Italian wine. Isn't that crazy . . . we went through three bottles and I feel great today.

I'm scowling, like fully giving my phone the biggest fuck-you my face can muster, my thumbs ready to delete the message, when Devin yells, "No fucking way."

I startle, my head whipping in his direction, as my phone drops into the abyss of the goddamn fog.

"Motherfu—" I grumble, not finishing the crudeness before I look over to Joe. "Turn it off, please. I just dropped my phone."

But nobody's paying attention to me; they're walking over to the craft services table. *What is happening?* I look around because I didn't hear anyone call dinner . . . or whatever the equivalent of that is when 10:00 p.m. is the start of your day.

"Hello?" I yell, but Derek points to the table.

"We got catering."

"And?" I whisper before letting out an annoyed breath.

My gaze drops back to the pillows of white smoke that hover around my calves. *I don't have feet. Jesus Christ.* I squat down, trying to feel around for my phone because I can't fucking see through the climate crisis they created.

But the moment my hand disappears, my fingers touch wet moss, making me jerk back with a gasp. Fuck. This is like those games at Halloween parties where you had to reach into a bowl and guess what you felt. And it was always peeled grapes labeled as eyeballs.

I loved *that*, but this . . . knowing there's real forest under my hand . . . with bugs and shit that live in dirt . . .

"Gross," I groan but commit to feeling around for the sake of my phone.

My hands find something wet again, but I keep patting around. I blow at the clouds in front of my face, trying to create some kind of path to see, but it's too thick.

"There are wagyu burgers," Devin shouts.

I flip him off under the fog, not even looking his way.

"Jesus, how far did this thing bounce," I whisper, getting down on my knees as I expand my search, crawling around.

"You look like you're floating," Derek shouts, and I notice the fog's covering most of my arms to my shoulders, but I keep sweeping the ground, my hands feeling dirty as the machines still work on overdrive.

"Hey, guys," I yell. "Can someone turn it off already?"

I don't wait to see if they heard me, stubbornly determined to find my goddamn phone. "I know you're here," I whisper, sliding my hand out and finally feeling something cold and steel. "Yes. Yes, yes, yes." I quickly crawl closer, over the cold ground, putting my hand over it.

A smile blooms on my face as I turn it toward everyone surrounding the catering to tell them I found my phone, when suddenly all my breath is sucked out of me and I'm pulled under, enshrouded in darkness under a cloud.

All by a hand gripping my wrist.

But before I can scream, I'm jerked forward, dragged quickly into . . . *Oh my god* . . . My body lands hard with a thud.

My head shifts side to side quickly, my nails instantly digging into the dirt walls I'm surrounded by. I'm blinking a hundred miles an hour, fight or flight manifesting as freeze because I can't move or even think.

Because I'm in a shallow grave.

I'll be buried.

My chest is heaving even though my breath is stuttered and shaky. I'm trembling as fear wracks my body. Every memory, every worry is hitting me like bricks until there's only one streamlined thought.

Billy's here. He's here. And he's come back to finish the job.

That's when my chest splits open from the terror that's been lodged there, and I finally scream.

I scramble to my knees, frantically clawing at the moss and ground as I climb up and out onto my hands and knees. Desperately gasping for air, sucking in the haze surrounding me before pushing to my feet to run.

Because that's the only thought in my mind.

Run.

My pulse in a full panic as my feet pound against the grass. I'm searching the distance in front of me, my vision blurred by watery eyes and speckled black dots as the scene before me ebbs and flows between present confused faces and a distortion by the past.

Because I'm back at Camp Weonoke. Back to that moment when I thought I would die.

I want to scream, *He's here. He's back.* But even as I open my mouth, nothing comes out. Or maybe it can't because I think I'm hyperventilating.

Oh my god.

My chest tightens, making me grip it as I stumble, feeling like I may pass out. I don't know what to do . . . or what's real . . . until my eyes land on his.

Chase.

He's here. Pushing past people, his steps picking up the pace as he rushes toward me, catching me as I all but jump into his arms.

My arms wrap around his neck as he grips the back of mine, holding me flush to him.

"Shh. Shh. Shh. Shh," Chase soothes. "What happened? What's wrong?" He pulls his head back to try and look at my face, but I'm too panicked to speak. "Evie . . . look at me. Everything's okay."

I can't. The fear is too much. My entire body's shaking and it feels violent. He tries to pull me back to see my face but I keep it buried because my mind is splintered.

The fear follows me, so solidly rooted within me that I can't hear the rational part of me say I'm safe. But somehow I instinctually know it because I'm with him.

So I won't let go.

Chase is my lifeline.

I grip him tighter and he doesn't move. He just lets me hold him, returning that fierceness back to me. His hands stay on me through the rough inhales and exhales that turn into cries and through the trembling I can't get a handle on.

He anchors me, keeping the world at bay as I focus on the steady thrumming of his pulse against my lips. I count to it in my mind, feeling my tears stain my cheeks and melt onto his skin.

I don't know how long we stand there, or how many people watch, but I just keep counting. Until my eyes flutter open as my heart begins to beat in rhythm with his and I swallow the tightness in my throat.

"Evie, baby. What happened?" he whispers to me so gently that I can feel how fragile I am in his arms.

"He . . . I . . . I was pulled under . . ." I stutter, unable to make out my words, my face still buried into his neck.

So I pull back slowly, our eyes connecting, as I try to tell him someone pulled me into one of the empty graves, but laughter comes from behind me.

Chase immediately looks over my shoulder, his brows pulling into a V. And I'm placed on my feet before I follow his gaze, turning around but keeping my back against him. No part of me can't touch him right now.

Joe, my colleague, is with a couple of the other guys from my team, and they're all laughing apologetically.

"Gotcha," one of them says as the other pretends to get pulled under. But it's as if they're trying to lighten the mood.

I shake my head, my dirty palms curling into fists as I try to process what's happening. And my ragged breath slows as reality takes a firmer grip.

It's a joke . . . Are they fucking kidding?

I drag my fingertips over the butt of my hands before wiping them on my pants, trying to get rid of the memories still gnawing at me from the back of my mind.

As if Chase senses it, his hand comes to my waist, and I let out a deep exhale.

"We didn't mean to scare you so bad. It was just a prank," Joe chuckles. "It's tradition."

He shrugs, and I nod, trying to recalibrate.

"A prank?" Chase's deep voice levels from behind me. "Are you fucking serious?"

I glance over my shoulder to see his jaw tense. He looks fucking murderous.

Joe lifts a burger to his mouth. "Come on, no hard feelings?"

But it hits the floor, smacked right out of his hand.

"What the fuck, man?" Joe rushes out.

"Sorry," Chase grinds out. "No hard feelings, right?"

Joe gulps, and the other guys shove their hands in their pockets, nodding sheepishly before they whisper more apologies to me.

But I'm turned around and pulled back into the safety of Chase's arms, and it feels like I can breathe again. So I do, slowly and deeply until all the fear I felt, while still lingering, quickly begins to get replaced by anger.

What a bunch of . . .

My thought is finished by Chase. "Pricks."

"Agreed." I say, letting out a whoosh of breath, before he releases me again.

I'm staring up at him, but before I can thank him, Derek and Devin rush over, their hands full with plates as they stare at me wide eyed, talking with their mouths full.

"Eves, you good? We brought you all the cookies you love. Fuck everyone else." . . . "Yeah, Joe likes them, too, but now he can't have any . . . What a dick. Want us to piss on his car? We will."

I can't help but chuckle, and it feels nice. Apparently, the sentiment is shared, because Chase does the same.

"I'm all good," I say, still sounding too winded. "I just got scared—a victim of a successful prank."

Chase scoffs when I say it. He's still pissed. *Good.* I'll get there fully, but I'm still shaken.

I motion to the guys, smiling up at Chase. "These are my assistants, Derek and Devin . . . Guys, this is my . . ." *My what? What is he? Because he's more than a friend.* "Chase. This is Chase."

"Oh shit," they say at the same time.

That's when all my thoughts catch up and spill out.

"Wait! What are you . . . How did you . . ." I take a deep breath, letting my mouth make friends with my brain. "Why are you here?"

Devin laughs. "She asked the same question in three ways . . . That's funny."

I ignore the Brothers Grimm, still staring at Chase, who finally looks down at me, the tension in his face relaxing as he gives me a grin. "I brought you dinner."

The boys nod, pointing to the catering on the table as I look over and laugh. For fuck's sake. Of course he did.

His heavy hand kneads my shoulder as he leans in closer. "Evil, you always complain about how the food sucks. So, I present a better burger with a spicy aioli sauce, garlic steak fries since you're on set with vampires, a classic Caesar salad, and the most delicious berry compote tarts, because I know how much of a lady of the night you are for them."

Devin takes my hand, tugging me forward as he rambles off about all the goodness waiting to be devoured. But Derek stays back, staring at Chase's profile. I look back, eavesdropping on the conversation for as long as I can.

Chase slowly turns his face to Derek's as Derek smiles wide and says, "So you're the dude."

It's as if they speak the same language, because Chase nods. "Yep. I am."

I don't know what that means, but I do know the one thing I didn't want happening is happening again.

Chase is having a moment. And it's a really big one.

Chapter Twelve

Chase

I never left.

Her location shoot was an hour away, but the plan was to deliver the food and come back. I mean, I'd hoped she'd introduce me around . . . as a friend. But I was also happy to just feed her.

Until I heard her scream.

I wasn't even in the park, but I came running because it sounded just like . . . *Fuck.* I can't even go there in my head, but I know she did because I heard what she said . . . she said *he.*

Evie was back in that night, even if only for a split second, which is why I never left. I waited around, really fucking tired, pretending to ignore all the security checks in the form of glances she gave me.

Because I needed her to know that no matter where she was, I was there too.

And when she packed up, so did I.

But now, watching her from the doorway as she stands aimless in the middle of her room, I'm at a loss for what to say or do. The night's caught up with her. All the adrenaline gone, and now only the aftereffects of her panic attack hang heavy on her small frame.

Evie's feisty and spunky and an absolute force of nature. But she still feels like the softest wind could knock her over.

With a heavy exhale, I uncross my arms, pushing off the jamb, and walk inside her room, saying something so I don't startle her.

"Hey, let me help you."

I come up behind her, my fingers gently hooking under the strap of her bag before I slide it off her shoulder and place it on her bed. She looks down at the ground and rubs her forehead, letting out a sigh.

"You don't have to do anything for me, Chase. I'm fine. You've done enough."

She says it as I walk past her toward the bathroom.

I can feel her eyes on me as I turn on the bathtub, filling it with warm water, testing it with the back of my hand to make sure it's hot enough.

"Bubble bath?" I ask, locking eyes with her.

She stares at me for a moment, like there are a million thoughts running through her, before she points to a cabinet, saying nothing. So I open it, finding some other jars labeled bath salt, as well as the bubble bath.

The sound of the water bubbles whooshes as I pour it all in and walk back inside the bedroom, extending my hand, motioning with my head for her to come with me.

Evie frowns, and I think she's going to push back, but she doesn't. Instead, she takes a hesitant step forward and slips her soft palm into mine.

"For the record, I can undress myself," she says quietly.

Her eyes lift, slowly meeting mine again. There's not nearly enough snark behind them for me to stop worrying, but I play along, saying something outlandish as I lead her inside the bathroom.

"Oh, I know. You used to strip in my dreams plenty."

She huffs a surprised laugh. "Is that so?"

I shrug, giving her a wink over my shoulder. "Duh. We're just friends now, so you don't do that anymore, which is why I said 'used to.'"

Or maybe I'm yours . . . *"This is my . . . Chase. This is Chase."*

She places her phone down on the counter, looking at the filling tub, seemingly lost in thought, so I start to walk away.

But she grabs the bottom of my shirt, not looking at me. And her voice is so quiet that it makes me want to get back in my car, drive the hour back, and punch that motherfucker in his goddamn face for that prank.

"Don't go too far, okay?"

I eat my thoughts and nod. "I won't. Promise."

As her fingers drift away, I have an overwhelming urge to pull her back into my arms like I did on set, but I don't think she'd let me anymore. So I walk back out, into the bedroom, hearing the door close softly behind me.

Fuck. I run my fingers through my hair as I look around the room, trying to think of what else I can do for her. There has to be something.

That's when a thought strikes.

"Hey, I'll be right back," I call out, walking quickly out of the room to grab my laptop and something else I think she'll appreciate.

I'm back in minutes, standing in front of the door, a little out of breath. Hopeful to make shit better for her, even though I know nothing ever makes what we feel *better*.

Except . . . The thought hits me hard because that's not totally true for me. I feel good when she's around . . . and I think about that night less.

Evie brings me ease.

I want to try and give that to her tonight.

"I'm back . . . Are you all bubbled up? Can I come in?"

I hear her huff a half-hearted laugh. "Yes. I'm indecently decent."

A chuckle accompanies my struggle to open the door. I can only use a few fingers because my laptop is in one hand, shot glasses are in the other, and a bottle of booze under my arm.

But I get it open, using my shoulder to push through, peeking my face around the door with a grin.

"Hi," she breathes out, lifting a toe out of the bubbles to touch the faucet.

Her toenails are painted red. And I can't describe what that's doing to me right now because if I did, I'd be standing here with an erection.

Especially since there's nothing but her head bobbing above a bathtub full of bubbles, those long braids all wrapped up on top of her head in a cute white bow.

"I come bearing gifts." I smirk, coming out from behind the door, showing my left hand first. "For a movie while you soak." She smiles, so I slide my right hand around the door, presenting the glasses. "For some chill because the night sucked."

Her brows rise. "Shots?"

I nod, shrugging to draw her attention to the long-necked bottle tucked under my arm. "Limoncello . . . We keep it classy."

She lifts her arm, water and suds dripping off before taking both the yellow shot glasses, letting me turn around to set up my laptop on the counter. But she lets out a shaky breath, so I turn back around and reach for my glass.

"Let's do these first?"

Evie licks her lips as I uncork the bottle and fill them. She hands me mine before our eyes connect. Goddamn, I will never stop thinking how pretty those eyes are. Her eyes are prettier than all my other *friends'* eyes.

Friend. That's a dumb word.

She raises it like she's giving me a cheers before knocking it back.

"Gettin' right to it," I tease before giving her the same nod of my glass, but before I can lift it to drink, she reaches out and steals it, gulping *it* back too.

"What the—" I fake protest, watching her wipe the back of her wet hand over her mouth. "I take it you needed a double?"

"Something like that," she breathes out, looking up at me. "Call it liquid courage."

I'd like to call it fucking hot. But that's not what she needs right now, so with that thought, I give her a wink and start to turn around to tend to the movie, but her voice halts my movement.

No, not her voice—her hand on the waistband of my jeans.

I blink down at her as I stand there in silence. She's just staring up at me, those eyes saying so much while her mouth says nothing at all.

To say I'm caught off guard would downplay how I'm also intrigued. I watch her swallow, looking for the courage to say what she wants. That's why she took my shot—her liquid courage.

But surely no matter what it is she wants to say, she knows I'll understand. That whatever she wants, I'd get.

I part my lips to tell her in case she doesn't, but her fingernails barely scrape my stomach. And that makes my breath come out ragged in the quiet of the room as I only manage to whisper, "Evie."

She says nothing. Just stares up at me.

We're breathing in sync, eyes fixed. And the drip of the faucet is the only sound in the room as her chest rises and falls.

The familiar pull I have to her starts to cloud my judgement, so I blink a few times, about to back away, but she beats me to the punch.

"You should get in." Her voice is husky and breathless.

Fuck draws out in my head. There's no way I'm hearing her right.

But I know I am. I felt it the moment she laid eyes on me just now.

She peeks up at me through long lashes, her bottom lip drawn between her teeth before it glides out slowly.

"What happened to being just friends . . ."

I ask, but I don't care about the answer.

The silence grows around us, as if it's stilling to make room for the electricity growing between us. When she doesn't answer, I test her resolve, rocking back on my heels to move away, but she grips my jeans tighter and sits up.

Goddamn.

Water sloshes, and my knees feel weak as water slides between her full breasts, soapy bubbles slowly falling from her nipples.

She's looking up at me, topless and brazen.

God never created a more beautiful woman.

"Get in, Chase. We can go back to being friends tomorrow."

I look deeply into her eyes, understanding exactly what she means—a one and done—but I shake my head anyway because now I do need to know why.

Both her hands come to my jeans as the shine in her eyes makes me feel how raw she is.

"There's too much going on inside of me. I'm still too scared, and for whatever reason, you're the only one that makes that go away. I don't understand it . . . and I don't want to analyze it. But you're the only place I feel safe. *You* take it all away."

We don't have to analyze it, because I understand it. Everything she's saying . . . none of it could ever make sense to anyone else except for us.

What she doesn't get is we feel the same.

Evie closes her eyes as if she's talking to herself. "I just need a moment . . ." Her lashes flutter open as she locks that exquisite gaze back on mine. "Please give me one."

I'll give her as many as she wants. Every day. For the rest of my life.

Because I'm crazy about the girl.

She never had to ask me twice. Period. The end.

Without another word, I step directly into the tub, T-shirt, jeans, and socks. She gasps up at my smile before I sit down, bounding water over the sides.

"What? You wanted a moment . . . How am I doing?"

There's relief in her smile as I slide my hand around her slick body, pulling it flush to mine.

"Do you remember how to do this?" I tease, my voice low and deep. "Since the official statement is we never happened."

We're face-to-face, her bare legs wrapped around me. Our lips barely touching as she reaches over my shoulders, gathering my wet T-shirt and dragging it up and over my back.

Water drips on my head when she pulls it over, before bringing her lips close to mine as she answers, "You're like riding a bike . . . The real question is, do you remember how to do *me*?"

She tosses my shirt on the floor, and the fabric hits with a smack. But my attention's on her as my stomach caves, tickled by the smallest amount of the curly hair she leaves unwaxed. Evie's breasts press against my chest as she drapes her arms over my shoulders.

Fuck, she feels good.

The corner of my lips pull into a smirk. "Evil, fucking you is the only thing I'm better at than cooking."

And I'll stand by that for life.

Her eyes are locked on mine, anticipating my move. But I take in a deep inhale-exhale as she searches my eyes, my palms exploring the slippery surface of her back.

I could explode and seal my mouth over hers. Kiss her roughly until her perfect pout is bruised and we're fucking like animals.

But I won't.

Instead, I lean in slowly, closing the millimeters that separate us, and kiss her, gently. Our warm lips press along with our bodies. And I feel her shudder before her wet hands weave through my hair.

She asked for me to take it all away, and the only way I can do that is to make it last until she's so fucking spent that all she can do is sleep.

And even then, I won't leave her.

My eyes are closed as her full lips part, welcoming mine to glide between them. We're slow and steady, the world fading into fuzzy edges and blurred lines as we kiss, lips gliding and slipping between the other's before I tilt my head and tease the tip of my tongue to hers.

A quiet moan leaves her throat before she wraps her arms tighter around my neck, dipping her tongue inside my mouth to dance with mine. Our breath mingles as we lose ourselves to this.

I swear to god, time stops. Because nothing outside this tub matters.

It's just her and this goddamn kiss.

My head rocks as we entangle passionately, deeply kissing to the steady rhythm of lust that dances over our lips. It picks up pace as she arches her body, pressing her bare breasts against my chest, and I squeeze her tighter in a hug, feeling how hard her nipples are.

I want to put one in my mouth and roll my tongue over it until she's breathing heavy and rubbing her legs together.

But I can't stop kissing her.

My hold loosens to let my hands explore her slick, sudsy body, running them down her waist to her ass.

She sighs into my mouth, circling her hips.

Goddamn. Everything about the way she moves her body and responds to my touch is divinely sexual. Evie is effortlessly erotic.

And all I want is her naked body on mine, skin to skin, completely connected.

My hands splay over her ribcage, lifting her off me because I'm still wearing my fucking jeans. She groans her dissent as our mouths break apart, our faces staying trained in each other's directions, still wanting more.

"Unbuckle," I make out before we're locked on each other again, lips sealed as if our lives depend on it.

We're more breathless this time, the kiss amping up to fevered and decadently impassioned as she reaches down under the warm water, fumbling around for the button on my jeans, before I feel the waistband loosen.

"Off," I growl, mad I have to stop kissing her again before I stand, and she squeals.

Water splashes up over her face as I shove them down my legs, throwing them to where my shirt's creating a pool on the tile. She playfully splashes back at me, so I rumble a growl, leaning down, ready to pounce, but Evie pushes to her knees in front of me. And I'm arrested.

She looks up at me with those amber eyes, slowing time as she reaches for the boxer briefs clinging to my skin before, inch by inch, she slowly peels the waistband, then lets the fabric drag roughly over my hips.

My jaw slacks, eyes hooded as I stare down at her beautiful face and watch her undress me.

The way her fingers make little gliding motions as she gathers the material gives me goose bumps. But as she pulls them down, the change of air hits the smooth tip of my strained cock, making me suck in a breath.

My hard length bobs forward, heavy and veiny, begging for her attention.

"I want to taste you," she whispers against my skin, pressing a kiss just under my belly button.

But as much as I want her mouth on me, I want inside her more. So I reach out, gripping her wrist, stopping her from taking the briefs down any further.

Evie licks her lips as I shake my head.

"No. That's for round two. Round one is us . . . me between your legs, our eyes locked, mouths hovered, while we make slow, sweaty love. And we don't stop until you come so hard, sound stops being an option."

I don't give her time to protest before I reach down, cupping my hands under her armpits and dragging her up. All the way up, so she's forced to wrap her legs around my waist.

"Okay?"

She stays silent, her eyes never leaving mine, but she nods.

"Good."

I right my briefs and step out of the bath. One strong hand on her ass, the other palm presses to her back, my fingers sliding up toward the nape of her neck.

Our gaze stays locked as I walk her out of the bathroom, wet socks and all.

My ass flexes with each sturdy step back into her room before I lay her down on the bed, keeping a hand on her heavenly body as I jerk my briefs down, kicking them off along with my socks.

She scoots back toward the headboard, and I follow, our bodies only staying inches away.

We're still staring into each other's eyes. And it's intense.

She shivers as I nestle between her thighs, letting my hard cock press against her clit. But she's not cold, she's overwhelmed by this feeling.

I am too.

I can't describe it. The way we just fit feels like an addiction I never want fixed. Her knees fall open as she slides her hands up my back while licking her lips and all I can think is *Goddess.*

Damn. A heavy breath leaves me as I curl my hands into fists around the comforter, the fabric gathering between my fingers.

"All I can think about is how tight and wet your cunt is for me."

She takes a quiet breath, tipping her chin to the ceiling and closing her eyes as she runs her hands up my chest.

I remember how warm she feels. And how with each stroke, she contracts, trying to keep me inside her forever.

My voice comes out rough and deep. "I *need* to fuck you, before I do anything else. But you don't come. I mean it."

I rock against her clit, hovered over her, giving her the friction she wants, before I'm rewarded by her gasp. *Top five sound.* Keeping my weight off her, I hold myself up with one hand as I reach between us with the other, taking my throbbing cock in hand, position it at her entrance.

She whimpers feeling my tip, and my jaw tenses. I circle it, teasing her, letting it push inside for a moment as I drag my hand down over my shaft before I deny her.

"Oh god . . . Chase," she breathes out seductively.

My eyes close, and her nails gently scratch up my back before I finally go home. She sucks in a breath when I slowly push my hard cock inside her, stretching her pussy around my size.

"Yes . . ." she pants as I reach down, pulling one of her legs up and over my hip, my fingers digging into her soft skin.

The feel of her slickness over my shaft takes my breath away as I bottom out. Fuck. She feels so damn good. So much so, I press my pelvis into her harder, wanting to go even deeper before I feel her contract around me.

"You're perfect," I whisper.

She says nothing, but her mouth is on my neck, kissing and licking before she sucks, hard.

That's right. Mark me, baby.

I slide my other hand up her arm, holding her wrist above her head. My eyes drop down the curves of her body. Her breasts are full, and her dark nipples pebbled. And there are goose bumps on her soft stomach that lead all the way down to where we're connected.

My eyes are fixed there, staring at her swollen clit peeking from between her curly hair, as I watch my cock draw out of her, only to push back in.

"You feel so good, Evil," I breathe out hoarsely. "I could fuck you for days at a time."

"Promise?" she moans. "Because your dick is magical . . ."

I smirk, connecting our eyes. "You like me fucking you, Evie?"

She nods, but I raise my brows, making her bite her bottom lip before she whispers, "Yes, Chef."

"Good girl."

Her body reacts along with her face as I roll my hips, giving her everything I promised. Breaths turn into panting. And wrists held hostage become held hands as we fuck. No . . . make love.

I'm making love to her.

Our mouths so close we're sharing air, our eyes connected so deeply I can almost read her thoughts. I'm taking my goddamn time.

The taut part of my stomach rubs her clit in such a perfect way with each stroke that I feel her wrap her other leg around me, but I told her not to come. And I meant it. We have other business to handle before she comes like this.

This was just a taste test to satisfy my palate.

I push in and out as she arches and mewls. Fuck, I'm almost trembling with the need to keep going, but I pull out, leaving her gasping and me growling.

"No . . . come back," she breathes out hard, but if I do, I won't be able to stop.

She keeps her legs wrapped around me, trying to reconnect us, but I ignore her, unhitching her legs before I sit up and flip her over without warning.

"Chase," she squeals, making me grin.

My hands are rough as I force her ass in the air and make my way down, positioning my face between her legs.

"Have a seat," I rumble deeply.

She sits, straddling my face, blinking down through those long lashes of hers as she bites her bottom lip. I know she's well versed in exactly what I mean. And to prove my point, Evie lifts one hand at a time, grabbing the headboard before she covers her wet pussy over my mouth.

Fuck. Me.

The heavenly taste of her lust hits my tongue as it thrusts inside her. I swear to god her pussy was made for me. I grab her hips to move her exactly where I want her, before I flatten my tongue and run it up to her clit.

"Oh my god," she moans, smacking the headboard.

I'm licking her clean and she's already trembling, trying to lift up. To make me chase her cunt to eat. But I hold her in place, trading off between laving her with my tongue and sucking her clit.

Damn. My cock's so hard it's almost painful, because everything about the taste of her is so goddamn good.

Evie is my favorite meal.

Her hips begin to rock and circle as I lick and kiss her pussy, making out with it while running my hands up and down her waist.

I will never tire of touching her.

She's soft and delicate, but rough exactly when I want her to be.

"Don't stop. Please. It feels so good," she pants, breathless and begging.

One of my hands slides up her body, cupping her breast before I pinch her nipple, rolling it between my fingers.

She gasps, covering her hand over mine, kneading it along with me.

I growl into her clit, flicking it with my tongue quickly before hooking an arm over her leg. My fingers spread her wet pussy open as I seal my mouth over it like a suction cup, doing figure eights over her throbbing center.

"Oh fuck . . . fuck," she yells, and I feel her stomach contract as her hips thrust in small movements, fucking my face.

The need to make her come is animalistic. A base desire. And it's all I can focus on. I want her come in my mouth and to feel her come undone . . . shaking and trembling.

"Oh god. Yes," she whines as her hand slips from the bed and into my hair.

Her clit is throbbing, a pulse thrumming inside it. I grip her hips hard, relentlessly devouring her pussy. All the while mesmerized, watching her as she tilts her head back, her beautiful tits on display as her whole body tenses.

Yes. Come on. Give it to me.

She slaps her left hand down on my chest, using it for leverage, while her right hand grips my hair as she fucking rides my face.

Fuck. It's the sexiest thing I've ever seen.

Her cries are stuttered, barely audible, as she thrusts her hips forward. I can barely breathe, but who the fuck cares. Let me die this way. I'd thank the heavens above.

I eat her out, growling, wanting her to shatter until she grinds into my mouth, sucking in deep breaths, chanting "Yes, yes, yes, yes . . ." and explodes.

"Fuck," she screams gutturally, quaking and tense.

I almost come with her because it's that sexy. Until her body retreats like she can't take it. *Fuck that.* I hold her in place.

"I can't, Chase . . . oh fuck . . . oh my god . . ."

My strong hands grip her waist as I lift her up, keeping my mouth on her. She whimpers and pants, only breaking away as she falls backward onto the bed.

I'm on her in an instant, because this time, I want to feel her come again around my cock.

Her eyes are wide and wild as she wipes the glisten off my mouth before pulling me into a long, deep kiss. Goddamn, I love that she'll taste herself. No boundaries between us is exactly how I want it.

I can't help myself, I want all of her, all the time. Without exception.

She reaches down, taking my cock in her hand, circling it as she strokes me, knowing I'm still coated in her. My eyes roll back into my head as my stomach jerks, because she's too good at that.

"Easy, baby . . . I like it too much."

She hums an appreciative moan as our gazes lock again.

"But it's your turn," she says huskily, lifting her chin for me to kiss her again.

So I oblige before I say, "Then, baby, take your hand off my cock and open your legs. Because I told you that I wanted to fuck you until sound wasn't an option."

This time I'm not gentle, thrusting inside of her the minute she spreads her legs. She gasps, gripping my wrists beside her head as I fuck her hard.

I'm thrusting inside her wet cunt as her body blooms underneath me. Nipples growing hard again, her lips parted as she exhales hard against the rhythm.

"Yes," she sighs. She slides her knees up and down my body, wrapping her legs around me.

Evie wraps one arm around my neck, pulling me closer for a kiss as she cradles my face. And the moment our lips meet, I pound into her harder, because she brings out the animal in me.

Every part of us is touching, and she's kissing and biting my bottom lip, her body begging to come again, but I'm not done enjoying myself.

I fuck her in long, hard strokes, rubbing her soft walls with my shaft as her breathing becomes more ragged and I feel my balls start to draw up.

I fuck her through rough hands all over me, insistent and pawing like she can't get close enough. Neither can I.

I fuck this girl until the sweat beads on my forehead and glistens in the small dip in her throat.

She can't keep me close enough as I draw in and out harder, faster, kissing her as I whisper how perfect she is.

"Chase . . ." she groans against my shoulder. "I'm gonna come . . . oh my god . . . I think I'm gonna come again . . ."

"That's right. Gimme what I want."

I can hear her trying to say my name, but nothing's coming out.

There's only silence and the smell of sex as we fuck harder and harder, chasing our pleasure. She's squeezing my dick so hard I can't miss that her body's ready.

We're kissing, my cock grinding into her, before she hooks her arms around my bicep. Her eyes lock to mine and I watch her fucking come for me.

She's trembling, her lips part, but no sound's coming out as her body stays locked on mine.

And that's all I can take.

I hammer inside her, feeling the sweet relief explode out of my body as I grunt and grab her jaw, keeping her eyes on mine.

Warm spurts fill her as my stomach jerks, but I can't stop fucking her, stroking my shaft inside her, softer now.

Our shaky breaths take turns as I lean down and pepper kisses over her jaw before taking her mouth again.

"That the moment you were looking for?"

"Yes, Chef."

Chapter Thirteen

Evie

It's still dusk out, so the house isn't completely dark yet, which made it easy for me to sneak out of Chase's bed just now.

The door closes quietly behind me as I tiptoe slowly over the tile to the kitchen for water. I can't believe we crossed the line not once but three times.

God. My head was so fucked yesterday.

There was all this latent emotional trauma having a dance party in my brain, and he was there . . . saving me, then saving me some more, because he kept it all at bay with only his presence.

Which doesn't make any sense, because he's the person I want to be around the least, but when he ran me a bath, all I could think was that I wanted him inside me.

But is that true . . . that I want to be around him the least, because it feels like a lie.

No . . . It was a dirty thought. But unlike the countless others I've had about him, it didn't pass.

I just kept thinking about it while I watched him pour in bubble bath and while he ran out of my room to grab the supplies I instinctively knew he was getting.

But I could only know something like that if I knew him . . .

Ever so slightly, I shake my head, trying to rid myself of these stupid thoughts as I open the fridge. No, I was just kind of spiraling yesterday, so when he walked back in and looked at me with those bright-green eyes and the most sincere smile, he wasn't just having a moment, he *was* the moment.

That's it. I used him to numb myself.

My hand closes around a bottle of water, pulling it out before I open it, lost to more of my thoughts.

But if that's true, then why does it feel more like I fell into him because I needed to? Like it was the only way I could heal.

Dammit. Either way, I shouldn't have done it. I knew better, and now I wonder if I fucked us both with last night's little escapade. He doesn't deserve that . . . *Oh my god, why am I caring about his feelings?*

This is Chase.

Silly, goofy, ridiculous . . .

I pause, my brows drawing together as my feelings begin to piece themselves together like a puzzle. Still, I try and hold on to my indignance.

No . . . This is Chase the . . .

My heart interferes with my head again, cutting off the thought. Holy shit. I think I might have a crush on Chase.

Or maybe I'm hitting rock bottom mentally. Frankly, liking him and a full breakdown aren't mutually exclusive, so . . .

No. This can't be happening to me.

I'm supposed to have an epic love story. That's the plan. In my twenties, I keep a roster. I live life to the fullest. In my thirties, I get serious, start looking for the one. And when I meet a man who I know possesses the qualities to be my equal, he will yearn for me.

Yearn.

And then like a scene out of *Pride & Prejudice*, he'll walk over a hill in a cashmere coat and fucking kiss me until I whimper.

Chase twerks in the kitchen while singing Shakira songs, doing the accent. He fucking asked a total stranger the other day if they could tell his Crocs were fake.

The fact that he wears Crocs in public automatically disqualifies him as my soulmate. Jane Austen would roll over in her grave.

And yet . . . I do. I have a deeply problematic crush on Chase.

How have I not seen this? *I'm so sorry, Janie . . . What have I done?*

Princess meows from where she's perched on the couch, so I walk to her, petting under her chin, wishing there was someone to pet me instead.

This is too much emotional turmoil. But what did I expect? To not fall for the person who's the human equivalent of a blankie for me.

Sometimes I'm the smartest person in the room, and other times I wonder how I make it through my day without dying.

And not seeing this coming is one of those moments. Because RIP my dignity.

On cue, Princess rubs her head on me, so I smile, thankful for a distraction. "Are you hungry, little tyrant? Let Auntie hook you up, because one of us should be happy."

Princess digs her claws into the furniture, so I pick her up and carry her with me toward my room before I hear a phone buzz. I shift my head to see it's Chase's, lying face up on the kitchen island.

Is it polite to look at someone's phone? . . . *No.* Did he leave it up for me to see? *Yes.*

Peach squirms, so I let her go, before she runs into my room and I let curiosity get the best of me, having a little peek.

Except all I can see is who's texting him but none of the message.

My brows raise as I look at the name. *Hookers* . . . If that STD gives me an STD, I will tell everyone I caught it at his restaurant. Ewww.

How is this the guy making me change my favorite color from green to red? How? I want answers from someone in this universe. Stat.

I can't like Chase . . . *but bitch, you do.*

The curtains in the living room are still drawn as I turn to look out of the windows, but I'm still so preoccupied, I just stand there in the dimness before I give my head a shake.

I'm grumbling and plotting his demise as I walk toward my room. The door's cracked open, but the light's on behind it. I always leave it on, but Chase must've done it for me this time before we went for round three in his room.

My palm slides against the grain of the wood, pressing it open as a crunch followed by a deep, menacing stuttered growl pierces my ears, making the little hairs on my neck stand on end.

Princess is in the middle of my bed, standing over a dark-red mess of black fur, her gold eyes locked on me as she chews on a long spindly tail . . .

Oh my god.

I scream and swing around, trying to hurry out of my room.

"Chase!"

I'm scrambling back as I hear two loud bangs next door. If I had to guess, one was him hitting the floor, and the other was him hitting the door because, as I think it, he bursts through it, eyes wide, hair a mess, his hand over his junk.

"Oh my god. Get dressed. Get dressed."

I'm already past him into the living room, so I throw a pillow from the couch at him. He catches it, using it to cover himself.

"What the fuck is going on? What's wrong? Why are you screaming?"

I shake my head, dancing on the balls of my feet. "There's something dead . . . . it's on my bed. Ohhh my god."

"What do you mean?" he yells at me again.

I let out a breath, shaking out my hands, and look around for Princess. "What I mean is Goldie's fucking cat left me a present. A dead rat, to be exact."

"Noooo," he drawls, taking a step away from my room as I nod.

"Yes." My head momentarily tips back as I pace by the kitchen counter. "This is why people shouldn't have a cat door. That monster's gone full predator."

Chase puts his hand over his mouth, then parts two fingers to whisper, "Are you sure? Go back and check. What if it's still alive?"

"Chase," I bark. "I am not putting anything out of its misery. Fuck." My eyes lock back to his. "Lion King over here needs to get it together. This is not cool."

"Well." He shrugs. "I blame your sister and Noah. They left her, and now she's got abandonment issues and decided to go full Dexter."

I scrunch my nose, looking serious. "Go check. You have to . . . It might still be alive."

"No."

"Chase."

"Absolutely not."

"Okay, then I'll call a guy I went to college with who lives out here. He's a firefighter . . . Come to think of it, he did this thing with a hose once . . ."

"Fine," he bellows before walking to the couch to grab another pillow and covering his ass with it. "Let me put on my doing-disgusting-shit pants."

A chuckle almost bursts from my mouth, but I keep it in as he walks back inside his room. Princess meows, and I shiver as I glare down at her where she's licking her paws in my doorway.

"Do I need to call the people from *Criminal Minds*, or have you had your fill?"

I turn my head, looking back inside my room, quickly doing the heebie-jeebies dance all over again before shaking my head.

This is why I will only own dogs.

Chase

"Oh my god, those are guts . . . Chase, those are fucking entrails."

We both jump back about ten feet from the bed before Evie turns in a circle, looking like she's going to be sick. I'm shaking my head as I wipe my forehead with my forearm.

I can't use my hands because we're both gloved up like mad scientists, equipped with yellow dish gloves and goggles we found while rummaging through the garage for more protection.

Evie's face-masked glare lands on the cat, who's standing in the crack of the door, cleaning herself.

"What is wrong with you," she snaps, but the cat ignores her, still licking her paw.

"Not an ounce of remorse," I add, letting out a harsh sigh. "This level of destruction is on par with hyenas or coyotes. You're a cat named after a *Super Mario Bros* character. What the fuck, bro."

"She's like a honey badger," Evie barks, sounding nasally because of the mask. "Or a capybara . . . Did you know those things are violently aggressive?"

I draw my head back. "Is that true?"

"Yeah." She nods. "I saw a documentary . . . or clips of one online."

I let out another deep breath and look back at the grotesquerie on the bed.

"Okay, come on. We gotta get this over with. Get it done."

I click my kitchen tongs together a few times, knowing I'm never using them again, but technically, they're not mine, they're Noah's, so whatever.

She's humming a squeal, dancing on the balls of her feet while standing in place, because she's dreading this as much as I am. But still, I inch closer, forcing her to do it at the same time. I can hear her breathing as she holds open a big black garbage bag.

It's the extra-large kind that supposedly doesn't break.

The closer to the bed I get, the more I'm regretting this.

Goddammit. Why are we doing this?

Oh yeah, because she's a lunatic who, after I said we should just pull the blanket and the sheets and toss it all out, declared we needed a goddamn funeral for the "*victims of this senseless attack.*" Her words.

My knees hit the mattress before I lean over it, and I stop to fake cry. I look up at the ceiling for a minute because I'm not cut out for shit like this.

It's like she can read my mind because she yells, "Chase. I swear to god . . . Men used to go to war. Pull it together."

I huff an empty laugh. "Joke's on you, buddy. Back in the *Game of Thrones* days, I would've been that sickly kid everyone was hoping would live just long enough to be king."

She jiggles the bag viciously, the loud whipping of plastic filling the room. I jerk my whole body in protest.

"Lock in, dammit," she barks.

I draw out a breath. "Fine. I'm fucking locked. Fuck."

We both let out a few harsh breaths before our eyes meet, and we inhale, then exhale together, our gaze never breaking.

"Okay," I whisper, and she nods. I finally look down at the carnage again.

It's time.

I extend the tongs on a shaky breath to pick up victim number one, swallowing, and try not to close my eyes.

"Get the bag ready," I say quietly, immediately wondering why I'm whispering.

Who's hearing me? Not the rats.

"It's open. I'm here," she counters. "Just do it already."

"Stop rushing me," I grind out.

Dammit. I'm a chef. I can do this. This is just like picking the lobsters or making frog legs. I even had to kill a live chicken once when visiting France. I can do this.

I slowly slip my extraction tool around the furry body, but as soon as I depress the tongs, I can feel the squishiness.

"Oh god," I grit between my teeth, my whole body shivering as I breathe through inflated cheeks, because getting the heebie-jeebies is an understatement.

I glance up, and Evie's looking away with the bag extended in front of her. But she's two feet too far to the left.

"Evie, I'm gonna drop dead rat on you if you keep looking away. Hold the bag in place."

She squeals, looking back at me, and that's when everything falls apart.

And I mean the damn rat.

The moment I pick it up, its body falls apart.

Evie screams. I yell, "Fuck this." And the tongs land directly on top of the murder scene.

She hops away, chanting *Oh my god, oh my god* over and over, abandoning the damn bag, her hands in fists up by her shoulders.

I take a bunch of steps backward, trying to keep my lunch down as I groan.

"Evie," I level, forcing her eyes on mine. "We're tossing it all. If you want to say a few words, this is the time."

She nods, finally on board, before she clasps her yellow-gloved hands together like she's praying. So I do the same.

"Okay," she says on an exhale. "Dear whatever or whoever is up there. Although definitely dear ma'am . . . please let these rats live their spirits out in a palace of cheese. And if they're set for reincarnation, let them come back as women in STEM who cure disease."

I open one eye, peeking at her, only to see her looking back at me.

"It seems full circle from the plague. Anyway . . . please let them be badass, and make sure Princess—" We both look at the killer cat. "Make sure she comes back as a rat."

"Amen," I say resolutely, hearing Evie say, "Awomen."

I chuckle before we both start pulling the sheets out from where they're tucked, tossing the ends toward the middle and folding the blanket over itself until it becomes a big pile.

I motion to her with my hand. "Gimme the bag."

She does, so I open it as wide as it goes before slipping it around the blanket until it's all inserted inside.

As I pull it away, Evie gasps, "Oh no. That's so gross."

My face snaps to the mattress. The blood from the rats not only went through the blanket and the sheets, but it seeped all the way into the mattress.

"That's not coming out with a Bissel," I offer to her scowling face.

"I am so not sleeping on that," she says, shaking her head. "There's no way, even if it did come out. This room is only eligible for participation in a fire, not my sleep."

I can't even concentrate on what she's saying because I'm too busy pulling the drawstring closed. Am I sweating? Probably. Goddammit, I hate this.

Something between a grumble and a whine tickles my chest as I pray that I don't feel anything when I have to pick this damn thing up off the bed.

"Door," I say, and she rushes there to hold it open.

This is why being a dude is the fucking worst. You always have to do shit like this—clean up the nastiest parts of life, all while being the guy who isn't scared of anything. It's BS. What was I supposed to do if these things were alive?

Get bit so she could run away, that's what.

I wrap my arms around the bag, picking it up because if I use the handle, it'll break. And I'm not capable of coming back from that. We'd just have to sell Noah and Goldie's house and get them a new one.

I'd have to be like, *Sorry, guys, I needed to make an executive decision on short notice. Hope it works out.*

I'm holding my breath as I make my way past the perp, still licking her paws like a fucking serial killer.

"Your Honor, she's guilty as charged," I breathe out before holding my breath again.

Evie follows me out of the room, glancing down at Princess too. "Yeah. It's the electric chair for you. No final meal."

She runs past me to the back door off the side of the kitchen, opening that one, too, as I walk as fast as humanly possible, seeing as I'm going to need to take a breath soon. But my feet don't fail me as I hustle through it and directly to the outside garbage cans.

The sunlight almost blinds me since the house is so buttoned up, making me squeeze my eyes closed for a second.

Evie must think I'm waiting on her because she breathes out *Oh shit, sorry* before running toward me and lifting the lid to the garbage can so I can toss the bag inside.

I'm still blinking when I toss it in and shiver. *Fucking gross.*

The moment she drops the lid, I suck in air, finally breathing again, and she smiles.

"We have got to stop trauma bonding," she teases, nudging me, but I give her a deadpan look before I laugh and take my gloves off, tossing them in the trash.

There's no reason for me to glance around, but I do.

She doesn't seem to notice, following suit and removing her gloves too. I run my hands through my hair and push my goggles to the top of my head.

"I'll make you a deal. Feel free to never call me for anything ever again. I'm done. You're too high maintenance. I gotta tap out now. I don't care how beautiful you are. I won't be bought by your impeccable face card."

She giggles, and I smirk, loving how she's letting me flirt with her, even though we're back to being just friends . . . I remember the rules. I don't like them, though.

"I really owe you one, though."

It's stupid, but I don't like being out here, exposed, for some reason. I think I'm just weirded out by the rat. But still, without asking permission, my now bare hands fall to her waist before I turn her around.

Again, she doesn't seem to notice my inner thoughts or my hands on her. And it's the my-hands-on-her part that's taking up space in my brain.

Maybe she's oblivious because she's too busy taking off her goggles. Or maybe it's because my touch is natural . . .

I'm staring at the back of her head and she's talking. But all I want to say is *Why are you fighting this so much?*

This thing that's always been between us, and not just because of last night, because that wasn't our first rodeo. It's the kind of pull people can't create.

"I cannot believe we have to sleep with a killer tonight," she mutters as I guide her back toward the door. "Who knows what could happen to us. You know, I read about a woman whose face was actually eaten by her cats."

I frown, closing the door behind us. "It's a good thing there's only one Peach in this house."

I don't say Princess because there's two of those.

Evie walks out of my hands toward the kitchen, glancing back over her shoulder at me.

And that's the moment it happens. I'm done. I'm not pretending anymore.

"Heads up," she levels. "I'm never going back in that room again. And I'm not sleeping in Goldie's bed, either, because I'm just as disgusted over what's probably happened on that mattress too. So, it's couch city for you."

"No."

She scowls, crossing her arms. "What do you mean no?"

I shake my head, walking toward her. Fuck it, I'm going to say the ugly truth whether she likes it or not.

"I mean absolutely fucking not."

She's backing up as I walk forward until her ass hits the barstool, so I grab her waist, sitting her on it before I cage her in. Both my palms smacking down on the island on either side of her.

"I mean that I'm going to sleep with my fucking girlfriend."

She draws her head back like she's wondering what the hell I'm talking about, so I clarify.

"We're not doing this anymore, Evil."

"Not doing what?" she says on barely a whisper.

I ignore her, dominating the conversation. "I like you, Evie Monroe. That's never been a secret."

Her lips part, then close. Yep. Stay quiet. It's my turn.

"And you like me too. Even though you like to try and pretend you don't."

She swallows hard.

"Fuck. I'm tired of trying to win you over, conning you into coming with me to the farmers' market or to my restaurant just to prove I'm not who you think I am. Because what I've known since the first time we met is that I'm for you."

Suddenly, she finds her voice again. "You lied? Oh my god . . . of course you did, because you're a guy with a group chat full of hookers. I told you last night—"

I cut her off.

"Fuck what you said. And don't talk about my girlie pops like that. That group chat is four women in their mid-seventies who ride or die for me. So stop avoiding what I'm saying. You're not hearing me," I level, dead-ass serious as I repeat myself. "I said—I'm for you."

Silence stretches out between us before she takes a shaky breath, licking her bottom lip to a shine as I look deeply into her eyes.

"Do you want proof?" My fingers only have to shift an inch in the direction of the phone before she shakes her head.

"No, it's too ridiculous to make up."

"Good. Then stop fighting this with all your bullshit reasons for me not being the one and just give me a goddamn chance already. I'm gonna surprise you."

She's barely blinking, but the look on her face was the same as the one when I pulled her flush to me in the tub.

"Because what did I just say?" I add, before she repeats it without hesitation.

"I'm for you . . ."

I grin. "Yeah, you are." I clock the goose bumps on her arm and the way she shivers before I add, "So be in my fucking orbit. And let me in yours."

"I think I'm going to pass out," she whispers, but I keep going.

"I'm a fucking catch, baby, and I've spent a year and a half begging you to snatch me up. So I'm done with the bullshit. I'm gonna fucking kiss you, and you're gonna let me. Not with the intention to fuck, but to just kiss you because I like you and you like me. And when I'm done, if you can remember how to tell me to fuck off, feel free."

Not a breath is taken before I seal my lips over hers, slipping my tongue inside without permission. I'm going to devour her fucking mouth. Her head tilts, welcoming me, and I can't help myself. I grab her jaw, making it deeper.

She lets out a sigh that almost sounds like relief, and it makes me hum a laugh. It vibrates my lips before she weaves her fingers through my hair.

There's my girl.

My. Girl.

Mine.

The world around us stops existing. All there is, is her mouth on mine and mine on hers. I don't even care if I can't breathe. I'd rather die connected to her than any other way.

She's had me hooked from the beginning, and I swear to god I'm never giving her a reason not to fall madly in fucking love with me.

The moment I pull away, the wetness left on my lips immediately feels cold. But the beautiful thing is, she whimpers.

Her eyes spring open as she stares back at me, breathless and also a bit dazed.

I know what I did, and so does she.

"Was there something you wanted to say to me?" I level.

But she nods, then shakes her head, then blinks a few times before she says, "What in the Darcy just happened?"

I grin. "Want me to do it again but come from over a hill?"

The laugh that comes out of her bubbles slowly before it picks up. She covers my mouth so I can't see her as she takes a deep breath and says, "Holy shit. Chase Beckett . . ."

There's a chuckle shared between us before she whispers, "I can't believe I'm dating Shrek."

I bite her hand, making her squeal, before I grab her legs and wrap them around my waist.

"Right now, baby, you're gonna fuck him too."

She laughs as I pick her up and walk her back to our bedroom to really seal the deal. Because hot damn, I just made Evie Monroe my girlfriend.

Chapter Fourteen

Him

The room's dark, but that suits me fine as I listen to their soft, steady breaths.

I've been sitting in this room for some time. Watching them. Admiring my work.

Maybe tempting fate.

It feels risky, but it isn't. Not when you know everything there is to know about a person.

Worst case, they wake up, and I gut them.

It's not the plan, but I've always found comfort in alternative outcomes. The blade in my hand dangles over the arm of the chair as I keep my breath matched to theirs, inhaling and exhaling at the same time.

The cat purrs, weaving between my legs, before I lean down and pick her up. She was such a good girl today, eating the present I left behind.

I tilt my head, staring down at her.

"We're alike," I whisper quietly. "I like to play with what I kill too."

I close my eyes, hearing the memory of her screams like a fear symphony. My fingertips slowly drag down over the cat as I savor it.

My body shudders because I can feel her fear so viscerally inside my body. The way she'll scream when I take away everything she loves.

Piece by piece. In front of her.

My eyes land on Chase—the protector. The pawn.

As if on cue, he pulls Evie closer to him, wrapping his arms around her as they sleep.

I wonder if he would be embarrassed if he knew how easy it was to get them here, since he's been trying to convince her for so long. All it took was a busted pipe here and a dead rat there.

The scare on location was serendipitous, though.

Frankly, what I had planned was much worse.

The cat lets out a quiet meow, grabbing my attention, so I look down, and realize I've stopped petting her.

I resume, still watching them.

Evie snuggles closer to Chase, draping her leg over his hip. There's not a spot on them that isn't touching.

It's perfect. Everything begins and ends with them.

The stage can only be set for grief once they're in place. Hate required it. Revenge deserved it. True fear sanctified it.

Without a second thought, I place the cat down on the floor gently and stand, slowly walking toward the end of the bed.

I could take the knife in my hand and stick it in her neck, so quickly she'd never make a sound. But her eyes would open as she slowly bled out next to him and I watched.

My eyes lower as I keep my breath quiet. I have an erection.

The knife twists in my hand over and over, feeling heavy, although it's not. It's the burden I carry to hold to the plan. To keep them alive until it's time.

There's no point in killing either of them until the band's back together.

I walk around the bed, my footsteps never making a sound, to where Evie's facing before squatting down.

She lets out another sigh as I bring our faces so close I could almost . . . I breathe her in, every inhale coming into my body, and with every exhale, I enter hers. Because I want to live inside her. Be the flesh she eats, the blood she drinks, so I can rot her from the inside until she dies.

Her breath smells like cinnamon and tickles my lips as I close my mouth, leaning in closer to let them brush hers.

"It's time to begin our game," I whisper so quietly she never stirs. "First one to the end of twelve days dies. Can't wait for the opening."

Chapter Fifteen

Evie

"Where are we going?"

Chase smiles back at me, motioning with his head for me to move faster, but I keep walking slowly, so he excitedly grabs my hand and drags me behind him down a sidewalk parallel to the beach.

"This isn't just a taco food truck, trust me. It's hands down some of the best Mediterranean fusion I've ever had."

I huff a laugh, really looking at his face, trying to find a flaw. I can't. It's annoying.

"Well, that's saying something, coming from you."

"The woman who owns it migrated here ten years ago, leaving behind a restaurant her family owned back home in Greece. But the story is she fell in love with this very handsome Mexican dude—her words—during a visit and never went back."

The way he's grinning makes me do the same.

"I'll give it to you, that's pretty romantic."

"Then they broke up."

I frown. "Not so romantic."

He winks. "Her true love is food . . . so still romantic."

He wags his brows at me, pulling me even closer so our joint hands are tucked up near his chest as I chuckle.

This sounds weird, but I like the way he talks about people. It's never some kind of ploy, like most people do just to highlight something about themselves. When Chase talks about people, it's like he's spotlighting them and celebrating their own uniqueness.

I never paid attention to that before.

The truck finally comes into view, so he pulls me faster, making me squeal before he sidles up to the metal counter protruding from the opening. I let go of his hand, noticing him looking back over his shoulder at me, so I turn my face toward the water.

I have to admit he makes me nervous, even after a week of playing house. Maybe it's because there's no more sarcasm to use as a shield or the truth to deny, making me feel exposed.

Although I do like being exposed in front of him, so maybe this metaphor is not working. Regardless, I'm nervous.

"Hey," he shoots out, forcing my face back to his. "Stop it."

"Stop what?"

He lifts a brow. "Stop acting like you're embarrassed to be with me."

What? I am not that. I mean, no more than normal.

I try and tug my hand away, but he doesn't let it go. So I rush out a harsh breath. "Don't talk about yourself like that."

"What?"

"What do you mean, 'What?' You heard me," I scold him. "Don't talk shit about yourself. That's what you're doing. You're not ugly. And you're insinuating that it's what I think . . . I don't."

He chuckles before snapping his jaw shut and kissing my hand.

"One, I don't think I'm even remotely ugly, and you know it. Two, how are you giving me a compliment that makes me want to jump off a bridge?"

I shrug and smile. "It's an art form. I'm very good at it . . . Top of my class, actually."

"Mmm." He smirks. "You're also good at gaslighting. Tell me something, if you're not embarrassed, then tell the world I'm your boyfriend. Do it right now. Yell it to the rooftops."

"Are you high?" I snap.

"On life . . ."

I scowl. He's so dramatic and insane that it makes me want to impulsively poke him in the eye, but I won't. I also won't make a fool of myself yelling that he's my boyfriend.

That's dumb. Tom Cruise did that bouncing on the couch, and look what happened to him. He got dawsoned up shit's creek.

He might've deserved it, though.

"Stop being dramatic—"

The middle of my sentence is cut off as I hear "Chase!" from a very peppy voice, and my eyes immediately narrow.

Completely without my permission, although anyone that happy deserves suspicion.

I look in the direction of the voice just in time to see a woman walk out from behind the back of the food truck.

Why does she look like she just stepped out of a surf magazine? This can't be the owner.

What is wrong with me?

I shove my hands into my back pockets, trying to fix my face.

Jesus, self-diagnosing the Billy shit was one thing, but I think I'm going to need actual therapy about Chase.

She smiles, and I'm almost blinded by her goddamn teeth. Okay, that's rude.

"Hey, you."

You? Who is you?

As in answer to my inner thought . . . *Oh shit, did I say that out loud? Noooo.*

Chase looks at me, grinning. I did.

"That's their daughter. She's a little younger than you."

What does that mean? Umm, sorry for aging. I guess I should just be buried or shunned in society for being twenty-six. Where are the villagers to stone me?

She tosses her golden locks over her shoulder in a really dramatic look-at-me, I'm-so-beautiful kind of way. Jesus, when people describe beach waves, that's her hair. She's the model.

Oh god. I'm being rude about a woman I do not know. I'm a girl's girl. But because of him, I've devolved into a gremlin. Eww. This is why he's the worst.

We should break up.

Without warning, she throws her arms open to wrap them around his neck. *I'll kill her.* But Chase jukes her like he's some kind of professional NFL player, swiping his shoulder left so she misses and falls directly into my arms.

Oh my god. My eyes lock on his, and I know he sees what I'm saying inside my head because he winces.

She pulls away, apologizing, so I nod, feeling just as awkward.

"Nice to meet you?" I laugh, and so does she, but it's fake. It's all fake.

I will kill him. Maybe even tonight.

She reaches out to playfully slap his arm, but he dips it again, making me give him a *what the fuck is wrong with you* look before it dawns on me. He won't let her touch him.

He won't let another woman touch him.

My mind is warring between celebration and chastising myself. I shouldn't love that as much as I do. It's ridiculous, but then us as a couple is too.

She takes a step back, giggling. "You're so funny. Always such a jokester."

A real fucking court jester. Maybe I can find someone to behead him.

"Coral," he says after clearing his throat. "This is my . . . um, my, umm . . ." He looks at me, his brows raised as if he's daring me to say it. To say I'm his girlfriend.

Ridiculous.

"I'm Evie," I rush out, finishing his sentence.

"She's Noah's wife's sister," he piggybacks, making me frown because does my sister know this girl?

And she never told me? *Oh my god. What is wrong with me?* I am the most toxic person. I literally just started dating him.

He looks at me with an explanation because, apparently, I need one? Yes . . . yes, I do.

"I brought the parentals here once."

It's when he looks at me that I realize I need to fix my face again. But damn, I'm one of those people who others can always tell exactly what I'm thinking by the look on my face. So today's going to be a challenge.

I quickly smile and say, "Hi."

It's definitely more awkward than I was hoping. Coral glances at him, pretty much ignoring me.

"I'm mad at you."

Are you? Are you? I think to myself in the most condescending tone as she continues.

"You ghosted me."

He shakes his head, then looks at me, but I give him zero reaction. He still stares only at me while he speaks.

"I catered a surf event that Coral manages when I first got here." He looks back at her. "I don't remember having your number, sooo . . ."

"Oh," she purrs, "we should totally fix that today."

I'll break his phone and throw it in the ocean . . . along with myself because I've literally lost my mind. If I don't stop this . . .

"Um." He looks between us. "How about we get some tacos before we catch up?"

She laughs and nods, waving us over to the food truck before she walks inside. I swear to god, she's the girl who makes her ponytail swish when she walks.

Chase looks down at me, giving me an empty laugh. "We never hooked up or anything."

"And I care why?" I snark, cutting my eyes at him, knowing I care because I'm a fucking loser that likes the guy who ghosted Coral.

Fuck. Me.

"Just putting it out there," he whispers as she walks inside the truck.

I shrug, really hoping for nonchalant, but I'm probably not even at fucking chalant. "I mean, I'm sure a lot of guys are into that type, so why wouldn't you be."

It's not so much a question but more inner rage.

Because I like him so much. And by like him, I mean he makes my heart skip a beat. Skip a fucking beat.

I didn't even know I still had one.

But I do, because it's fluttering over his stupid smile and his dumb clothes and even the way he laughs at all his own jokes, but mostly the way he always looks at me like I'm the only fucking person in the room.

Still, I'm not yelling that I like Chase Beckett for everyone to hear.

Because this is the worst day of my life. I'm the hot girl crazy about the guy who embodies the Sandler *sabadooo*.

I gasp quietly. Is he right? Am I embarrassed? But I already know the answer.

Little Miss Irritates-the-Shit-Out-of-Me shows up at the window, perky and adorable, smiling directly at Chase, interrupting my thoughts.

"All right, hot stuff, what can I get you?"

Cyanide.

I don't mean to make a sound, but I do, and it's a chortle. It's unladylike and draws his eyes to my face.

"Is it funny somebody called me hot stuff?"

I narrow my eyes on him as Beach Barbie volleys between us. "I mean, kinda. I guess you are to some . . . from like far away. Or when they haven't met you."

What am I saying? What am I doing?

But I know what. I'm mean flirting. I can't help it. He brings out the worst in me.

I'm also marking my territory.

He grins, slutting out that damn dimple.

But Coral pipes up, souring my mood again. "I think hot definitely describes you."

I want to immediately say *nobody asked you, Coral,* but Chase leans in toward me, crowding my personal space. I don't move.

"She thinks hot *definitely* describes me."

Oh, you motherfucker. Taunting me? The audacity.

"I guess one person's trash is another person's treasure."

He lets out a quiet exhale, biting his bottom lip, but he doesn't take his eyes off me as he calls off an order of tacos. I barely pay attention to what he says because the way he's looking at me is making my stomach flip and other parts stand at attention.

I'm so fucked. Or at least I'd like to be.

"It'll take about fifteen," Coral offers. "How about a beer while you wait? I've got your favorite in the back."

How do you know his favorite? I'll never let him drink it again.

His eyes tick to her for only a second as he says, "Sounds good."

She winks at him and turns around to get it, so I raise my hands as I give him a dirty look.

"It's okay, I'm not thirsty."

Chase chuckles, not saying a thing as she comes back with the bottled swill and hands it to him. He put some money on the counter, but she balks and pushes it back to him.

He doesn't take it, though, and that makes me smile.

I'm about to turn around and head to a section of tables by the beach, but he says "Hey," catching my attention. I watch him open the bottle on the metal counter, then use the bottom of his shirt to wipe the rim before he hands it to me.

"Ladies first."

My lips part, mostly because his charm is beginning to win him points.

"I thought we'd share it since I have to drive," he offers coolly.

Oh. I pinch the cool neck between my fingers before bringing it to my lips and taking a drink. *Okay, he can keep drinking it. It's delicious.*

I hold the glass to my pout for a moment before lowering it, licking what's left behind as he takes the bottle from me.

Holy hell. Coral could be watching . . . She could be crying for all I know, because I can't take my eyes off his Adam's apple and the way it bobs as he takes a swig.

I'm going to lick that later.

"Come on," he says to me, motioning to the benches before looking over his shoulder to Coral. "Tell your mom I said hi."

She doesn't get a chance to answer because he starts walking, fast enough to make me spin around and immediately keep up.

Jesus. If I'm not careful, our "how I met your mother" story will include how I fell for his BDE so hard that I almost tripped over it chasing behind him at the beach.

Neither of us says anything as we sit down, only glancing at each other but not lingering. We just sit in silence as he hands over the beer and waits patiently for me to pass it back.

But the pause in conversation feels too pregnant, probably because I think watching him just *be* is knocking me up. That's the thing about finally admitting the truth to yourself. It's like taking a screw out of a dam.

I'm flooded . . . mainly with thoughts and prayers for my future because I can't stop staring at his goddamn beautiful face, thinking about how truly attracted I am to him in spite of what's on the inside . . . actually more because of it.

The sound of waves crashes onto the shore next to us, and the occasional seagull calls, but we stay silent. Chase puts his hands behind his head, leaning back against the seat on his side as his eyes finally connect with mine, and he lets out a deep exhale. His stubble shines, and it's hot. How did I ever think that was unattractive?

I didn't. I just lied to myself.

His eyes lock on me, a smirk on his face. But I can't tell what he's thinking.

I hate it. I want to know.

"Do you like the beer?" His voice is too deep, but I nod, trying not to smile because I feel my ears getting hot. "Good . . ."

I hand him the beer before resting my forearms on the table. I don't know why I'm suddenly so honest. But somehow, it feels like the perfect time and place.

"You know, I've never really said thank you. I don't like to think about any of it—that night . . . Halloween. And I don't really like to talk about it, either, but what you said to me, Chase, that meant everything to me."

He frowns, probably remembering the memory. How could he not? It's burned into all our brains.

"You didn't have to do that for me, especially since I'd been so mean to you leading up to that point. But . . ."

He chuckles, but his smile doesn't meet his eyes. It hurts him too.

I can feel my hands starting to shake, so I blow out a shaky breath. "You made me feel safe and brave. I wouldn't have survived without you. Thank you for saving me and then bringing me back to life."

I know my eyes are shining, but I won't cry. "I'm sorry it took me this long to say it, but I've liked you since that day in Goldie's kitchen when you started talking about Lisa Bonet. I was jealous you weren't talking about me. So I decided to hate you. And when you got me the fish . . . I treasured her. You were all I could think about at the wedding."

The hint of a grin on his face stays in place as he searches my eyes, probably wondering where this is all going.

"You said I was embarrassed of you. That's not true. I've always been embarrassed about how much I like you and scared to death that you'd never like me back as much."

It feels like there's a weight in the center of my chest that is lifted.

He puts the bottle down and reaches across the table, scooping up my hands and bringing my palms to his lips, kissing them.

"I'm gonna love you. That's how fucking all in I am. Just don't tell my girlfriend . . . it may scare her away."

My heart stops beating. *Oh my god.* Before I can say anything, the moment's interrupted by Ariel's cousin, Coral.

"Four lamb tacos, ready to devour."

I can't help but laugh, because of course this is what happens. He laughs, too, like he's thinking the same thing.

We both watch as she places our cardboard plates down before asking, "Anything else?"

"No." Chase grins. "I think that'll do it."

Donkey . . . that'll do, donkey. Get out of here already.

"Wait . . . you forgot." She holds out her phone, and I freeze, scowling. You have got to be kidding me.

He chuckles. "Oh, um. Yeah, I don't think my girlfriend would appreciate that."

Without hesitation, I say, "I'm the girlfriend," and point to myself before smiling and repeating it even louder so most of the beach hears.

Chase is grinning ear to ear, staring at me as I mouth, *Happy?*

"Sorry," she whispers, probably thinking I'm unhinged. I am, but only over him. "I didn't realize. My bad."

My mouth opens, but Chase speaks for me. "No worries. See ya around, Coral."

He looks across at me, still smiling wide. And I know I'm doing the same because this man just basically told me he almost loves me, and I believe him.

"You're not going to promise it back, are you?"

"No," I breathe out, picking up my taco and taking a big bite, before I talk with my mouth full. "But I can definitively say that I love this taco."

He laughs, deep and full. "Of course you do. I told you it's the best."

We eat in comfortable silence, sharing a beer, but what he doesn't know is that I do think he's the guy I'll love, and it'll last forever. But where's the fun in letting the cat out of the bag?

If I've learned anything from the great romances over time, it's that timing is everything. So the day I know I love Chase Beckett will be the day someone will have to rip him out of my cold, dead hands.

Chase

We're walking hand in hand back to the car after a mic drop lunch. And not just because the food was good. I told her I was falling in love with her . . .

It's too fast, but I didn't even know it before I said it.

But the minute it tumbled out, I knew I meant it.

I think I've genuinely liked her for so long and fallen so hard that all it took was her finally giving me a chance to have all the feelings hit hard.

I smile at my beautiful girl as she points to a building off in the distance, talking about some famous murder that happened there.

I'm nodding, about to ask a question, when my attention's stolen by the gathering momentum in the distance.

A car alarm.

My brows draw together as she rattles off something wild.

I know it's wild because she always talks with her hands when she gets excited. But I'm still only half listening because I'm looking over in the direction where I'm parked.

That better not be my car.

"Dang, someone's car's going off," she says casually before going back to her story, and then her eyes get big. "That's not yours, is it? Because aren't we parked over there?"

I slow down and lift my keys, having thought the same thing. I click the alarm icon on my car fob. Unfortunately for someone else, the sound continues.

"Not mine," I say back to her, smiling.

My phone dings in my back pocket, then again and again . . . and again.

"What is happening?" she laughs, lifting her brows at me.

I chuckle, letting go of her hand to pull my phone free. "The girls are doing an F1 driving experience. I have a feeling I'm getting pics."

She shakes her head. "Break this down for me . . . because I wholeheartedly believe you about them, because strangely it's on brand for you, but like—"

I throw my arm over her shoulder so that the phone is closer to her face, my messages open, a group photo of them on the screen.

"Right after the *Friday the 13th* of it all," I breathe out as she glances up at me, "I went through a dark time. I did a lot of really impulsive shit. I think I was trying to remind myself I was alive and in control. Anyway, one of those things was skydiving."

Evie's scrolling through the pictures of us on the plane, smiling.

"That's where I met my ladies."

She snuggles in closer to me, clearly loving this, pointing to the first name that's popped up as we weave between cars.

"Tell me about Birdie."

"Ohh, well." I tilt my head with a grin. "Birdie, or Roberta as her driver's license says, had ten husbands in her lifetime. All of them now deceased, and three of them named Patrick."

"Birdie has a type," Evie teases, and I nod.

"And Gail?"

"Gail's spunky, a little bit of a hippie. She has pink hair and a fourteen-year-old grandson who teaches her all the newest slang. She puts it to good use, too, as if it's her word of the day."

Evie giggles.

I stop us, waiting for a car to pass us in the throughway, glancing down to watch her read the messages as her shoulders bounce.

"The way Joyce wrangles everyone is so funny. Do they live together like the Golden Girls?" She lifts her eyes to mine again as she asks.

"Joyce is the most rational, but I think it's because she's a retired clinical psychologist. She actually helped me a lot when shit went south for me."

Her head cocks up, her pretty face bathed in concern.

"How bad were you?"

Watering down the truth has never felt like an option with her. Not the way it does with everyone else. So I answer truthfully.

"Bad. But I'm pretty sure it's the same answer any of the four of us could give."

"Specify."

"I was stuck in a cycle of fear and anxiety. Just waiting to die. Wondering if I was living a *Final Destination* life or if some night I'd be walking to my car and bam, somebody would gut me. I couldn't sleep or eat. Let alone cook. So yeah, like I said . . . bad."

She grabs my shirt, right above my jeans, stopping me from stepping into someone's side mirror. I maneuver around it, coming to a stop between two identical black SUVs as I turn and face her.

"I didn't know," she whispers, leaning forward to kiss me right in the center of my chest.

With a finger under her chin, I lift her face, holding her eyes for a moment before I cradle her face and kiss her, letting my words play out on her lips.

"It wasn't for you to know."

She pinches my chin between her fingers and gives me her best impression of a goddess as she bats her lashes at me.

"It is now. Got it?"

"Yes, ma'am. But I'm good now . . . really good. And hey, you know, if you ever wanted to talk to Joyce, too, I could make an introduction. I went first, so you can trust her."

Evie smiles and nods in that way she does when she's trying not to give away what she's thinking.

"Yeah, that could be cool."

I don't think I'll ever get over earning her trust. It's the greatest privilege of my life.

She looks down for the phone and takes it from me, hooking her arm through mine, and we continue on our way to the car.

"Mimi?"

I wait to answer because that car alarm is getting louder and louder . . . and I know it's not my car, but what if it's next to my baby and scratched it?

She nudges me for an answer, so I snap back and pay attention.

"Aww, Mimi—she's like a little ray of sunshine that likes to read very smutty books about werewolves and to send me recipes she finds online to help my career. Sometimes they're even by me."

She's chuckling as we single file it through a few more cars, that alarm now blaring. *Man, it's way too close to where I'm parked.*

Evie's voice is raised as she jokes, "Welcome to Hollywood, the live-action version of *Grand Theft Auto*."

I crane my neck, trying to see past a white SUV that I'm parked behind, finally breathing easy because I can see the Volvo next to it is the culprit for my worry. Its headlights are blinking on and off, all the sound coming from it.

My head falls back, and my shoulders sag as I smile back at Evie. "Not gonna lie. I was a little worried about my girl."

Evie rolls her eyes. I don't hate it. I've got a thing for her eye rolls . . . *I've got a thing for her.*

I'm grinning, a pep in my step as we finally clear the cars and my Mustang comes into view. That's when everything hits me all at once. Like a goddamn brick.

Oh fuck.

"Chase," she yells, gripping my bicep, but I'm frozen, my chest already heaving. The sound of the alarm sounds over and over like the pounding in my chest.

I can't even process what I'm seeing. *Oh my god.* This is not happening.

"What the fuck," I breathe out, walking toward my previously pristine Mustang, Evie still holding on to me. "No, no, no, no . . ."

My shoes crunch over the glass that's everywhere. The windows are destroyed, cracked and completely blown out. So much so that the front windshield is shattered to the point you can't see through it.

Evie's hands shoot to her face as she stands in place, shaking her head.

I walk to the hood, running my hand over the huge craters dented all over it. It's like someone took a fucking bat to my car.

"What the fuck," I bellow as my hands run through my hair.

There are a million thoughts racing through my mind. The most prominent being *Goddammit*.

Evie walks past me to the open passenger-side door, peeking her head in before locking eyes with me. "Don't even look inside."

I frustratedly punch the air, groaning loudly before barking, "Fuck." Then I look at the Volvo and yell, "Shut up already."

Evie winces sympathetically at me, making me drop my eyes to the ground.

My blood is boiling, and I'm so pissed. But I can't fucking lose my shit in the middle of a parking lot. It's unhelpful in the journey of adulting. So I wipe my hand down my face and try to collect myself, taking a few deep breaths.

But then I hear her yell.

"Fuck you, Volvo . . . and Volvo owner. Nobody needs this soundtrack for our misery. Your car's dumb, and the color looks like piss."

She's nuts, which makes me grin as I look over at her. And as I do, the damn alarm stops. Her eyes pop open wider, staring back at me as I make the same face.

"Way to handle it, fella," I say on a heavy exhale as she winks, before I stare at my car again and add, "We should take pictures before I call the insurance company."

Without a word, Evie follows my lead, taking photos with her phone from the opposite side of me.

"Jesus," I sigh, looking at the headlights, which are now nonexistent, and the tires that are flat.

If I didn't know any better, I'd think this was personal. It feels it.

As if she's thinking the same, her voice flitters over the wreckage. "Why would someone do this? Who hates you?"

I squat, taking a closer picture before hearing her voice again from the back of the car.

"Hey, Chase . . . you should come back here."

A deep groan rumbles my chest as I stand and walk around the car, over the glass and past the open driver's-side door, which makes me nauseous because the leather seats are shredded.

I hate people.

"They didn't even fucking steal anything," I grit out, walking her way.

Evie's chewing her middle fingernail as I close the distance, and she points to the car.

"Shit," I rush out, reading what's keyed across the back of the trunk amid the red paint splashed across my back window.

Evil Will Die.

"Come on," I shout, throwing my hands up and turning away from her before I face her again, pointing at it. "Why would someone do this?"

Evie crosses her arms, shaking her head. "We should call the cops," she whispers, drawing my attention.

She's scared. Of course she is. It's only been a week since that bullshit at her work. But this is . . . this is just someone being a dick. Even as I think it, I'm not totally convinced either.

Still, I don't want her to be afraid.

"Baby," I call to her, opening my arms, signaling her to walk to me and snuggle in. And she does.

"It's okay," I say, kissing her forehead. "It's nothing more than some asshole fucking up my car because he can. It's LA, after all."

My eyes fall to the destruction again, and it sounds weird, but I'm getting déjà vu. I rub her shoulder, glancing down because she hasn't answered.

Evie's gnawing at her lip, staring at the car, worry behind her eyes before they pop open wide and she looks up at me.

"Umm . . . What are the chances, while you've been doing all the PR for the restaurant, you posed in front of your car?"

I shrug, not following. "What? Why?"

I'm not making the connection until she says, "The paint . . . isn't that like one of the vigilante moves for people who hate animal cruelty? They throw it on fur coats, right?"

My mind never even went there, but she looks a lot less afraid, so I'm game.

"Did you talk shit about vegans in that *LA Times* spread?"

I breathe out heavy. "Define shit?"

"Oh my god," she rushes out, pushing me away like she's solved the crime.

"Come on . . . I always talk shit about vegans. And yeah, I got my fair share of emails saying meat is murder, but I didn't take it seriously. There's a whole-ass vegan option on the menu. Gimme a break."

Her brows rise. "Well, you might want to start taking it seriously. For a multitude of reasons. The main one being . . ." Her eyes shift to my license plate.

I hate to say it, but she's starting to make sense. I did pose with my car in that magazine article. And I do talk shit.

Goddammit. That stupid plate. Oh man, I knew that plate was a bad idea. No, I didn't—I loved it. But it's made it real easy to find me.

Still . . . the feeling in my gut won't go away.

No, I'm being paranoid thinking anything else. This makes sense. She's right. I've done this to myself. But still, fuck them.

"What about not being cruel to this animal," I bite out, pointing to myself. "You know, if they ate more meat, then they'd be too lethargic to fuck up my car and become felons. Meat saves the world."

She starts to laugh, then stops and walks over to me, forcing me to look at her. But I'm pouting, trying to keep my eyes on the ocean.

"Look at me," she presses, but I don't, so she tries to shake me. "Look at me."

I do, directly into her eyes.

"The good news is, I bet you have excellent insurance—"

I pop my shoulders and begrudgingly nod as she continues.

"—and you're rich . . ."

That earns her the dimple.

"—so come on, let's lock it up . . ." I raise my brows, and she nods, realizing how futile that is. "Or leave it as it is and go back to the beach. I'll buy you another beer while we wait for the tow truck . . . I might even let you make it to first base under the pier."

A grumble comes from deep in my chest.

"I'm sorry about your car," she whispers, lifting to her tiptoes, giving me no other choice but to kiss her.

I let out a deep breath, pulling away before draping my arm over her shoulder and letting her lead us away as I throw out, "Hey, you wouldn't know anyone who could give me a ride to work tomorrow?"

She laughs and glances up at me, reaching up to interlace her fingers with mine.

"You're in luck. I do know a girl who could give you a ride. But only for the right price."

Our steps match as we walk.

"Oh yeah, what's she charge?"

She bites her lip, doing a poor job of hiding her smile, before she levels, "Your heart—"

My face whips to hers, because for the first time in our history, Evie just said something cheesy and adorable on purpose.

I shrug. "Never mind, I'll walk."

Her mouth falls open, eyes wide as she slaps my chest, but I grab her face and kiss her.

How is it that ten minutes ago I was ready to lose my shit, but now I can't think of anything else I'd rather be doing?

Chapter Sixteen

Evie

"Chase." My palms slap down on the kitchen island as a deep exhale escapes me. Actually, it's more of a moan. "That's so good. Right there."

His deep voice vibrates in all the right places. "Devi impastare, tesoro. Non fermarti ora." *(You gotta knead, baby. Don't stop now.)*

My eyes tip up to the ceiling before squeezing closed because I can't concentrate. I'm not sure I even know my name. "You're torturing me. Goddammit."

Another moan falls from my lips, although it sounds more like a whimper.

"Evie . . ." he levels.

My name is said as a warning. But his voice is so commanding that it makes my fingernails curl into the flour spread on the counter, under the doughy mess I stopped rolling around two minutes ago.

"Shhhh," I beg. "Shut up, shut up, shut up."

He tsks. "Se te lo ripeto, non ci sarà il dessert." *(If I tell you again, there will be no dessert.)*

I drop my head and meet his gaze from where he's sitting on the kitchen floor. Between me and the counter. Fingering me and teasing me with his tongue while making it really fucking hard to concentrate on anything other than getting off.

"I'm pretending you're telling me to concentrate on coming."

"Dough. Knead it," he growls in English, pressing his lips to my clit like a chaste kiss.

Fuck. I shake my head, half crying and fully panting as I open my eyes and stick my hands back on the stupid bread dough.

"Happy?" I snap, but the moment I do, all my breath is stolen from me. "Oh fuck."

My stomach caves, because Chase just thrusted two fingers inside me, gripping my bare ass with his other hand.

"That's not how you answer me," he croons, blowing on my clit.

"Yes, Chef," I rush out with a shiver, lifting to my tiptoes as he makes a come-hither motion inside of me, rubbing the perfect spot.

My voice is a squeak. "Oh god, that's so good."

As a reward, he runs his tongue slowly over the throbbing little beggar, making my entire body convulse as he squeezes my ass to remind me to knead.

This is my own fault.

I woke up all hot and heavy this morning from my dream and stupidly said, *Wanna play Top Chef?*

But instead of rolling over on top of me, he hauled my ass out of bed, set me on a barstool, and began making bread. And now he's forcing me to finish while he finishes me.

His tongue leaves my clit as he says, "The secret is to make sure you roll in a slow motion . . . like this."

My lips part as his thumb begins massaging my clit in slow circles. I don't know if my hands are copying him, but I'm doing something, because I feel my body rocking.

Or maybe that's because I'm desperate to orgasm so I'm fucking his fingers.

"You can't put too much pressure . . ." His fingers move together with his thumb, making me pant as I knead this damn dough. "You want to make sure it's just enough, or you could ruin it."

Jesus, my legs already feel like jelly and my lungs feel like I can't suck in enough breath. Because he's so fucking good at this.

He never lied when he said he fucked me better than he cooks . . . because I'd give him all the Michelin stars. All of them. I'd take them from other restaurants to give to him.

My mind is a scattered mess, unable to keep itself on the goddamn dough because Chase just keeps stroking and fingering me. Over and over. In the most erotic rhythm.

I'm lost to the feeling of the way he fucks my cunt. The draw of his fingers against my entrance before he presses them back inside, massaging my G-spot each time.

He bites the inside of my thigh, and my body quakes before he starts to kiss and suck a hickey onto my skin.

Fuck, that's sexy.

He's so close to my clit that it amps up my lust. I rock my hips while his fingers do their work. My eyes close, my fingers pressed into the soft dough as his voice touches my skin.

"Je veux te marquer pour que tout le monde voie que tu es à moi. Tu auras de la chance si je ne te baise pas si fort que tu sentiras toujours comme moi." *(I want to mark you so everyone can see you're mine. You'll be lucky if I don't fuck you so hard you'll always smell like me.)*

Fuck. I can feel my body building toward my orgasm. It's gathering, swirling in my stomach, climbing higher and higher.

I'm breathing hard as his fingers massage me and his mouth stays just out of my reach. Dammit, I want his tongue so bad. I keep rocking my hips, begging for it.

"Kiss me," I mewl, pressing my hips forward again.

"Ti bacerò finché non avrai un orgasmo così forte che potrò leccartelo via dalle cosce, tesoro." (*I'll kiss you until you orgasm so hard I can lick it off your thighs, darling.*)

Oh fuck. His mouth sends me over the edge, and not just the words. Chase slowly runs his tongue directly over my clit.

A wave of pleasure hits me as I suck in a breath and demolish the bread between my fingers.

"Chassuhhh . . ." I grunt on a very unladylike moan, squeezing the dough between my fingers and bending over him, my face almost hitting the island.

But I barely finish, my chest heaving as I'm dragged down his body. His tongue licking my cum off my thighs before my knees touch the floor.

"Come 'ere," he says, ragged and deep. "Get on . . ."

He's already pulled down his briefs, freeing his rock-hard cock as I straddle him, reaching out to position him at my entrance before it pushes inside me.

I can't help but gasp, because Chase isn't just long, he's thick. The man has big dick energy for a reason.

It doesn't matter how wet I am, he always makes an impression.

I lean forward, placing my elbows on his shoulders as I steeple my hands above his head. He kisses the tops of my breasts, pulling one of my nipples into his mouth before I rock my hips, riding him.

We're surrounded by flour spilled down the counter and pieces of dough on the floor, but neither of us cares. Because all that exists is our bodies, sweaty and flush to each other as I lift and grind back down.

"You're fucking beautiful, you know that?"

I smile, kissing along his forehead. He lifts his face, forcing his lips on mine. Chase brings a hand to my ass, gripping it hard before he takes over, lifting me up and down quicker.

Fuck.

He's breathing into my neck now as we curl into each other, fucking harder and faster. We're nothing but hot, shallow breaths and beads of sweat just unwaveringly locked on each other, chasing our release.

The sound of me, the lust I'm coated in, smacks and spreads out between us as Chase lifts his hips to meet the way he pulls me down onto him.

"Fuck me, baby. Fuck me good with that tight pussy."

Damn. His dirty mouth does something to me. Every time.

"Chase. I want to come again . . . make me come . . . please," I breathe out heavily.

I honestly don't know if I can, but I still want him to try, because the need's growing. We're moving in unison, the fullness of him inside me so intoxicating it has my head falling back as he draws his tongue up my throat.

A soft moan escapes before our mouths meet again, kissing deeply as I grind down each time he lifts my ass.

"Goddammit, Evie," he growls, breaking from my mouth and pressing hot kisses down my neck as I weave my sticky fingers into his hair. "You feel so fucking good."

He's panting, swallowing hard, his hot breath dusting my skin as we move faster and faster.

Yes. Oh god.

The tingling starts in my stomach, bleeding out and down through my center as I breathe quickly, panting. I can't take it . . . it feels overwhelming. My clit throbs, wanting more friction as I ride him, clinging to his body.

"That's it, baby, come on . . ."

I whimper, my fingers curling into his hair, as I rub myself against him while stretched open by his hard cock. His arms wrap around me and he growls, bucking his hips to meet me at each movement.

Our cheeks press together as stuttered cries begin to fall from my lips. Oh god . . . I'm coming.

"Oh . . . oh . . . oh my . . . fuck," I moan, contracting around his cock, coming hard.

That's all he needed, because Chase groans loudly into my shoulder, holding me to him tightly. I can feel his cock pulse inside me as he fills me.

Thank god for the pill . . . No little Chases yet.

Did I just say yet? Jesus Christ.

I feel him smile against my skin before we peel ourselves away, each of us still breathless.

He stares into my eyes and brushes a braid out of my face.

"You're gonna be the death of me."

I shrug. "Seems fair, since I've been wishing it on you for so long."

He laughs, and I can't help but just stare, because if I'm being honest, Chase feels a lot like *I've died* and gone to heaven.

"Be honest, did I ruin the dough?"

I already know the answer because it took us forty-five minutes to clean up the mess, but I'm still amused at how unsettled he was over ruined bread dough. You'd think I started a pyramid scheme and stole money from a children's hospital with all the *What a shames* said under his breath.

"Yes," he levels, looking back at me in the bathroom mirror.

I blink, putting a hand on my hip. "Okay, next time, you make me something . . . anything while I blow you, and we'll see how well you do."

He grins, bringing his hand to the top of his towel. "Go get a stick of butter—"

I laugh, playfully shoving him before I walk out of the bathroom and plop down on the bed in my towel.

"Hey, you never told me if you successfully kept today a surprise from the guys."

Chase peeks his face around the doorjamb. "Yeah, they don't have a clue. It's getting delivered and installed later tonight. Nobody will be there . . . except for me."

Obviously. He's so cute.

"I think it's so cute that you had, like, a family portrait made for the kitchen. Ten bucks says Leo tears up."

He laughs from the bathroom before he walks out, talking. "I mean, some of these guys have been with me since the beginning in Boston. Come to think of it, Eddie's really the only new guy."

I'm putting lotion on my legs as he saunters past me to his dresser, looking sexy enough to eat with a towel around his waist. I fall back on my elbows and smile.

"Slut."

He grants me that goddamn dimple and winks. "Aww, thanks, baby."

He grabs his underwear and pulls it on before I get back to the point.

"How did you guys meet? You and Eddie . . . because he doesn't strike me as someone you'd normally be friends with. He's kind of unfriendly."

"I think it's cause he's British."

I laugh. "That's what I thought. But British people are exceptionally funny, and he didn't laugh at my jokes . . . not once. I don't know, he just seemed off . . ."

He looks at me like *Oh* before selecting a T-shirt.

"You can blame a guy named Tommy—he's who recommended him. I was doing an appearance with some other chefs. I knew I needed someone new since my old sous had kids, and he wouldn't want to leave and come to LA. So Tommy recommended him. I flew out, we had dinner, he had excellent taste and seemed to know a lot about me, so it seemed like a good fit."

He pulls his T-shirt over his head. "Would you want me to get someone new, baby?"

I blanch, surprised by the offer because he's dead serious. Chase is staring back at me as he buttons his jeans, not a trace of humor or malice written over his face.

"You'd do that?" I breathe out. "You would fire somebody simply because I don't like them."

He grins and shakes his head. "No . . . I would fire someone if you told me that your gut said they weren't cool." He walks toward the bed, leaning over me and kissing my forehead. "I trust your judgment, Evie."

And that, ladies and gentlemen, is the difference between a boy and a man.

I roll my lips together, trying to hide my smile before I say, "Just tell him to laugh at my jokes, and we'll be cool."

Chase laughs, pushing back off the bed. "Stop making me fall for you."

"No promises."

My phone buzzes somewhere over on the bed, so I roll around, trying to find it, until I lie back and hold up the message to my face.

> **Erin:** Call when you
> get here. We had
> a weirdo on set.
> Security will score
> you in.

I instantly sit up, looking at Chase, then read him the message.

He starts shaking his head. "You're not going in."

My hearts warm at his response, but I roll my eyes. "Shut up. There's security everywhere. And it's not a weirdo for me. It's a weirdo for Jenny, aka Muffy."

"No. Home," he presses.

I know why he's being so protective, but I also know I've never felt stronger over the past two years than I do right now. It's so anti-boss bitch to think this, but Chase fixed something broken inside me.

Because he let me feel it all and never wavered from his post. I feel protected and reminded that we made it out of that fucking horror story into a goddamn rom-com.

And now I just want to live my life, with a healthy amount of caution, but to never go back to where I was.

Explaining that to him is another story. Especially seeing as the stubborn lines on his forehead are on display.

"Hear me out . . ." I say with a grin. "Yes, she had some guy send her a bunch of strange shit, like teddy bears with their hearts cut out." I hold up a hand as he scoffs. "But nobody witnessed it . . . and don't forget she's the girl who needed to commune with the werewolf suit. So, grain of salt . . . plus, I think she's on hallucinogens."

He crosses his arms. "Like I said . . . stay home."

I scoot off the bed to stand in front of him. "And like I said . . . no. I'm not living in fear anymore of what could happen." My hands land on his waist, and I give him a little shake, barely moving him. "I mean . . . if I did that, you wouldn't be here."

He leans down, nipping at my shoulder as I continue. "I promise it's safe. There's security, and I've got the Double D's. No more living in the past."

"True," he grumbles. "But I'm not sure those two could find their ass from a hole in the ground."

My eyes pop open, and he shrugs. "I heard that one from Gail."

"It's solid."

He grabs the front of my towel, looking down at me sternly. "Listen, missy. Promise me you'll check in. And if you need me or if anything weird happens—"

I cut him off. "I'll call you. I promise. But it's time for me to start living my life and not look over my shoulder anymore."

He lets out a deep exhale as I grin, and my voice becomes very flirty. "You know, I'm kind of inspired by this boy that I really like . . ."

There's a lift of his brow. "You are, huh? He must be really handsome."

"Incredibly . . . like way hotter than Matt Damon."

Chase wraps his arms around me in a bear hug, then motions for me to keep going as he walks me backward toward the bed.

I start listing actors, but by the time I make it to Charlie Hunnam, we're kissing again, and I'm definitely going to be late to set.

Chapter Seventeen

Evie

Getting into work went off without a hitch, and I even texted Chase to let him know I was safe and sound.

Because that's what good girlfriends do. God, that's still so weird.

Even though I still haven't told my sister. So it's not totally official.

Chase and I actually decided not to because we thought it would be fun to surprise them. Because we're terrible people who love to shock the shit out of those we love.

Plus, we deserve a grand introduction, since Goldie's been working on this union for like ever. So when they show up at the restaurant opening, we're going to act casual, and I'll be mean until he leans down and kisses me.

We've actually got a bet going as to who says *No fucking way* first.

I chuckle to myself, faintly hearing my name called before it finally catches up to me, forcing my face over my shoulder to see the director waving me over. He's standing with the vampire lead next to a tree.

Deep breaths. Every conversation with this guy is more annoying than the one before. I make my way over, mindful to keep a smile on my face.

"Hi. What can I do for you today?" *Since you literally ask me ten thousand stupid fucking questions every day.*

"Well," he huffs. "You could start with making the blood realistic." He points to a streak of red on the vampire's shirt and then to the vampire's nose.

My brows furrow.

The vampire, whose name is Paul—not in the movie but in real life—shrugs. "Yeah, that's my bad, Evie. I accidentally ran into the tree and gave myself a bloody nose."

I look at his white ruffled shirt that looks more like what Prince wore in "Purple Rain" than anything Lestat would dare to don, knowing damn well we never applied any blood to his shirt. So that is, in fact, his real blood.

And it's ten for ten in the dumbass-questions department, but good luck to me to try and tell this director that.

I open my mouth, but the backup director for a Tums commercial speaks first.

"I need the blood on his shirt to look like the blood on his face. It doesn't look like that . . . Do you see it . . . Do you *see* it?"

He's obnoxiously pointing. It's making my eye twitch.

"Your finger's in the way," I level, ignoring Paul's chuckle, especially as I add, "No. I don't see it."

I mean . . . I could've said . . . I should've said yes. But, fuck this dude.

He's already out of breath, the rant readied as he throws his arms in the air.

"Does anyone understand how important this movie is? Does anyone understand what we're doing here? This will be a significant moment in vampirical culture."

"He made that word up, right?" Paul whispers, looking at me.

I nod, then roll my eyes. "I'll be right back. I'm gonna go make some fresh fake blood to apply on you for the first time."

Paul gives me a sympathetic smile as the director keeps raging, but I turn around, uncaring, and walk off set. I pull my phone out of my back pocket, grinning because I know we're going to break soon as I hear, "Get me the werewolf. He understands."

I'm not looking up as I text Chase to come by and slap a burger out of that jackass's hands, too, making myself chuckle as I picture it.

Me: Failberg really lost it today.

Chuckles the clown: What happened . . . did he find his Were canoodling with someone else?

Me: I swear they're dating. Nobody can convince me otherwise.

I look up at the sky, noticing the sun setting. It's pretty.

Chuckles the clown: Are you looking at the sunset . . . because I'm looking at it.

Jinx. God, he's so romantic sometimes. I start to respond, but another text comes in.

Chuckles the clown: Wanna meet at sunrise and fuck in the pool?

I take it all back.

Me: Yes.

I smile, putting my phone back in my pocket as I walk. Too much pep in my step. If I'm not careful, my meticulously created badass-girl image will be ruined because I'll be skipping all over the place.

The good thing is my work trailer is the furthest away from set, so nobody will see me.

Although, I simultaneously hate and love it. It's inconvenient when we're bringing shit to set, but it's nice to have the separation so I can work quietly.

Not that it's ever quiet with . . . speaking of . . . I look around.

"Where the hell are the Double D's?" I say under my breath.

As I say it, three extras walk out of the makeup trailer, giggling. Their faces are red as Devin follows them out. Well, I've discovered where my puppies went.

I smile to myself, not bothering to whip them into shape. *Oh, I really am getting soft.* Whatever. I finish my walk, taking the steps to my trailer quickly, before tugging the metal door open, but as I walk inside, the room is pitch black.

My heart kicks up a notch, the way it always does when I'm faced with the dark. But I meant it when I said today I wanted to move on, so I exhale a really deep breath and walk inside, letting the damn door close behind me.

I'm standing there, acclimating, letting myself just breathe. *It's literally just a dark room. And plenty of fun shit happens in the dark all the time.* I can't help the smile that forms on my face as I think of last night with Chase.

Really, really fun shit happened last night.

I reach up to the wall and begin feeling around for the switch before it transforms into a nervous giggle because I know I'm fine, but Rome wasn't built in a day.

At least I'm not having a panic attack . . . I'm just a normal amount of scared. Well, maybe a little bit more than normal, but I know it's irrational.

I frown, patting the wall down . . . actually not irrational. I almost got murdered in the dark. Then again, those orgasms last night also felt like I might die.

I'm pretty sure this isn't what anyone meant by the term "sexual healing." But whatever works.

I'm definitely not sharing this on Reddit, though.

As I find the switch and flick it up, I suddenly feel flesh—a hand.

I gasp, my shoulders hitting my ears before I start laughing hysterically, knowing exactly what I'm feeling.

The smile on my face is wide as I stare at my Thing hand. The one I made years ago and hang next to a light switch because the jump scare never gets old.

I just never have my lights off. So the scare doesn't get me.

My phone buzzes in my pocket, but I ignore it because there's a rap at my door. I turn, opening it.

The head of security's standing in the door, a guy in his mid-sixties who went gray a long time ago and refers to old movie stars like we should all know who he's talking about.

"Hey, Rick, is there a problem?"

"No." He shakes his head. "I'm just keeping an eye on all the trailers. The young guys are patrolling. What with all the Jenny nonsense, we have to keep our eyes peeled." He leans in and whispers like he's telling me a secret, so I do the same. "Between us, sweetheart, it's a setup.

She's trying to get herself on some TMZ thing. You know, to make her famous."

My mouth falls open, and my eyes spring wide. "God, I love a good goss sesh. No. Way."

He nods, then snaps his fingers. "By the way, I found some footage of an extra taking your fish."

I stick out my bottom lip because I miss Ruth Bader.

"Yeah, the Double D's told me."

He laughs at the nickname. "Yeah, but I found some more. It's a better shot of his face. I'll be around all night if you wanna take a look."

I pat his arm. "Heck yeah, Rick. I'll come by later. I have to make new blood first."

Maybe Scooby ganging it isn't such a bad idea.

He turns around, waving at me as he opens my trailer door. "Oh yeah, 'cause this movie's getting an Oscar."

I laugh as the door bangs shut, leaving me alone to create fresh blood because, apparently, realism has left the building. But humor still reigns supreme.

Chapter Eighteen

Chase

"You're alive," I joke, hearing Noah laugh on the other end of the phone.

"I don't know about alive, but at least we're on the same soil. Not gonna lie, the Cinnabon in JFK was a sight for sore eyes."

"Filth. But welcome back anyway, brother. Never leave me again. I had no one to talk to."

I'm a big fat liar. Huge. Giant.

He chuckles. "Do not bust my balls for not calling. I'm on my honeymoon."

I stop at a red light as someone with house music blasting pulls up next to me. So I turn my head and yell, "I'm on the phone. A little consideration."

Maybe it's my fault for getting a convertible as a rental. But I needed a pick-me-up since it'll take a month to restore my baby.

"What did I tell you about yelling at strangers while you drive?"

"These fucking kids nowadays . . . and listen, technically, your honeymoon is over. So it's time to give me attention. What time do you guys land in the a.m.?"

I'm hoping it's sometime after sunrise, because that's not the version of our surprise romance Evie was thinking of when she made a plan to spring it on them.

"Well, currently, we're sitting in a lounge, exhausted and trying not to get too drunk so we don't fall asleep and miss our flight. But if all goes well, we'll be home in about six hours. Give or take a tailwind."

I count on my fingers. It's eight thirty right now, but he's East Coast time . . .

"Midnight, dummy," he shoots out, making me laugh.

"God, it's nice to have the nerd back. I've been doing too much heavy lifting as the personality hire of this group."

I hear him repeat what I said to Goldie, who laughs, and it makes me think of something Evie said earlier, so without thinking, I say, "Listen, my girl . . ."

Fuck. Oh, I promised I wouldn't screw up the surprise.

Noah scoffs. "You have to stop calling *my girl* your girl. She's my wife, so my girl."

Saved by my personality. Of course that's what he thinks.

I roll with it. "Fine. But tell me how many times she complained I wasn't there to feed her."

He grumbles. "I'm gonna kill you."

I laugh too maniacally. "I knew it."

"Honestly, I'm kind of surprised that I'm talking to you right now. Speaking of Monroe women. I figured Spartacus would've killed you by now."

She's trying to, but it's a death I'd take over any other.

"Nah, we figured out a way to get along . . ."

"As long as nothing got broken in my house, I'm glad you worked it out. I'll call when we land."

I pull into the back parking lot behind the restaurant, remembering I had something to say.

"Hey . . . hold up. Did you get my text?"

There's rustling like he's getting up from a seat, and then I hear him tell Goldie he'll be right back. I press the button on the car to put the roof on.

The second it's done, his voice is low, but there's less noise. "Yeah, I did. I was gonna talk to you about it when I got home because I'm with Golds. But what's going on?"

I shake my head, staring at the street I'm facing.

"I don't know . . . it's just something in my gut. Today, Evie told me the movie's having some trouble on-site with some weird guy. And she doesn't know I know, but a couple of weeks ago, Ruth Bader got stolen. And then my car . . ."

I clear my throat, hearing how crazy I sound, before I send him a picture of the damage. Still, no matter how many times Evie cursed the red-paint vigilantes, that fucking pit in my stomach wouldn't leave.

It's why I was so worried about her going into work. But if anyone can either talk sense into me or say run, it's Noah.

"Look at what I sent. I think I'm just being paranoid, dude. It would track, considering . . ."

"Yeah," Noah says, huffing a laugh. "I fucking get that more than anyone. Damn," he breathes out when he sees my car.

"And that's one of the reasons I can't shake the feeling. It's the kind of damage . . ." He knows I mean his old apartment. "The car threw me. I know Evie thinks it was because of my stupid article, but all I said was that I love a good steak and would never bring myself to embrace a fake. My car was personal . . . and now with the shit on set . . . Something's off."

He grumbles like he hates what I'm saying. "And nothing weird has happened at the house or anything? Like anyone on the property or shit being misplaced?"

I scrub my hands over my stubbled cheeks, briefly thinking about how I tried to shave this a.m., but she all but wrestled the razor from me.

"I mean, nothing unexplainable . . ." I narrow my eyes. "There were rats on the bed . . ."

Noah groans. "Yeah, Goldie said Princess brought in a treat. That cat hates me. At least she isn't shitting in my shoes again."

I'm nodding, wanting him to talk me out of this or this out of me. But it's like there's something right in front of my face, and I'm missing it.

Noah reads my silence wrong, saying, "You don't think it was Princess? You think someone was in the house?"

"No . . . no," I rush out. "I was just thinking that I'm missing something, but, dude, listen to us. We're two theories away from connecting Princess to the grassy knoll."

He lets out a breath. "You're right. We sound crazy."

"No, as Joyce would say, we sound traumatized."

"Yeah," he agrees.

"Nobody broke in," I say like I'm the one trying to convince the both of us now. "Who's getting past all your locks to leave rats on her bed? Because if that were true, then the theater wasn't a prank either. And my apartment was a fucking setup . . ."

I mean it to sound ridiculous. Like lunacy. But I'm gripping the steering wheel as my face darkens. I open my mouth to tell Noah to say I'm being paranoid, but a text comes through.

> **Evil 😈:** They're serving croissant sandwiches. And they're not fluffy. You'd be so pissed.

She's so cute, but seeing the text makes me frown because her name in my phone is right above the picture I'm still open to—of the back of my car.

Without a second thought, I screenshot it, sending it to Noah. I'm silent, waiting for the screen to say delivered, because it's becoming real fucking hard to think this is all just a coincidence.

"Evil will die . . ." I whisper, knowing he's seeing what I am. "Look at her name, Noah."

"Fuck . . ." he answers quietly.

"Am I paranoid? Say I'm paranoid."

My heart's beating out of my chest. This shit can't actually be happening again. Lightning doesn't strike the same place twice.

"I can't," he rushes out. "Because I am, too . . . but we don't know anything, especially *who* we're dealing with. If anyone. We could be wrong."

"We could . . . but if we're not . . ."

There's silence, and I know he's going over a thousand different scenarios just like I am.

"The most important thing is if someone is watching, we can't let on. So we don't tell the girls. It's gotta look like business as usual. We don't want someone going rogue on us."

I nod before I say, "Agreed."

"I'm going back to the lounge to keep an eye on my girl, and I suggest you do the same. Evie's yours until we get there."

"She's mine even when you're here."

I don't care about the fucking surprise anymore.

"Heard. Chase." He pauses, the gravity of what we're thinking settling in. "We don't know what this is, but I believe your fucking gut. Just promise if anything goes sideways, swing first and call the fucking cops second."

"I got you."

We both hang up before either of us says goodbye, and I take a deep breath, quickly texting Evie back.

Me: don't eat that
shit. It'll be in your
stomach for years.
Here's an idea . . .
when I'm done
here, I'm gonna
drive up and hang.

We'll drive home together when you're off with a quick stop at your fave donut place.

Evil 😈: Stop talking dirty to me.

I let out a heavy breath, because if our nightmare is angling for a sequel, I've got way more to lose than just my life. I've got Evie.

Let's hope this is nothing, I think as I turn off the car, pushing the door open with my foot before exiting. I'm glancing around the parking lot, noticing there still isn't another car.

It's always weird to be here before the opening, because it's like the calm before the storm, but right now my eyes aren't just looking for the art guy . . . I can't shake the idea that I'm not alone.

I stand quietly, taking in the night. A couple's walking together across the street and there's a stray cat on the wall. It's an otherwise normal night.

My eyes narrow as I hear Noah in my mind again. *The most important thing is if someone is watching, we can't let on.*

"This guy better hurry the fuck up," I say to myself, jingling my key chain as I start toward the restaurant door.

I look at my phone for the time as a breeze blows, but I'm fifteen minutes early. We'd said nine because the delivery guys couldn't be here until after the shop closed. I was happy to oblige, considering it was a rush order.

A heavy exhale leaves me as I stop in front of the door, glancing over my shoulder into the darkness. I'm fiddling with my restaurant keys, looking for the right one before I reach down for the handle.

My hackles rise when I hear a car rev, darting my attention to someone pulling out from a parking spot too quickly.

"Dick," I whisper, holding the knob as I bring my key to the lock, but when I stick it in to turn, there's no tension.

What the fuck?

It's already open.

My heart begins thrumming faster as I quietly shove my keys back into my pocket. I swallow, looking around again as a thousand thoughts war inside my head.

Anyone could be inside . . . I should just call the cops, but . . .

If there's someone inside who might be trying to hurt us. To hurt my girl. I'm handling it. Tonight.

I glance over my shoulder once more, an ominous feeling settling in my bones before I slip inside.

The kitchen's pitch black, mainly because the front windows have been papered with a sign about the opening in a few days. So I stand for a moment, letting my eyes acclimate before I cautiously take a step forward, keeping my footsteps quiet while I look around.

But nothing seems out of order.

I glance at my knives, wrapped in their leather casing, still sitting where I left them. And the metal counters gleam even in the darkness as I let my fingers skim the surface while taking one silent step after another.

My head shifts to the wall cutout that's open to the front of the house. I don't see anything, especially in the dark, so I squint and stand still, waiting to hear something, anything.

I don't.

The tension in my shoulders begins to drift away because I'm starting to think that maybe I forgot to lock the fucking door.

I mean, I have been pretty distracted.

And when I left here the other day, my face was buried in my phone, watching a video Evie sent of some phony pretending to be a chef while fingering food.

It was a disturbingly up-close shot of outrageous shit getting done to an orange before he chopped it up to use as a garnish. But the part I liked was the text. It said: *Do this to me when you get home?*

I was all fucking in. And to her surprise, I made it a fruity threesome. No orange or tangerine was safe. Even a grapefruit had stories to tell. So I can't really blame myself.

My hand runs through my hair as I let out an audible breath, standing with my hands on my hips for a second as I look around.

It seems I've created my own drama.

Which is the kind I prefer, seeing as I'm far too intimately aware of the alternative. I walk to the wall that leads back to where the sinks and baking ovens are, only half thinking that I still haven't checked there as I flick on the lights.

The fluorescents flicker slowly, turning on as I push through the set of double doors, this time not bothering to be quiet. Because nobody's here, my paranoia just making me check.

But as I do, my feet skid to a stop as everything happens in slow motion.

A wrench hits the ground, and the sound feels like it's happening in an echo chamber, pinging and clanging before the world speeds up again and I'm rushed by someone in a black hood holding a hammer.

And the world goes black.

Chapter Nineteen

Evie

I look down at my phone again, seeing there's still no text back from Chase. It makes me wrinkle my nose before a half-frustrated huff whooshes out. He was supposed to be here. And I texted him hours ago to let him know I'd be off soon, but he hasn't gotten back to me yet. He must still be caught up at the restaurant.

Truthfully, it's not unlike him to get sidetracked by food . . . or maybe Goldie and Noah got in already. I look down at my phone again to check the time. No, they should be landed or landing right now.

I'm about to send him another text when I'm interrupted by Derek's voice. "Hey, boss."

I look up and smile. "Hey back. Where's your sidekick?"

He grins, hitching a finger over his shoulder. "Helping Erin with some lighting. He'll be here soon. She's actually had us doing a bunch of shit today. We didn't want to tell her it wasn't in the intern contract because, honestly, neither one of us read it."

I laugh. "Well, if you had, you'd know chasing tail all day wasn't in there either."

He laughs, looking guilty. "Yeah, Devin said you caught us. He saw you see him."

I shake my head, handing him my masticated brush clumped full of fake blood, and point to the tree I was decorating.

"When Devin makes it here, you guys finish that off. I need to grab a cookie and make a call."

He gives me a thumbs-up before I chuckle, walking out just as the man of the hour comes running in.

"I was just talking about you. The orders are with your brother, Romeo."

He shrugs in an excited, boyish way. "Just say I'm your favorite already. Don't worry, I won't tell the others."

I leave my puppies behind, my phone already in hand, ready to call Chase.

I know I'm being ridiculous, but I don't like that he's not calling me back. It makes me worry. His number's already ringing in my ear as I see Rick, the security guard, wave me over to his trailer. So I nod, taking a detour heading over.

Chase's voicemail comes on, making me groan as I end the call at the same time Rick looks down at me.

"Uh-oh, bad time?"

I shake my head. "No, it's fine. I'm just mad at everyone. But that happens all the time."

He chuckles, opening the door to his trailer. "Well, come on in, and let me show you that video I was talking about earlier."

My brows rise in agreement as I walk up the stairs and inside, the door clanging shut behind me.

Rick leans in like before when he was telling me a secret. "Don't worry, I don't think it's weird you have such affection for fish. Plenty of people are lonely, and animals, even fish, can help get us through hard times."

Fantastic. Somehow, this feels worse than being called a crazy cat lady.

"Thanks, Rick. I'll really keep that one deep in my heart."

He smiles like he's done his good deed for the day as he walks over to a laptop.

I point to it. "I have to be honest, I pictured, like, multiple screens and a whole setup for security."

He shrugs. "That's only in the movies and TV . . . and maybe on sets with an actual budget. You know I still moonlight at OfficeMax on some nights."

I press my lips together before I say, "You know, Rick, I didn't know those were still around."

He nods as he settles down in his chair, opening his laptop.

"You'd be surprised how many people try to break in for some Post-its."

The device comes to life, and I have to smile at his screen saver—*RuPaul's Drag Race*. Love that for him.

I stand behind him, looking over his shoulder.

"Now, the picture's a little small, but I bet I can . . ."

I jump in before he finishes. "No worries. I'm just hoping I'll recognize him so I can track him down and get my goldfish back . . ." Now's the time to slip in that I'm not sad. "You know, my boyfriend actually got me the—"

"Okay," he rushes out, cutting me off, finally figuring out how to make the picture full screen.

Looks like I'm doomed to stay the lonely fish lady forever. It's just remarkably sadder and weird.

He hits Play, so I watch the screen before I hear him grumble to himself about needing to fast-forward. There's no way I'm jumping into this generational gap and helping him figure it out.

The man is owed his dignity.

I brush my braids over my shoulder, watching as people come and go on the screen and costumes are carried, all at six times speed, before he says "Dang it," followed by "Well, shit. Now it's too far forward again."

I'm trying so hard not to laugh, but I'm failing because this couldn't get any more zany if it was written. God, Chase is going to eat this up when I get home tonight.

"Here we go. It's right here," he levels.

I lean in closer over Rick's shoulder, my eyes trained to the screen as I see a guy in a black hoodie turn the corner, holding my damn fish tank.

I gasp. "There she is. What a motherfu—" I catch myself, not wanting to say that in front of Pop-Pop.

"Mmhmm," he hums, making me like him even more. "Here it comes. When he turns this corner . . ." He's pointing to the corner of the screen.

My eyes narrow as I stare intently.

"There." He pauses the video right as the man's face comes into view.

Rick is talking, asking me questions. I hear him, but I don't. Because the hairs on the back of my neck are standing on end, and my breath . . . Oh god.

I stumble back away, my hands shaking. There's no way. I'm not seeing what I think I am.

A memory hits, taking me back to that night.

Remus looks up and smiles at me before the man steps in behind him and takes him by the chin. And the knife slices straight across his throat.

Rick turns in his chair, making it squeak, pulling me from the recesses of my mind. He looks at me, confused as he stands and reaches for me. But I step further away.

My throat is tight as I shake my head and scramble in my pocket for my phone, pulling it out and trying to swipe it open.

"Are you okay, honey? What's wrong? You look like you've seen a ghost."

I blink up at him, the frame still frozen in the background, before I look down at my phone again, just as my sister's name populates.

Everything in my head comes out in a stream of consciousness. There are no breaks between my words as I tear out of Rick's trailer, hearing him yell to me, but I'm already heading to my car.

"Goldie, he's alive . . . He's fucking alive. I can't believe this—I saw him on the video . . . I saw his face. He was supposed to be dead, and he's not dead. You need to get here. And Noah needs to get Chase. He's not answering. Noah needs to call Chase because oh my god, he's alive, Goldie . . ."

"Evie!" she screams, snapping me out of my panic and stopping me in my tracks. Her voice is laced with tears, unsteady as she levels, "Open the message."

My blood turns to ice as I swallow the lump already formed in my throat. It's as if my mind's already figured out something important I'm missing in the moment.

"Goldie . . ." I whisper, but she repeats herself, so I pull my phone away from my face. My hand's still shaking as my chest begins to tremble with the sobs gathering there.

There's one unread message. *What the fuck? I didn't even hear my phone ding.* I swipe it open, hitting the video link.

And the world around me goes dark, until every single piece of me feels like it's shattered, so I look to the sky and scream.

Chapter Twenty

Him

Leaves rustle and gnash under the weight of his body, and a groan escapes him before his whimpers mix with his own harsh breath.

He hurts. I made sure of it.

I drag his body by the ankles over the ground as dirt and sticks leave a wake behind him.

"Evie," he whispers.

I often wondered about this moment, picturing it almost sentimentally in my mind. It always felt strange to think of it that way, because how can I feel sentimental about something I've never done?

But that's how intensely I've yearned for their deaths. How viscerally I live out this moment in my mind.

This is my legacy. Just like death will be theirs. It's fucking poetic.

He groans again, his weak hand trying to latch onto a passing tree, but it's no use.

"We've reached our destination."

I drop his heavy feet to the ground, causing a thud, a reverberation of his impending death, through the forest, before I squat close to his face.

Blood trickles from his nose, the tight skin around his bottom lip popped open like a can of biscuits.

He calls her name again. And I laugh.

"Even in this moment, one that should elicit your life to flash before your eyes . . . you're only thinking about her."

Poetic. This is exactly where I want you.

I suck in a breath of the crisp air. "I shouldn't tell you this. I'm going to kill you and let them watch."

My eyebrows rise in surprise because he groans, trying to fight, but I pull out my phone and lift it for the perfect angle, readying the camera to film.

"Say murder."

Chapter Twenty-One

Evie

I barely get my car into park and my keys out of the ignition before my sister comes bounding from her house, but I'm doing the same, bursting from my car and meeting her in the middle of the pathway. Our arms instantly wrap around the other, tears already staining each other's shoulders as we hug fiercely.

She pulls back, the palms of her hands wiping my cheeks as she keeps repeating, "Are you okay? Are you okay?"

I nod because I know she's wondering if I'm hurt, and I am; she just doesn't know how yet.

"Baby," Noah whispers, looking around. "Inside the house." He ushers us in, but I point to my car.

"There's a bag in the back . . ."

Noah doesn't hesitate as Evie and I rush inside the house. I'm through the door as I ask, "What did the police say?"

She frowns, immediately letting me go before walking to the fridge and grabbing me a bottle of water. "Here, drink this."

"I'm fine. I want to know what the police said. Do they know who sent the link? Can they locate him? Do they have a lead on Remus?"

All my questions are laid bare in front of her as I stare unblinking, waiting for answers.

Noah walks back inside as she lets out a breath. "The link—"

I draw my head back, confused. "What about it?"

"We called and spoke to a detective, but when we tried to send the video of . . ." She chokes up, and I have to look away. So I take the bottle from her hand to give me something to focus on, or I'll scream again.

She sniffles, pulling herself together, and I blink, listening to the plastic ring around the cap pop while trying to ignore the visions of Chase's body being dragged, bloody and beaten, playing in my mind.

Noah runs his hand down her shoulder, finishing her sentence. "We couldn't send the video . . . The link doesn't work anymore."

I shake my head, pulling out my phone and swiping straight to my messages before, with a tremble, hitting the link. But they're right, it doesn't work.

"What the fuck," I shout, turning toward the kitchen island because I feel like I'm going to break. "But what about Remus . . . They have to look for him."

Nobody answers me, so I turn back, locking eyes with my sister.

"Did you tell them about Remus?"

She's staring back at me, searching my eyes before her lips part and she says, "No."

My chest caves with the exhale I let out. "I don't understand . . . Why wouldn't you tell them? Goldie . . ." She looks at Noah, and I feel irate, so I yell her name again. "Goldie."

Her head whips back to me, her voice almost as loud as mine. "Because he was just the camp counselor, Evie . . . and I saw him die. With my own eyes." She stabs her finger at the floor. "I stood in front of him and watched him bleed to death."

"Goldie . . ." Noah whispers, trying to comfort her, reaching for her hand, but she pulls it away.

"No, Noah. Chase is out there. Someone has him, and she's still back there, in that night . . . Remus isn't alive. Jesus. He was just some poor guy who got caught in the crosshairs of a lunatic's revenge. You know that. This is her panic, and it isn't helping."

Her voice trails off as she turns away from me, walking toward the windows in the living room with her arms crossed over her chest.

"Fuck you." The room is silent as she turns back, and we lock eyes. "Fuck you. You think I'm crazy?"

She spits back with just as much venom, "I think you thought Billy was back at the theater. I think you haven't dealt with the trauma. And I think you're making this about you. You don't even like him, but I can't take care of you right now, Evie. Chase—"

"Is mine," I snap, cutting her off. "Chase is mine . . . and I'm not crazy. It was Remus, Goldie. And it doesn't matter if he was just the counselor. He's connected in some way. So you can either help me find the goddamn love of my life, or you can get out of my fucking way."

The feeling of my eyes welling stings, making me blink, allowing a tear to escape, but I wipe it viciously from my face. I'm not sad because they think I'm the product of my fear. Maybe I am, but I'm not afraid for myself anymore. I'm only thinking about him.

There's nothing but silence as her brows draw together, and she and Noah exchange glances.

I walk to where Noah dropped my duffel bag and clutch the handle, dragging it back to the kitchen as I start opening and shutting drawers, grabbing the biggest knives I see before adding them to my arsenal.

Goldie walks toward the kitchen slowly. "When did you guys . . ."

I don't look up as I speak. "Why do you care?"

The clangs of silverware and the slams of drawers almost drown out my rage as I take what I need from each one.

"Will it make you less of a bitch right now?"

Noah blows out a harsh breath, drawing my eyes, before he stands between us so we can't look at each other.

"We need to work together. We're all on the same side because, clearly, we all love Chase."

Reluctantly, I nod, and I see my sister try to look around him before retreating and turning back around.

Noah looks down at the duffel. "What's in the bag?"

"A crossbow . . . from set."

"Jesus Christ," Goldie rushes out from behind him, so I smack my hands against the counter.

"Then what's your plan? Huh?"

Noah's much calmer than me or Goldie, probably because he's been here, done this two times more than we have. The distance between us is closed as he strides over and sits on a barstool, looking me in the eyes.

"We're going to keep calling the cops until somebody fucking listens to us. And I think we should try and talk to whoever saw him last . . ."

"I saw him last . . . It was me." My voice gets shaky, seeing him in my mind, and it drops me to my knees.

I crouch, gripping the open drawer with all my might because Chase's favorite knives are inside. He keeps them here because he said all his best dishes are for me. A truly fragile breath exhales between my lips before I make my way back up, slowly reaching inside and pulling them out.

"Who else does Chase spend time with?" Noah presses.

My eyes close for a second before I pull it the fuck together. "I don't know . . . nobody. His kitchen . . ."

That's when a thought hits.

"Eddie," I blurt out. "His sous chef . . . He knows Chase's whole schedule. And he waited for the guy who installed the cameras . . . Maybe he'd know something . . ."

His eyes grow wide, picking up exactly what I was thinking. He snaps his fingers. "Fuck yeah. We need that footage. That's something the cops *can* use."

I nod. "Um . . . his laptop's in our room." I point to the door. "His contacts are on it."

He's on his feet, talking over his shoulder. "Listen, I'm not taking Remus or someone who looks like him off the table . . . but how well do we know Eddie?"

Goldie breathes out Noah's name, but he ignores her as he walks into the bedroom and out almost just as fast with Chase's laptop in hand.

"Rexy, everyone's a suspect," he levels at her. "We don't know who we're dealing with, so all I'm saying is, could Eddie be someone we only recognize as a problem in hindsight? Because Chase felt like something was happening . . . We talked about it today."

It feels like a bomb just dropped in the room. *Chase thought something was happening . . . What does that mean?*

It's as if Noah can read my face because he adds, "We agreed not to tell you or Goldie until we were sure there was something to tell."

"Okay, hate that, but go on," I answer.

Goldie walks up next to Noah, staring at his profile, and adds, "Same."

He ignores both of us and continues. "The car felt personal. It reminded him of when we found our apartment in shambles." He looks at Goldie. "And there's been a suspicious guy on Evie's set. And her fish was stolen. He was even suspicious about the rats and his apartment . . ."

She looks around as if she's suddenly scared to be in her own house, but Noah grabs her hand. "We're safe here. I promise."

"He knew?" I don't know why I care so much about Ruth Bader right now, but I do. It's the one thing I latched onto.

Noah nods. "There was nothing substantial. It's all explainable shit, but he kept saying that he just felt like something was coming . . ."

I breathe out, feeling so heavy I'm not sure I could move from this spot, so I stare down at the counter.

"He was right. As usual."

But still, the thought strikes that he'd love this moment—hearing me say he's always right. *You better live, you son of a bitch.*

"There's also . . ." Noah's voice cuts off as Goldie whispers his name.

But I'm frowning, locked on an idea that's swirling like it's on the tip of my tongue, but I can't articulate it as I half-heartedly say, "Also what?"

My head springs up as the thought hits me, but Goldie shakes her head. Except she's looking at Noah.

I ignore that for a second as I pull my phone from my pocket, immediately scrolling to the numbers, and tap the one I need, typing quickly. The swoosh sounds before I place my phone back to the counter, face up, and dive into what I just saw.

"What's going on? Why are you shaking your head?"

She glares at Noah, who shrugs. "You need to tell her, Golds . . ." Her arms cross as she looks unconvinced.

So I snap, "Tell me what?"

A whoosh of breath leaves her as she faces me. "I got an email yesterday. It was sent from that PI company Dad hired. They found some info that never made it my way . . ."

"Get to the point," I level.

"I have a brother," she answers.

I swallow, all the wind knocked out of me. *What the fuck is happening?* I don't know what to say as an empty huff bursts from my chest.

"Did you tell the cops about that?" It feels mean because I meant it to be.

"Yes," she throws back, brows drawn before scoffing at me like she's insulted.

I shake my head, so angry that it feels like I'll never forgive her.

"That's why you think it isn't Remus . . . I'm not crazy. You just know it's your brother."

The guilt behind her eyes answers for her. But Noah speaks up.

"We don't know anything. Especially if the report's even real. Someone's been fucking with you and Chase. How do we know this isn't the same? Look at what's happening. If I wanted to pick us off one by one, this would be a good way to start."

My phone dings, immediately grabbing my attention, and everything we've been talking about comes full fucking circle.

I turn my cell around so it's facing them before I slide it across the counter. Noah catches it, and I watch their eyes lower to the picture I asked Rick to send.

A grainy black-and-white screen capture of Remus stares back. He's wearing a hoodie while holding Ruth Bader, but it's as if he wanted to be caught, because he's looking directly at the screen, smirking.

Goldie gasps as Noah says, "What the fuck."

But I nod. "Meet your brother, Goldie. Because he's alive."

Her eyes try and meet mine, but I can't even look at her. So I turn away to stare at Noah instead as he says, "Imma send this to myself."

He does, motioning like he's sliding my phone back to me, but Goldie nabs it. I'm watching her, two silent tears tipping over from the corners of her eyes, each at different times before they crookedly make their way down her face.

"I watched you die," she whispers, holding my phone up, staring at the photo.

Goldie's chin quivers before she rubs her lips together and brings the back of her hand to her face, wiping away the sadness.

"It'd be great if my relatives would stop coming back from the dead," she says, finally looking at me.

And this time, I don't avoid it.

I nod. And we both break, walking around the counter, hugging again, saying sorry for all the things we didn't mean.

"I didn't think you were crazy."

"Yes you did . . ."

"Okay, maybe a little."

"I'm sorry your brother's potentially trying to kill us."

"I'm sorry he kidnapped your boyfriend."

That's the thing about me and my sister. It doesn't matter how many fucked-up relatives she has popping out of the woodwork or what life throws our way. I love her with my whole being. I'm her ride or die for life.

Nobody comes between us.

And if they did, we'd get grounded as adults, for life.

One loud clap next to us makes our heads whip to Noah, who's standing in the middle of the room with my duffel over his shoulder.

"I sent everything to the cops. And I'm glad you made up. But we got another text."

Goldie and I let go of each other and rush to our phones.

Unknown: No
cops or he dies.
location ping

My head lifts, Goldie and I looking at each other as Noah says, “Looks like we’re going on a road trip.”

Chapter Twenty-Two

Evie

We've been driving for hours past the location I've been spending all my time lately. Hours through pitch black and into sunrise. But it's hard to make out where we are, sitting in the back seat and looking out the window, because all the land in the middle of nowhere in California looks the same.

It's just dirt, speckled with trees and cacti. I haven't seen a landmark or building for miles. And a part of me is scared to death we've been sent on a wild goose chase.

But what was the alternative?

There is none. Because it feels like someone's set a clock, and it's ticking down, and we don't know how much time is left.

"Where the fuck are we going?" Noah mutters to himself, checking the directions he has connected to the car again.

My eyes stay trained out the window, looking for something to make this drive make sense. But all I keep getting are flashes of memories with Chase—us in the kitchen, him dancing around . . . that day at the farmers' market when I think I knew somewhere in the back of my head that I was going to fall for him.

He shakes his head, so onto me, and raises his voice. "Hell has frozen over. She wants to talk about me, everyone."

"Shut up," I rush out, reaching up to cover his mouth, but he grabs my wrist, lowering my arm gently. "Sue me. I'm fascinated. I kind of always thought you were a rich-boy douchebag whose only saving grace was that he wasn't an elitist. But it turns out you're a nonelitist rich-boy douchebag who speaks three, almost four languages and saved your grandma from a fire . . . that you started."

The way he laughs is like an explosion. It's loud and intrusive, but if he was a wine, he'd be a really expensive bottle with a bold flavor.

And I can't help myself—I pull out my phone and take his picture. When he looks at me, I shrug and say, "Proof of life . . . for our guardians."

I shake my head, making the thoughts go away because I'm acting like he's gone. I don't mean to, but that's how fucking scared I am that we're too late. That he's . . . *Don't think it. He's not.*

"You're sure we're going the right way?" Goldie whispers, giving me a reason to focus on something else.

Noah lets out a frustrated groan, gripping the steering wheel too hard.

"Yeah, I'm following the directions. But what the fuck is all the way out here?"

He's not mad at my sister; he's feeling exactly what we all are—scared. Because we don't know what's going to happen.

What I do know is the further we drive, the bigger the pit in my stomach grows.

But I need to stay positive. Not let fear get the best of me.

Chase is alive, and we're bringing him home.

I close my eyes, this time trying to picture him in my mind, him smiling at me the way he always does, because it's always the thing that keeps me calm.

"Have the police messaged or said anything?" I ask Goldie, already knowing the answer because I asked the same question an hour ago.

I open my eyes, watching her check her voicemail anyway, then shake her head. Noah was smart to pass on Eddie's info, along with

Remus's photo, leaving them with Goldie's number. Just in case he gets any more texts.

I take a deep breath, my eyes drifting back out the window, when a half-collapsed shed catches my eye off in the distance. I stare at it, my head following it as we pass by, before I immediately look out the other side to a section of high desert that's more lush.

Way more. *Oh my god.*

"You guys . . ." I whisper, but I'm ignored.

"We have to make a left here," Noah says over me and begins slowing down.

I know this place. Fuck.

The moment he turns, the tires hit gravel, and my heart stops beating. I know exactly where we are, and I'm the only one, just me.

"Oh my god, is this . . ." Goldie breathes out, not finishing what she's saying, but she doesn't have to because the answer is yes.

The car pulls to a complete stop as nausea roils through me. I never wanted to come back here.

Noah and Goldie stare forward, their eyes tipped up, staring at what I already know is there. And still, my hands grip the backs of the seats as I scoot to the edge of the leather, eyes locked on the same thing—the Camp Weonoke sign.

It's still arched, standing tall, marking the replicated entrance to the place that lives in all our nightmares.

My voice comes out as barely a whisper. "He's brought us back to where it all began."

Nobody says a word. Maybe out of fear or rage. But either way, we all know our worst nightmares are about to be relived.

Noah restarts the car and puts it back in drive before we slowly roll under the sign, only the sound of the gravel echoing around us. I try not to look at the tagline, *Adventure Awaits*, because there's nothing about this adventure that I'm looking forward to other than getting my goddamn boyfriend back.

"This is fucking sadistic," Goldie breathes out.

I can hear how scared she is. *Same.*

The thing about this set is it's one of those locations that, from the outside driving by, looks like some kind of desert oasis with a spot of tall trees that make it impossible to see in.

Because of that, it's dark inside . . . which is why production rented it.

The lighting always made it look like nighttime.

On cue, the sunlight begins to fade, becoming sporadic streaks through the trees until it becomes night. But not real night—the kind of set with movie lighting. It's on and illuminating our way.

What the fuck.

The tension inside the car is so thick you'd need a chainsaw to get through it.

"We just need to focus and keep our eye on the prize," Noah says, feeling it, too, as we pull onto the set.

I look down, noticing my hands slightly trembling, so I make fists and flex them. No way. I will not panic. I will not lose it.

"I know it said no cops, but . . ." he adds, my sister and I jumping on him at the same time.

"No!"

He holds up a hand just as we begin to drive through the middle of the camp.

"Oh god," Goldie whispers. "I never wanted to come here. I avoided it at all costs."

I can't help myself. I'm looking out the window. A weird array of mixed memories begins popping up, some from when I was working and others from real life.

My tongue darts out over my dry lips as I blink a few times, realizing I'm staring at nothing, losing myself to my thoughts.

"I can't believe you worked on this, Evie," she whispers to me.

"People do crazy shit in the name of trauma . . . Let's just be glad I didn't write a movie about it."

A burst of laughter rips from her chest before she catches herself. I touch her shoulder, and she squeezes my hand. If there's one thing we never lose, it's our uncanny ability to wallow in dark humor.

Noah drives all the way to the far end, parking next to the cabin that was built as the duplicate for my and Goldie's original one.

He puts the car in park before killing the engine, not looking at us as he says, "All I was saying is that if we find him, we should call the cops while we're here. Not wait until we split."

Goldie shifts in her seat, looking back at me, and we telepathically, eyebrows raised while shrugging, weigh it out before we nod and agree.

"The problem is," I say quietly, feeling like I should. "We have to find him. And I don't know about you guys, but I have no idea what the fuck to expect. I mean, we're literally back to the future."

"Do we just get out?" Goldie throws out, looking around before she looks between me and Noah. But none of us are sure.

"Remus is really bad at this villain shit," I say back.

Noah's door cracks open first, so Goldie and I immediately follow, sliding out and taking careful steps away from the car.

We're each looking around, on high alert, trying to expect the unexpected. But for some reason, I'm getting angrier by the second. Because we're being toyed with like this is a game.

I can feel it.

And if my gut feelings are good enough for Chase to believe and fire someone over, then they're good enough for me. I shake my head.

"Something's weird. It feels like we're being watched, but for what? Why bring us all the way out here for nothing?"

I walk out into the middle of the dirt road, cupping my hands over my mouth and yelling, "Where are you, you little fuck? Because we showed up."

Goldie rushes me, jerking my hands down. "What are you doing? He could be anywhere."

"He knows we're coming. And no, he couldn't be anywhere," I snap, pushing past her and heading toward one of the cabin doors before I raise my foot and kick it like I'm trying to break it down.

It doesn't move.

"Nothing's real here. I know . . . remember. This is a mind game. He's fucking with us, like a cat with a mouse."

"Or a rat . . ." Noah offers.

"Yeah," I throw back. "Let's not turn up dead on someone's mattress. Deal?"

He nods, joining me. "If there's only a few places he could be, that means we just need to check them one by one. Because Chase has to be here, right?"

I don't answer because I don't know anymore. The thing none of us wants to think or even say is that maybe this is where we die too. Not where we find Chase.

"Where should we start?" Goldie aims the question at me, reaching for my hand as she walks toward me, but the sound of static fills the air.

Our heads lift as we all freeze.

It's the kind that happens when you turn on an intercom system, like the one used to greet campers. We're eyes up toward the sky as deep, mangled words mixed with a demonic melody begins to play.

Almost like someone's turning a record backward slowly.

It drifts over the camp, haunting and foreboding, making goose bumps explode over my arms, before it begins to speed up and suddenly play normally.

"What the fuck?" Noah rushes out as he steps toward Goldie.

But I feel like I'm having an out-of-body experience.

I remember that day during production when someone had found this song on the internet. They brought it to the director, and he literally played it over and over while shooting the opening of kids arriving at the camp.

I had to run off set that day and puke.

"It's the Weonoke theme song," I say, looking up at my sister's disgusted face.

She's already put it together. But the longer it plays, the more I start to realize the voice is different.

"That wasn't the same person singing when I heard it," I mutter, not really for anyone other than myself.

"That's my mom's voice . . ."

Goldie looks at Noah, her face ashen, and my eyes dart to him as well. *Oh my god.*

He's shaking his head, his arm raised shoulder level as he points to the sky.

"Why does he have her voice?" It comes out hoarse and raw as he says it. His knees buckle, but he catches himself.

My pulse begins thrumming faster, because *how does* Remus have Noah's mom's voice? She's dead.

Goldie runs, grabbing onto him, keeping him on his feet as he wraps his arms around her. "It's my mom, Goldie."

She shakes her head, holding him tight. "It's not real, Noah. Like Evie said, he's fucking with us. That's not your mom." She forces him to look at her before kissing his lips. "It's not."

I'm watching them, trying to swallow because I can feel that familiar sense of panic right at the edges of my mind. It's waiting, looking for the opportunity to sneak past my defenses.

But I can't let it.

Chase is out here somewhere.

I wag my finger, turning in a circle, looking around. "No. This sick bastard is trying to break us," I spit. "We need to look for Chase. Now."

Nobody answers me. So I whip my face toward them.

Noah looks shell shocked as Goldie keeps reassuring him, so I walk to the trunk of the car, barking, "Noah. Open it."

He pops it open for me just as the song stops, and I can hear him let out a whoosh of a breath. Jesus Christ, I can't even imagine what he feels, but . . .

"We need to keep our eyes on the prize . . . right?" I say over my shoulder to him, reminding him of his own words.

Noah nods to me before turning his attention back to Goldie, kissing her gently.

I hate how much my heart is racing and how clammy I already feel, because the panic keeps growing, and I'm worried I won't be able to stop it.

I'm about to say something to my sister when I freeze again, because this time, a voice comes over the loudspeakers. It's masked by one of those voice changers that makes it sound like a child.

"Hi, sissy." With each word, the voice gradually grows deeper until it's . . . familiar. "Do you recognize my voice?"

Oh my god. Goldie gasps and my heart stops.

Remus.

He really is her brother. And he's here.

"Welcome to Camp Murder, where all your nightmares come true and serial adventure awaits."

Jesus. He's going to torture us with our worst fears. First, Noah with his mom, and now Goldie. I blink quickly, too quickly because I can feel the flutter in my chest, the tightness growing.

My biggest fear is losing Chase. And something tells me he knows that.

My eyes are fixed to the duffel in the trunk, tears beginning to prick as I try and breathe. But I can't. I can't . . . Oh god.

I can't lose him. Not like this. We just got started . . . *Please, not like this.*

Black spots begin to accompany the burgeoning tears, and although I can hear Goldie and Noah speaking, it's like I'm trapped underwater and I can't get to the surface.

My fears are dragging me down inch by inch. Oh god. I won't be able to help him. He'll die because of me.

The hairs on the back of my neck stand on end as my eyes close. I reach for any part of the car to keep me steady. I'm desperate to escape from what's happening, but that fucking voice on the loudspeaker won't let me.

"It's time to get to know each other, campers. Even though I already know so much about you. Let's play a game."

Stuttered breaths begin to leave me as I hear my name, but I shake my head. *No . . . no. I need to focus on something . . . anything. I need . . .* Chase.

He comes into my mind so clearly. So vividly that it makes me gasp. His green eyes are locked on me as he smirks. Just the way he did when I saw him back at the theater for the first time. His head tilts as he crosses his arms.

"Don't get meek on me now . . . Where's that bite I like so much?"

It's as if I've been yanked from under, pulled above water. My eyes spring open, a smile on my face as I take another deep breath. I uncurl my fingers from the grip I had on the car, settling back into my body, my panic subsiding.

Goddammit. He's always fucking saving me. Such a dick.

"Fuck this. No more," I bark, shedding off the last of my panic and doubt, saying the rest over my shoulder. "Can we please kill some psycho fucks? Because I want my boyfriend back."

"Yes," Goldie answers, raising her voice to the sky. "And fuck you, Remus. I only have a badass sister."

We nod at each other, the strength inside me doubling by the second before I'm opening the duffel bag, everything but the kitchen sink staring back at me. I brought it all. Even Chase's favorite knife.

And that's my first choice.

But I also double back and yank the crossbow free just as that creepy-ass voice says, "We're gonna have so much fun. Cross my heart and hope you die."

"You die, motherfucker . . . not us," I whisper, facing my sister and Noah, who are staring back at me as I hold up each of the weapons in my hand.

I shrug. "Just in case the die part of the game comes first."

"Who are you?" Goldie mutters, walking past me to get a weapon too. "Buffy?"

"No, a woman scorned," I breathe out, mentally going through the places that are real on set.

Noah's thinking what I'm thinking because he looks at me, holding a cleaver. "Where to first?"

But I don't get to answer because the deep boom of electricity getting shut down starts at the front of the camp.

Light after light is slammed off, as the sound gathers speed. Doof . . . doof . . . doof . . . doof. Doof. Doof. Doof.

It all goes off until we're in pitch black, and that damn voice whispers . . .

"Hey, Evie, are you afraid of the dark?"

Chapter Twenty-Three

Him

"Wakey, wakey."

No matter how many times I've slapped his face, he's still groggy. But I suppose that's the downside of a hammer to the head.

I let out a deep breath as I stare at him, scrunching my nose up because this room smells dank and like mold.

"Wake up," I say sharper, slapping where it's already red.

Moaning accompanies his eyes finally fluttering open. Attaboy. His head flops as I reach out next to me and pick up the silver duct tape.

I'm waiting for the realization to hit. For him to understand what's about to happen before I rip a long strip. Letting the sound punctuate the fear in his eyes.

"What the f—" he breathes out before I press it to his face quickly, smiling down as he struggles to keep saying something . . . anything.

"Huh? . . . I can't hear you. Oh wait . . ."

The moment I know it's stuck to his skin, I tear it off.

He grunts, turning his face sideways, but I'm already prepared with another piece, forcing it onto his face harder this time.

"Now shh. Don't interrupt me. I have so much to tell you."

His eyes water as he strains against the chair he's tied to. A loud bang rings out because he all but lifts it off the floor, growling at me.

I take a step back, impressed.

"Wow . . . I bet you're a beast in bed. I mean, I kinda know . . . I watched. She does this thing right before . . ."

Another loud bang. "Oof, so feisty. But you're going to need to calm down and let me explain what's going to happen before you hurt yourself."

He's staring at me with so much rage as I drag a similar chair across the concrete floor, letting it scrape the ground the whole way, before flipping it around to straddle it.

My arms fold along the rusty top, and I rest my chin on them.

"Okay . . . Where should I start? How about at the part where you die?"

Chapter Twenty-Four

Evie

Oh. My. God. I can't see.

"Looks like it's your turn to get fucked with," Noah whispers. "We're here, Eves. Don't worry. We got your back."

My pulse is racing. I can feel it in my temples as Noah and Goldie each touch my shoulder.

The lights are out, leaving us bathed in darkness. They went out so fast that my eyes blink rapidly, white stars behind them. We're frozen in our places, waiting for our respective visions to acclimate.

Only the sound of our combined breath. But my hands grip my weapons.

"Can you see anyone?" Goldie barely whispers, but neither of us answers.

Because honestly, I'm not just waiting for my vision to acclimate, I'm waiting on my newfound courage to do the same. But that's the thing about the dark. It brings out all the hidden monsters and makes you see things that aren't there . . . like terrified faces behind windows that aren't real.

Except, I can still see them. Those memories are burned into me. Etched into my bones, and it's making this camp look way too much like two years ago, when I was scared and running for my life.

Sawdust looks like the dirt on the ground, and the prefab walls look like real wood ones. So much so, my damn hand twitches, because I swear I can still feel the way the wood splintered into my skin when my palm smacked against it.

I let out a shaky breath. "This is unhinged . . ."

"I don't know what scares me more . . . knowing what to expect, or not knowing when it's coming," Goldie whispers back.

I nod in agreement. She's right. I don't know which is scarier either. But the one thing I do know is someone's dying tonight, and the three of us are hoping it's Remus.

"Campers," that fucking voice says enthusiastically, making my shoulders jump. "You have fifteen minutes to find what you came for . . . and then we come find you."

Jesus Christ.

My stomach caves as my chest starts to rise faster. That clock I felt ticking earlier comes crashing down.

There's only fifteen minutes to find him.

The heavy weight of how fucked up this is hits me hard, square in the chest.

We need to cover as much ground as possible. Noah's and Goldie's hands are off my shoulders as I spin around, thinking, trying to come up with a plan.

"Fuck," Noah breathes out as I immediately shift my face to his.

"Agreed."

"What do we do?" Goldie whispers.

I feel like I'm having a heart attack. My chest is heaving, my pulse hammering. I can already feel the sweat trickling down the back of my neck. But I'm not hot.

There's scared, and then there's this, but the only answer is to find Chase.

That's it.

"We split up," I blurt out, hating the idea but knowing it's all we've got.

"We are not splitting up, Evie," Goldie snaps back.

"Agreed," Noah throws in as quickly as she's done. "That's what he wants . . . for us to be apart."

I ignore them and keep talking.

"The only buildings that are real, are the cafeteria." I point to it. "Remus's office." I point to that too. "Our cabin." Goldie shivers. "And the boathouse."

They look over their shoulders in that direction.

We're all having déjà fucking vu right now, I'm sure of it.

I blink too rapidly, trying to stop hearing Goldie crying in the back of my mind. But it only stops when she grabs my wrist. I shake my head, tugging it away carefully so as not to slice my leg with Chase's knife.

"We only have minutes, Golds. I'll go to Remus's office. Noah, you go to the cafeteria, and Goldie, take the cabin. We'll meet back in the middle for the boathouse if we don't find him."

I don't want to do this, but time is of the essence.

My sister whispers her dissent, but before I can run away, Noah grabs my arm.

"He would never forgive me if something happened to you."

Our eyes lock, and the sincerity in his makes my heart sink. Chase would hate him forever. But sometimes we have to make tough choices.

It's like he can read my mind, because he adds, "We stay together, or we follow you. Your choice."

I scowl. "That's not a choice. That's the same thing, worded differently."

Only seconds tick by as we stand off, but it's enough that I can feel my anxiety spike. He's leaving me no choice. But Noah knows that. *Goddammit.* He's officially my least favorite.

I push past him and my sister, giving in, and head toward our fake cabin first.

"Come on," I hiss before crouching down as I take the stairs quietly. Fuck, they even creak in the same spot as the real ones.

My mind begins to war between the past and present, drifting back there again until Noah's hushed voice pulls me back.

"Let me check to see if it's clear."

I stand off to the side of the door, my crossbow ready as Noah runs to the window, peeking inside quickly before nodding at me. With a deep breath, I grab the handle and turn it, pushing the door open.

A whizzing shoots past my ear, making me blanch and stifle a scream. The silver glint of a butcher knife bounces off the floor as my shoulders lift to my ears, and my head whips to Goldie.

Holy shit.

"What are you doing?" I rush out. She winces, looking horrified as I stare at her, my entire body locked in position. "Chase could've been tied up in there."

Noah's eyes are like saucers as he looks back and forth between us. But she's panicked. Shaking her head before she covers her mouth, speaking through her hands.

"Sorry . . . sorry. I got attacky. I was thinking that someone was waiting for us."

My weapons rest on my knees as I bend over, breathing heavy. Finally exhaling, my muscles unknot themselves.

This is not the kind of calamity we need right now.

Noah goes to her as I try to ignore the misfire of my goddamn heart. I look around the room, confirming it's empty . . . again, then close the door.

My eyes land on my sister. "Let's not kill the fucking guy we're here to save, yeah?"

She nods, hugging her husband before she whispers, "What about the bathroom?"

"Not real," I say back, heading down the stairs.

"Remus's office?" Noah says quietly, and we follow.

We're hurrying as quietly as we can, our heads turning toward any noise as we rush. The dark makes it colder, or maybe that's the adrenaline coursing through me, because I'm covered in goose bumps. My hands still trembling. Truthfully, they haven't stopped since we arrived.

I hate this. Straight up capital-H hate, but it doesn't matter what I feel because I can't even imagine what Chase is feeling.

The picture I'll never forget—him bloodied and semi-unconscious, being dragged—owns my thoughts again. Tears shine in my eyes, I can't help it . . . He called for me, said my name.

Fuck.

I'll find you or die trying.

"Do you see anyone?" Noah says over his shoulder, so I refocus and glance back over mine. There's nothing.

Just that quiet, eerie silence that happens right before hell unleashes. Like the calm before a storm.

"No," I whisper, feeling like even that's too loud.

I duck under a tattered camp flag hung from its post on the porch of a cabin as I wave Goldie closer to me.

We're near the office, and she knows it, too, because she reaches for my arm.

Fuck, these memories are like machine gun fire, barraging me and wearing me down. I can't escape them. No matter if this shit . . . this campsite, is real or fake. The people who died were real. And my fear is fucking real.

"Eves," Goldie breathes out.

But she doesn't need to finish that sentence because I'm already hyperaware of the fact that we're in *the* spot.

The one where we were forced to choose the right path between freedom and death.

A crack of a twig makes our feet stop. Halt on instant command. Noah stands in front of me and Goldie protectively, but we turn our backs to him. Each watching to see what or who is coming.

I swallow hard because, this time, I can't stop the memory playing out in real time as I stare into the darkness.

"Can you tell which ones are fake?" Goldie whispers.

I shake my head as I run my palms over my cheeks. I can't tell. And the panic is building so fast it feels like I can't stop it.

"Do you have a designer tell? Look for that?"

My sister's saying it over and over, and the others are talking at me too. But I can't tell. I can't fucking tell.

"No." I don't yell it, but it feels like it. "I can't tell."

There's no pulling from the memory. I'm back in it. The present is the past, the past is the present. It's existing together.

The gravel underfoot gives our movement away as we take small steps, trying to make sure nobody's coming for us.

Because if there's one thing I'm sure of, Remus isn't waiting until the time runs out. He wants us all dead.

We did kill his father, after all.

"We can't keep fucking standing here. We're sitting ducks," Noah hisses. "The voice said they would look for us. We gotta move."

He starts to take off again, but what he just said hits me like a brick.

My hand springs forward, grabbing his wrist and tugging him back. "Wait."

"We're running out of time . . ." he counters, but I don't let him go.

I shake my head. "Repeat what you just said . . ."

He huffs in frustration as I drop his arm. "What? That that crazy motherfucker will be coming to get us?"

My mouth opens, then closes as the realization I've had sinking into my gut leaves me scared to fucking death.

"No," I whisper shakily. "The voice said, 'We . . . come find you.' Who the fuck is *we*?"

We stand in silence as blood drains from their faces. Goldie starts shaking her head in tiny beats. "I don't understand . . . does that mean he's back? That Billy . . ."

But I don't get a word out, because in answer to our questions, three spotlights turn on.

One at a damn time . . . whipping our heads first to the north, directly in front of us. Then to our left. And the last to our right.

My blood runs ice cold. This isn't happening. No. Not again . . .

"Goldie," I breathe out, needing someone to confirm I'm not hallucinating.

But I'm not. Standing in each of the spotlights is a man dressed in all black, wearing a matching hoodie. I hear Goldie's stuttered breath and Noah's *motherfucker* somewhere around me, but I'm focused on the blocked pathways.

This is how he's fucking with me. It was never the dark . . . That was just the foreplay before he tortured me.

Because behind the hoodie, each of the figures is wearing a grotesquely distorted prosthetic mask . . .

Of Remus's face.

I feel sick. As if bile is crawling up my throat, because they all have a fake slit on the neck. Like the one we thought was real when blood spilled out over the floor.

It's like they skinned him to wear him.

Goldie starts to cry, and it's not unlike the first time when it was me who was spiraling. Noah tries to comfort her. But I take a step out alone.

I stare at each of them.

"He's literally re-creating the whole night," I level. "He wanted us back in the most horrifying moment of our lives."

My eyes narrow as the handle of Chase's knife circles around in my hand. Over and over, as I keep staring between them, feeling two years ago so viscerally that it's hard to breathe.

But maybe that's okay.

Maybe this is what it means to overcome something. You don't forget the fear, or stop feeling it, you just figure out a way to use it.

I take a deep breath, thinking about what's happening—*time's a-wasting.*

Fuck that. *You don't get him.*

Remus may have faked his death the first time, but I'm going to help him live more authentically this time.

"If this is like last time, that means only one of these is the real guy," Noah grits out.

"But which one?" my sister whispers.

My eyes close, letting the memory take over. Not fighting it. Using it.

"Can you tell which ones are fake?" Goldie whispers.

I shake my head with both hands on the sides of my face as I look to the masked men and blow out a harsh breath.

"Do you have a designer tell? Look for that?" Noah urges.

"No," I draw out. "I can't tell. Fuck."

"Come on, there's gotta be something," Chase adds.

But I start to cry again. "I don't . . . oh my god." My breathing starts picking up pace as I keep looking between the paths. I'm panicking. I've never felt like this. Like I can't stop the fear from getting the best of me. But it's taking me under.

"I can't tell. Oh my god. I just don't . . . I just don't know."

Chase pulls me close, wrapping his arms around me, whispering into my ear.

"You don't have to know. I promise you I'll save you and Noah and Goldie. If it's the last thing I do, I will save the people you love. Do you hear me?"

I'm saying I'm sorry *over and over, but Chase isn't listening.*

"Promise me, you will only think about yourself and live. Just live, Evie. For me."

A smile blooms over my face as I shake my head, and my eyes glisten. I was thinking about everyone else, and he was only thinking about me. Even back then.

It's my turn to save you.

"Evie," Goldie presses, so I look at her.

"No," I level calmly. "I can't tell which one's real . . . but I know what can . . ."

I lift the crossbow and fire to the north.

She shrieks as the sound clicks and whizzes, her shoulders jumping. Noah pulls her face to his chest, but I'm staring straight at my arrow.

A loud thud, followed by a white fog that dusts the air, giving away that it's fake. The dummy falls to the ground.

"Boathouse, now."

We run. The all-too-familiar sound of our feet pounding the ground echoes around the false night. Our labored breaths mingle as we race down over the dirt and grass.

Noah yells "Four minutes" behind me, but I can't move any faster, so I stretch my arm out, giving him my crossbow like a baton, letting him pass me.

Someone has to get there.

The sound of my panted breaths echoes inside my head, the only thought being *Please, god, be there.*

My feet are slowing on their own as I watch Noah sprint. But suddenly my eyes shutter, everything happening in slow motion as my mind tries to process and act at the same time.

There's a click in the distance, followed by a sharp explosive sound. And it sounds like it's slicing through the air.

My mouth falls open, eyes growing wide as terror takes over my body, because my sister screams.

Noah looks back, screaming her name. But I can't move as my entire body shakes, trembling and in shock.

Because Goldie drops to the ground.

Noah scrambles over the ground, back to her side, dropping the crossbow. As he immediately presses a hand to her shoulder.

I can't make out what he's saying, because he's sobbing through his words. Screaming for her to keep her eyes open.

I'm trying to say her name but I can't.

Red begins to bleed through her shirt and my eyes fix to it.

She's been shot. The thought is chanted in my head as time begins to speed up along with my breath as reality kicks back in.

Noah cradles her in his arms. "Baby," he shouts, but she's limp.

My hands cover my cries as I fall to my knees, digging my hands and nails into the dirt to crawl to her, but Noah looks at me, bellowing, "Evie . . . go! Go, go, go . . ."

I don't want to leave her.

"No," I rush out, crying as I reach for her, but her tearstained face lifts, her voice weak.

"Evie, get Chase."

I'm immediately nodding. Listening to what she's told me to do. Because Noah has her. He has her. He'll take care of her.

Her eyes stay on mine as I stand, walking backward a few steps, and I watch Noah pick her up to run her to safety. Then I turn and run toward danger.

And I run like the goddamn wind straight toward the boathouse. Without worry for myself, praying with every step that he's there.

Also knowing that without a shadow of a doubt, this is part of Remus's plan.

The boathouse was where Billy was tortured and almost drowned. This is where he wants me to find him.

Because in the end, it was always going to be brother versus sister.

The moment I hit the door, all the fear over the last two years settles inside my bones, mutating, turning into rage as I bust through, locking eyes with *him*.

Chapter Twenty-Five

Chase

If they open the door, I fall in.

If they open the door, I fall in.

When they open the door, I die.

I'm staring at the wood grain ten feet from the cause of my death because I'm taped to a fucking chair, gagged, ankles tied together. Rigged to fall and go under the water behind me.

My chest shakes with every breath I take, mainly because of the physical pain but also because I can't stop staring at the goddamn wood-grained door, hoping it's not her who opens it.

If there's any god in the universe, he'll use whatever power he has to ensure it's not my baby. *Please don't let her carry this for the rest of her life.*

I pull against the restraints again, still not giving up. Even as the duct tape over my mouth stings the open wound where my lip's split.

Fuck. I've spent hours going over and over why this is happening and trying to break free. That must mean I'm at the bargaining stage of death.

I strain my arms again, trying to twist my wrists, the tape pulling at my skin as I sit bound, waiting.

Just fucking waiting to die. It's happening. This is how I'm going to go.

For a while, I thought about my family and my niece . . . wondering how they'd find out. If they'd blame me for not calling the cops when I had the chance. Then I drifted to the guys at the kitchen, wondering if they'd keep me alive through the food. Take some recipes out into the world as it existed without me. But I kept coming back to Noah and Goldie . . . *and her*. It's always her. Because she's my heart.

The one reason I have to keep struggling until the bitter end.

I squirm, trying again to pick at the duct tape around my wrists, but I can't get enough of it to tear. *Fuck.* Harsh breath rushes from my nose before I close my eyes, ready for what's to come.

My baby's beautiful face materializes in my mind, and like a movie, I see all our moments, even the ones she didn't know we were having. The way she rolls her eyes when she really wants to give in and blush. Or the way she always sits up straighter in her seat when I put a plate in front of her, like each meal is the most exciting thing she's ever experienced.

But my favorite memory is the way she looked at me the last time we woke up. She didn't say anything, just stared into my eyes, and I knew she was going to love me for our whole lives.

I just didn't know it was ending so soon.

The words can't come out, but I think them in the hopes that somehow they'll find her one day.

I haven't left you since the day we met. And I will love you past the day I die.

I keep my eyes closed, finally allowing myself to be at peace, before they shoot open because the door bursts open. And our eyes meet.

"Chase," she screams.

Evie.

And then water rushes over my head as I plummet to the bottom of the lake.

Chapter Twenty-Six

Evie

I don't think before I act.

I run, diving into the man-made lake where Chase just fell in. He was bound, his chair connected to a tension wire that snapped the moment I opened the door.

Cold water rushes around me, murky and dark, as my arms push fast, dragging through the water as I kick like hell. I'm swimming harder than I ever have, following the glimmer from the metal leg of the chair all the way down fifteen feet to the bottom.

This isn't a real lake, just a fucking hole in the dirt. But we could still drown and die in this watery grave. Water whooshes around me, my eyes straining and stinging as air bubbles surround me, tickling my skin as I go deeper.

He hits the bottom, kicking up the dirt around it as he lands on his side, and I all but scream underwater.

Oh god. He can't die like this.

My lungs are already starting their protest because I was already spent from running, but I won't stop until I get him out.

I reach out, kicking the last couple of feet before I grab him. He's struggling, his hair lifted off his face as we stare at each other, but I can't lift him off the ground.

My face shifts around. I'm frantic, my lungs beginning to burn, as I swim around him, trying to pull the duct tape off his wrists.

Goddammit.

Screams that are caught in my throat warble underwater as my body twists because I can't fucking get the tape off. Chase's eyes stay locked to mine, and I shake my head, because he's telling me to leave him.

I can't. I won't.

He motions with his head, but I don't listen, still looking for a way to free him. But he does it again, and this time my eyes follow.

Oh my god.

His knife.

When I jumped in, I had it in my hand, but I must've let it go, and it followed me down. I swim to it quickly, kicking and turning my body, desperately wanting to take a breath before I reach for it, pulling it out of the dirt.

Burning seeps over my chest as I bring the blade to his wrists and cut through the tape like butter.

Chase's arms rip from the chair, flying at his side as he frees the tape around his mouth. It twists, floating in the water next to us as I swim to his feet and cut there too.

We're encased in dirty water, pushing against the ground, kicking and fighting, the knife abandoned again as we swim to the top.

But I feel like I'm not going to make it.

My arms begin to slow, my eyes locked on him above me. Chase looks down and reaches out, grabbing the back of my shirt and hauling me with him.

Water breaks and splashes around us as we breach the smooth surface. Sucking in sweet, blessed air. He's gasping and coughing, as I do the same.

We're alone, wading, my arms already sore as we stare at each other.

Because we're alive.

Sobs begin to rumble my chest as I break. But it's not sadness. It's relief. I'm so fucking grateful that he's okay. I got here in time.

Chase wraps a strong arm around my waist, keeping us both afloat as I hug him, my face in the crook of his neck. The tears won't stop.

I feel him swimming us back to the edge, and I look up into his eyes.

"Missed you," he whispers with a grin.

I kiss him, hearing him hiss because his lip's split, but when I pull back, his hand cradles the back of my head, keeping me in place.

We sigh into each other, savoring the moment.

But it's over too fast, because we're still in danger. He pushes me up onto the dock first before I turn and lie on my stomach, reaching down to help him out as well.

Water's dripping from us, pooling around our feet, and my clothes feel too heavy as we stand silently, the euphoria of our reunion wearing off.

"We have to get out of here," I whisper.

He starts to say something, but there's a creak outside, coming from the side of the building.

Shit.

I bring my finger to my lips to tell him to be quiet, but he's already looking around for another way out. Except there's only the door.

And that's half opened, still swaying from bouncing off the wall. Another creak. Someone's coming.

Our fifteen minutes are up.

I come close to Chase's ear and whisper, "We need to get to the car. Goldie was hurt, but I think Noah will be waiting for us there. It's Remus, Chase . . . he's the one—"

Chase grabs my face, turning his quickly to stare into my eyes. "No . . . baby, it's not. Evie . . ."

But before he can finish his sentence, the door slams against the wall, and a set of familiar eyes walks through the door.

Followed by another.

My own eyes are saucers, and it feels like the wind's been knocked out of my tired lungs. "What . . . what are you doing?"

Derek and Devin stand together, smiling before they exchange a glance, Derek taking the lead.

"Surprise, Evie. Betcha didn't see that coming."

Chapter Twenty-Seven

Evie

I can hear myself breathing because, no, I didn't see that coming.

Chase squeezes my hand, centering me, and I give him a squeeze back.

"She's shocked," Devin says, putting his chin on his brother's shoulder as they both stare at me.

My mind is working overtime because I don't understand . . . What are they doing here? How . . .

"She is," Derek answers. "What a moment." He breaks out into applause, extending his hands as if it's for me.

"What's happening?" I rush out, trying to process what I'm seeing.

Chase starts to speak, but Devin holds up a gun around his brother's arm and points it at him.

"Shh, this is *her* moment. No cheating and feeding her lines. You already know the plot."

Fuck. He shot Goldie. How are my Double D's the people who set us up? Because clearly they have.

"I don't understand . . . You're working with Remus? Why? What did we ever do to you? I thought we were—"

Devin lifts his head off Derek's shoulder and goes back to his side.

"Were you going to say friends?" He slaps Derek's shoulder while still gripping the gun. "I told you she really likes us."

"I'm ashamed I doubted it," Derek levels. "But authenticity is rare in this business. Look at us, always having to sneak around and hide our affection for the macabre."

He reaches into his back pocket, tugging out the fucking *Texas Chainsaw Massacre*–style flesh mask of Remus, and pulls it over his head. He holds up his hands as he shifts the face back and forth between me and his brother.

Devin lifts the gun, putting it under his chin, pretending to shoot himself as he says, "It's macabre, for sure. A lost art, really."

I grimace. "You're crazy. You've been working together with a guy who faked his death to try and kill us all? That's not macabre. It's psycho."

They look at each other before Devin reaches for his brother's cheek, patting the mask. "I know . . . I was rooting for her to get the twist too. But give her a minute—I told you that storyline needed more fleshing out. And you're going to hate me for saying this, but I still think there's something elegant and sexy about the villain's monologue."

"Storyline? This is entertainment to you?"

My head feels like it's going to explode as I volley between Chase and the guys, desperate for some explanation, but more so hoping Chase is quietly trying to figure a way out of here. He gives me a small shake of his head before his eyes tick to the other side of the room.

Derek pulls off Remus, dropping it to the floor.

"Evie. Catch up," he snaps. "You're smarter than this. There is no Remus—he died the first time around."

I can't even process what they're saying, but I cut him off. "I don't understand . . . because I saw him . . ."

"Or you saw what we wanted you to see," Devin offers.

I stare down at the mask on the floor and back at them as silence fills the room.

Oh my god.

They were the ones who first told me about the footage. They led me to it. Son of a bitch.

A thousand thoughts race through my mind, and they're heavy and suffocating as I think through all the little things I missed—their curiosity with my history, the way they never even flinched when I got scared that day on set, or how I only saw one of them at a time before Chase went missing.

They have access to my phone, to all our numbers, because I gave them my code.

Jesus, I made it so easy for them to get to us. *Holy fuck.*

"But why?" I whisper, fear coursing through me.

They smile. But it's different from the countless other times I've seen them do it. There's no light behind either of their eyes. It's as if whatever mask they've had on is gone.

Devin presses the corner of his lip between his teeth, using the barrel of the gun as he tilts his head.

"Because every thriller needs a good bait and switch."

My brows draw together. They're talking like it's a . . .

Chase's voice finishes my thought.

"They're making a movie," he says quietly, garnering a tsk from Devin before the gun is aimed at his head.

"Stop fucking up my script. I'm a writer, Chase. We hate last-minute changes." Devin's voice is strained with anger as he stabs the gun forward. "You already committed that offense once when you showed up at the restaurant, and this makes two. Another, and she'll be picking brains out of those braids for days."

Derek piggybacks on what he says. "Don't you see? We made it up. *We* sent the email to Goldie . . . and doctored the video. She doesn't even have a brother. It was just the right amount of drama and suspense. Especially since we secured this set."

He motions around as it all starts to fall into place.

They're not just villains. They're the producers of fear. Because while the idea of Remus after us is horrifying, he's the devil I knew. This is something I could've never imagined.

Devin takes a deep breath, locking his eyes on me. "It all happened really organically . . . We were just in the right place at the right time."

"Destiny, if you will," Derek adds before they begin taking turns to unveil this horror.

"Because we were there . . . two years ago, at the camp."

"Saw it all . . . every gruesome detail."

"It was inspiring. Seeing a monster like Billy, live and in action. Wow."

"The bar was set. It was better than any slasher film before it," Derek says, before he shivers like he's excited.

Sick fucks. They're fans. Horror enthusiasts with just the right amount of psychosis to want to ruin our lives . . . again.

What the fuck.

Devin wags his eyebrows. "We actually got some of our first footage of you that night. It's amateur camerawork, but we've gotten way better since then." He looks at his brother, his eyes wild. "Show her."

Derek pulls out his phone, turning it around to face me.

My brows furrow because I'm suddenly watching myself inside Goldie's house . . . but from the outside. It's the day I first came home to Chase cooking.

I shake my head because I feel blindsided. They've been fucking watching us.

He swipes to a new video, but it's him holding dead rats above my bed, teasing Princess. "Whoops, not that one." He swipes to another. It's me and Chase the night we almost kissed at his restaurant.

"Show her my favorite . . ." Devin whispers.

I'm squeezing the fuck out of Chase's hand because rage has replaced the shock.

They've been pulling strings since the beginning. This role—the girl who has panic attacks, the one still afraid of the dark—she's been nurtured. Groomed for this performance.

But I'm not that girl anymore. That's their fatal flaw. It's what all horror movies do wrong. They make the woman a victim, someone defined by her fear, and then some dude comes to save her.

Not this time, fuckers.

Chase gave me the space to heal myself, but I saved me. I found the tools and the will. And now I'm going to use that rage to kill these two assholes.

I'm nobody's victim.

Cinderella's saving the prince and getting the hell out of here.

My eyes shift back to the screen, watching myself leading Chase to the bathroom at my fucking sister's wedding.

The couple on the screen is laughing, but the couple standing here is murderous.

He ends the video, turning his phone back around.

"It gets rated R after that, and we don't know who's watching right now."

He points up, and my eyes follow. There's a tiny red dot by the ceiling. It's a camera.

My pulse is thrumming so fast I can almost hear it as my blood turns to ice, but not out of fear.

Derek smirks at me. "You're live . . . Well, not totally. It's set for the world to see in one hour. Don't you love technology? This is what sets us apart from other movies. Because, frankly, after watching *One Killer Night*, we knew we could do it better."

"No offense," Devin throws out, but Chase scoffs.

I throw my hand over his mouth to make sure he doesn't speak. He looks ready to fucking end it all, but I shake my head.

We did not almost drown to have our dead bodies thrown back in.

Derek crosses his arms with a big nod of his head. "Easy, big guy. We're not being rude to her. So protective." He winks. "We just wanted to be the first people to make a sequel better than the original."

"This is so beyond twisted. It's pure evil."

"And evil is forever, Evie," Devin barks. "This is our legacy. Nobody will ever beat it. Name another movie in history that people get to buy tickets to the live ending. We're revolutionary."

"No, you're certified. What is this . . . daddy issues? Mommy issues? Your nanny not give you enough attention? You think you'll get away with killing us." I point to the camera. "You're supplying the evidence for the electric chairs. If you're lucky, they'll let you sit next to each other."

Devin points at me with the gun, making my body tense as he shouts, "This is why I loved her for this, Derek. Such passion. She's feisty, and honestly, there isn't enough strong female representation in film anymore. Hollywood hates women."

Chase tries to pull me behind him, but I won't move.

"*Me too . . .*" Derek hangs out there like he's waiting for us to get the joke, before rolling his eyes. "Y'know . . . the movement . . . it's a play on words? For fuck's sake, I love women. I'm an ally."

"You're trying to kill me," I level.

Derek's head draws back before he looks at his brother. "Tell her."

Devin shrugs his shoulders a few times like he's excited. "See, the thing is, Evie . . . only one person lives . . . and it's not any of the rest of us."

I swallow, feeling like I'm in an alternate universe as Chase stands closer, looping a finger around a belt loop of my pants. *Good call.* I really want to lunge at someone right now.

"We'll kill your family . . ." Derek says as Devin finishes for him, "And then you'll be so angry that you'll kill us while the world watches. You won't be able not to, because what kind of friend, sister, lover would you be?"

Derek holds up his hands, shaking like he's trying to razzle-dazzle. "We get our final girl, and our names will live on in infamy. Tell me you don't love it."

Devin reenacts a mic drop but doesn't drop the gun, before he quickly adds, "The working title is *Cross My Heart and Hope You Die* . . . but let us know if you don't like it, because we won't be able to change it in post."

What the fuck is the only thing I can think. It seems to be the most accurate question for everything they say. I keep opening and closing my mouth, glancing at Chase, whose eyes are locked on the guys.

I'm trying to buy time for a plan to formulate.

"Oh, she's nervous for her big moment," Devin says, sucking in a hiss of a breath.

Derek claps his hands together before doing an impersonation of Kris Jenner with his hands coming to his knees. "You're doing great, sweetie."

Think. Think. Think.

We have to get out of here, but there are two lunatics in front of the only exit, and they have a gun . . . A gun they'll use on Chase.

Just not on me . . .

. . . because I'm the final girl.

I'm wading through the thought slowly because a plan *is* forming. One I hope Chase will pick up on.

We're standing there, Chase and I still dripping wet, before I reach behind myself and gently push his hand off, taking a step forward.

"No."

They frown, Devin looking at Derek before he says, "What do you mean, no?"

"I mean no, I won't be your final girl. And no, I won't kill you."

Derek laughs. "Of course you will. Have you been paying attention? We've been watching your every move, Evie. I can almost set a clock to those little panic attacks nobody knows about. If you think we can't control you, then ask yourself how we knew what to send Goldie to make you two fight. Or how littering her inbox with shit about Italy would get her to go . . . Guess you don't have to be blood related to both be easily influenced."

Devin looks me up and down, popping a hip effeminately. "It's comical because you think you made these decisions yourself, when in reality, they were selected for you by the people in this room, from the voices in our heads."

Derek chuckles. "*Devil Wears Prada*. Insane reference."

I huff a laugh. "Think what you want about me, but I'm not participating in some D-rate piece of shit. I'd rather you shoot us both right now."

My eyes lock on Devin, whose jaw is tensed, his trigger finger far too itchy as he points it back at Chase for the third time.

But Derek smiles before he sighs and lowers his brother's arm so he's not pointing the gun at Chase anymore.

"Sorry, my brother can be a little hotheaded . . . Creatives are eccentric. But that's moviemaking for you. Something I know you understand, Evie. We're the same . . . you and us. This is bigger than just one person. Be a part of this movie."

"What's in it for me?" I snark, truly going for it, because making them believe I understand them is our only shot at what I'm thinking. "I'll be a hero, but alone with blood on my hands."

They raise their brows at the same time, surprised by my answer, but I don't stop there.

"Plus, I know you fancy yourselves moviemakers and scriptwriters, but maybe instead of having let the crazy out so soon, you could've honed your craft . . . because you've got a plot hole."

"No, there isn't," Devin shoots back just as fast.

But Derek holds up his hand for me to continue.

"I'm supposed to be so emotionally affected by the death of my sister and Noah—" I can't even glance back at Chase as I say, "—and my boyfriend, that I go wild and end you two."

"Yeah," Devin rushes out again, clearly offended by my doubt.

I shrug. "Then where are they? It's just me and Chase here. Even if you said you'd killed them, I wouldn't believe you. And that kind of rage is more of an in-the-moment kind of thing. So . . . where are the motivators? Because last I checked, you shot my sister, and I don't see Noah."

My head shifts around as I highlight my words with sarcasm.

God, let this work. Let this fucking work.

Devin scowls at me, tapping the gun against his leg as Derek glares. They're standing there quietly, trying to assess my motive for saying what I've said. Weighing out whether or not I'm wrong.

I pull out my final card. "You know I'm right. Without them, all you have is a shittier version of *The Blair Witch Project* and a bunch of headlines that say: Wannabe filmmakers go off the deep end. Your masterpiece will be a zero on Rotten Tomatoes."

The seconds feel like hours before Devin turns to him, his voice hushed but insistent.

"You told me to shoot. You told me to kill Goldie . . . but she's right."

"Shut up," Derek bites back. "If you hadn't been caught by Chase, we could've stuck to the first script."

Devin tosses his hands in the air, instinctively making Chase and me duck before I weave my fingers between his and squeeze to get his attention.

The two of them begin to argue as I give Chase a look, then the gun, because Devin's not paying attention, his arms moving all over as he yells at his brother.

We break away, inching closer to them, my heart in my throat. Even my hands feel clammy, but this is our only shot at getting away.

I motion with my head to Devin so Chase knows who to go for.

Neither of them pays attention as we take careful steps closer and closer. They're just blaming each other for not knowing where Noah and Goldie are—relief courses through me—and for Chase's failed drowning.

Insults are being lobbed back and forth.

"If you think she's right, then fix this!"

"I will," Devin shouts. "You always do this to me. Expect genius at a moment's notice. You're so selfish. I wish Mom hated you so I could've pushed you out of a tree and been the good son."

"Fuck you," Derek yells. "I carry you . . . I'm not the one who couldn't kill the friend. Eddie's death would've been a perfect distraction. I even had to flush her fish, you pussy."

Jesus Christ. They killed Ruth Bader. Motherfuckers.

Chase and I exchange a glance before I let out a quiet, shaky breath, bobbing my head in three counts before we go all in.

Chase lunges at Devin as I leap toward Derek. A loud thud, followed by the skittering of the gun, sounds to my left, but my fingernails dig into Derek's face, scratching across his eye as I open my mouth wide and bite his chest.

I'm feral, all the rage built inside my body exploding, but he's so much bigger than me. It was never the plan in my mind to win this fight, only to give Chase enough time to get the gun away from Devin.

I know he can. Because he's always my hero. And that's not changing today.

"Evie," Chase yells as Derek grabs me by the neck and tosses me to the ground.

All the wind's knocked out of me, but I'm staring up, watching Chase barrel through him, lifting Derek off his feet before he slams him down to the ground.

Before I can suck in even a molecule of more air in, I'm lifted off the ground, held in Chase's arms as he takes quick steps out of the goddamn boathouse and back into the dark, running.

My lungs try hard to fill as I hold on to him, but all I can manage is coughing out stuttered huffs until they finally relax and I can breathe.

"Are you okay?" he says for the fifth time.

I nod. "Yes." But I'm still panting, trying to make up for the loss.

My head shoots over his shoulder. "Where are they?"

Chase barely slows down as he places me on the ground so I can run, too, while he answers, "I don't know. I knocked Devin out, and the gun's in the water. But I only dazed Derek . . ."

"We have to get to Noah and Goldie. They have to be at the car."

I look over my shoulder again, and Devin and Derek are standing in the doorway, like two hellhounds out for blood. But it's only for a moment, because they break and sprint toward us.

"Chase," I scream. He takes my hand, pulling me along faster.

The world's a blur beside us, his grip on me like a vise as we run. The moment our feet hit the camp, I point toward the car.

"The trunk . . . There are weapons in the trunk."

I can barely speak because I'm heaving breaths. There's no more left in the reserves of the reserves. He lets me go as I scramble for the driver's-side door handle. I'm praying I'll find keys when I open it and my sister with Noah.

But as I tug the door open, the car's empty.

Fuck. Where are they?

Chase is rounding the car to the back. I look up to tell him I don't see my sister, but my eyes spring open, not enough air in me to scream his name, because time's run out.

The boys went a different way.

Derek's behind him, a metal wire in his hand, his arms lifted in the air as he closes the distance. He's about to put it around Chase's neck, to kill him.

I stab a finger in the air, squeaking out my words, stumbling against the car. "Behind you!"

Chase's head whips over his shoulder, but as he turns, he collides with Derek, and the trunk flies open. The wire scratches the metal, piercing the air as they fall against it.

Derek howls but not because Chase hurt him.

But because the arrow I released from my bow nicked his shoulder before making a wet thump behind him.

I'm trembling, standing with the crossbow as Chase and Derek follow my line of sight.

Devin stands, his mouth hung open, the arrow lodged straight through his mouth and out the back of his head. He blinks, blood trickling over his bottom lip as a gurgled sound accompanies his stumbled step.

He drops to his knees before falling face first into the dirt.

Derek screams, running to him, crying out his name over and over.

"You killed him. You killed my brother," he screams.

But I toss the crossbow I found in the back seat down to the ground. "I was just sticking to the script, asshole."

Chase closes the trunk, a meat cleaver now in his hand. He looks back at me over his shoulder.

"Close your eyes, baby. You've seen enough for today."

Derek's yelling and sobbing, but I turn around, closing my eyes and putting my hands over my ears as I start to hum "Baby I Love Your Way" by Big Mountain.

But I know when it's over because I feel the cleaver hit the ground.

Chase's arms encircle me, keeping my face hidden before I look up at him splattered with blood.

Normal people would be falling apart. Normal people would be scrambling to call the cops, but there's nothing normal about us.

We're just two traumatized versions of Romeo and Juliet who would kill for each other.

"Sooo," I breathe out, taking his hand as we turn away from the carnage, my eyes lifting as I hear sirens off in the distance. "This feels like the wrong time to say this, but I love you."

He grins, showing off that dimple. "Thank fucking god, because I'm not sure I could best murder."

His hand cradles my face as he stares down at me, then frowns, letting go to grab my still-damp shirt and wiping his mouth on it.

"Gross," he says, looking back at me again, retaking the *I'm about to kiss you* position before he does just that.

He kisses me long and tenderly before pulling back. "Hey, you probably already know this, but I love you too."

This is where the movie would end if this were fiction, but instead, I scream . . . because Noah flies out from the cabin, with the knife Goldie threw earlier in his hand.

"Fuck . . . youuuu." Chase jump scares, almost breaking my arm to put me behind him.

Noah's chest is rising and falling at breakneck speed, his pulse visible on the side of his neck, as we all stare at each other before he looks at the crime scene behind us.

"Oh . . ." he breathes out, still a little breathless as he lowers the knife. "Okay. So, handled."

Chase nods, running his hand through his damp hair. "Yeah, but I may never make lamb chops again."

Goldie's voice comes from the cabin, so I rush to her, wrapping my arms around her. "Oh my god, you're okay?"

She nods weakly. "It's gonna take more than that to kill me. I'm the main character."

Damn. She has no idea how close her joke is to the truth.

The boys take a seat on the steps as my sister and I hug on the floor in the doorway, and art imitates life imitating art all over again.

Police descend, ambulances tear in behind them, and even the familiar sound of a chopper kicks up dust around us. But the four of us sit, looking between each other.

"Can I say it?" Chase grins as Noah chuckles.

I nod, rolling my eyes. "Yeah. Do it."

"Cue the credits."

I hate him. And god willing, I'll never have to live without him.

Chapter Twenty-Eight

Chase

Me: Girlie pops, you will never believe what happened to me!!!!! You're gonna wanna sit down . . .

Joyce: Oooo, spill the Lipton.
Mimi: It's tea.
Joyce: I know that.
Gail: Jesus H. Joyce, Mimi means the saying is: Spill the tea not Spill the Lipton.
Birdie: @everyone we need to listen to Chase.

Joyce: You can't @ everyone in a text. That's for Facebook.
Gail: And it's annoying there too.

Me: I almost died guys. We literally got attacked again. *inserts picture of himself*

Joyce: Good lord!
Gail: Holy fuckballs!
Birdie: Even almost dead you look so handsome Chasey.
Mimi: Who do we need to call? I know a guy from the deli . . . I think he's connected.

Me: No need . . . my girl saved me. Emphasis on the

MY girl. *inserts another photo of him and Evie*

Gail: I knew you'd do it! She's a lucky girl.
Mimi: You've made an old woman cry. When's the wedding?
Joyce: Jesus slow down Mimi . . . let them breathe. We're glad you're both okay. We love you Chase.
Birdie: We should go to that psychic again . . . she can predict their future.
Gail: The only thing she's predicting is that she's full of shit because she's constipated.
Mimi: Doesn't matter what she says. Look at those faces. I know

soulmates when I
see them.

“Soulmates, huh?” Evie smiles, her chin rested on my shoulder.

“Obviously.” I turn to face her, cradling her face. “I love you, Evil.”

She shrugs, exhaling softly, that wry look in her eyes. “Yeah . . . I love you too, Chuckles.”

Goddamn. Now that’s a happily ever after . . . at least right after I kiss the girl, it is.

Epilogue

Evie

"This is the opening of your restaurant, Chase. We can't have sex in the bathroom."

I laugh, trying to push him away because, like the inappropriate perv he is, he followed me in here.

"Why," he whines before drawing his head back as if I've insulted him. "Are you trying to tell me that it was okay at Goldie and Noah's wedding, but it's unacceptable at my restaurant? What's wrong with my restaurant?"

"Of course that's what you took from what I said. Stop making 'missed the point' your brand. I'm gonna need you to use the two brain cells you have left."

"Stop talking dirty to me. You know how hard that mean-ass mouth makes me."

I laugh, covering his mouth with both of my hands because he's not allowed to speak anymore.

"Chase Beckett, we are not having sex in the bathroom when both our families are out there, along with your Hookers and conservatively sixty other people waiting outside to celebrate your achievements."

He drags my hands down his face, gently biting the sides as he stares at me with a hard glare, then tilts his head. "What about just the tip?"

I giggle and accidentally blurt out "Fine" before I immediately correct myself, shoving him away. "I mean no. Oh my god. How is this my fate? Why did the universe choose this karma for me?"

He growls in a sexy, animalistic way as he pulls me toward him, scooping me off my feet and into a hug, our bodies flush.

"Because the universe knew you deserved to be loved like this. You're my forever. Completely and holy—and I mean that with an *H*, not a *W*—because I worship the fucking ground you walk on, Evie Monroe. And I always will."

I stare into the moldy-color eyes, which truly is the most spectacular color of green. And he stares back at me.

It's strange to think that my butterfly effect started from a horror story.

All the way back to when my sister was hatefully conceived and then mercifully left on the steps of a police building. Had that not happened, she never would've wished for me, and I never would've been born into the most beautiful family, eventually leading me to hate every man because they never measured up to that kind of wonderful. Until him.

Because he doesn't just make me feel safe; he allows me the space to be strong.

Chase always says *To be seen is to be loved.* And while he's always seen me, the part that makes me feel loved is that he celebrates what I see in myself.

Chase takes my hand in his, lifting it to his lips, pressing a kiss before he smiles.

"Hey, I know how much you hate surprises now. So just a heads-up, in about ten minutes, I'm going to ask you to marry me, and you're gonna say yes."

I blink in shock and awe. My lips part, and then I smile, too, saying "No," making him frown before I add, "I'm gonna say, 'Yes, Chef.'"

It's easy to think that after everything that's happened, our legacy would be hate or fear, but in the end, love always wins out.

And there's nobody in this life I love more than Chase.

Bonus Epilogue

Evie

Five years later

Emerson swings between Chase and Noah as Goldie and I trail behind in the park.

"Again," Emerson says to her dad, beaming.

But Noah laughs. "You sure you're not tired yet? Because my arm sure is."

He's teasing her, but Uncle Chase is nodding. "Yeah, what'd you put in that little pink backpack? Bricks? You're strong, girl."

She giggles, shaking her head and the white bows that are in it. "I already know that, Uncle Chasey. Daddy says when I grow up that I'm gonna play for the Parrots."

"Patriots," Noah corrects, making me and Goldie laugh.

Her daughter might look like her, but she acts just like me. A little spit ball who's more professional wrestler than princess. My niece is amazing, what can I say?

"I still can't believe she wanted Chase to pick her birthday brunch venue," Goldie whispers to me. "It's unfair that she likes him more than the rest of us. I'm the mom, for fuck's sake."

"Swear jar," Emerson, or Emmie, yells over her shoulder as Goldie gives me a hard stare.

They named her after Noah's mom, something our mother loved beyond words and promptly got to monogramming every piece of fabric around her.

I chuckle, remembering my sister showing me a frilly custom diaper cover. *Why?* she'd said.

God, watching her become a parent has been so surreal, especially after everything we've gone through. But over the last five years, life's been the healing we all needed.

It's like that nursery rhyme, first comes love—Emmie—then came marriage . . .

Chase and I got married back in the village his grandma was from. The whole town came out, which made for a helluva party.

Thankfully, this time, he didn't set a grease fire. But watching my family mix seamlessly with the one we've created—Golden Girls, kitchen sous (I even like Eddie now), rowdy sommeliers, and even my favorite Italian Stallion . . . it was honestly to date some of the highest of highs.

Then came a baby . . . as in another restaurant baby, back in Boston. Which was perfect because I finally felt strong enough to go back to work, with the help of my favorite honorary great-grandma to our future babies, Joyce.

So now we get to be bi, as Chase loves to tell people, until I interject with *coastal* . . . He's never stopped being a jackass. And I've fallen deeply in love with it. So it works.

Life feels beautiful and the good kind of messy again, surrounded by people we love, *our family*, no matter where we are.

Goldie hooks her arms through mine. "You've got that wistful look on your face again."

I smile. "Can't help it. I'm happy."

The moment I say it, the universe conspires to drive home the point because "Work Bitch," *the clean version*, starts playing loudly from the brunch restaurant we've been walking toward. One by one, drag performers, donning all the different Britney eras, file out.

Emmie screams and starts jumping up and down in a circle, her little arms moving like dance is her life.

Oh god, he called it . . . he'd said, *The holy trinity for every little girl is hair, makeup, and a dance party. What's better than a drag party?*

Chase starts dancing with her, singing every word, covering her mouth when she starts to say *bitch*, while Noah laughs. Goldie's smiling ear to ear as I stare at my husband.

We've been through hell, and maybe it took that to get here. I don't know. And I don't care, because either way, I'm going to love him for the rest of my life.

And one day, he's going to make an incredible father. A smirk plays out on my face as he locks those gorgeous, sexy green eyes with mine.

On second thought, maybe we'll take Britney Jean Spears's advice and get to work on those babies . . . starting tonight.

A little version of Chase fills my mind, and I shiver. I'm not sure that's a jump scare anyone's ready for.

But you know what? Hell yeah.

Acknowledgments

What an incredible treat writing this duology has been. I'm so moved by all the readers' enthusiasm and the welcome to this genre. Thank you so much for reading!

Now for the people who had their hand in the cookie jar. Ha ha, that sounds appropriately rowdy and on brand for me.

Maria Gomez and Lindsey Faber at Montlake—I love this little team. You are the loves of my editorial life. Thank you for all your dedication and commitment to ensuring my voice is always heard!

My beautiful, talented, and hilarious agent Stacey Graham—it's wild that you're so wise and yet not a speck over the age of twenty-five. So weird and unusual.

Caroline Teagle Johnson—such a perfect complement of a cover to the first!

Sarah Pederson—quite literally the Goldie to my Evie. Love you beyond measure. Even though I will never forgive or forget the Uber where I became your mother. A plague upon that dude's house.

Serena McDonald—thank you for always rooting for me and reminding me of everything I forget!

Gretchen Eddy—this is my acknowledging you reading *Fourth Wing* on my bed as I read you every other line, scurrying around like a little writing mouse to finish before my deadline. Lol.

Sandy—thanks to you, people can read what I type. God knows my drafts would be a stream of consciousness otherwise.

To my betas and my sensitivity reader, Bria—your feedback was an immeasurable gift.

Special shout-out to Charlie for being the only person out of about twenty to come up with a banger of a name for this book! You're an eleven-year-old icon!

Last but not least, my friends and family—I'm so lucky to have people around me who always cheer me on and irrationally believe that I will be the largest success in history. You guys make me think I can do anything. And I love you for that. But the truth is, I'm only cool because you love me. (I never change this dedication because it ALWAYS applies.)

May everyone find a family that loves them as much as mine loves me.

Thanks for reading. Xoxo, T

About the Author

Trilina Pucci, a #1 Amazon and *USA Today* bestselling author, is a connoisseur of pop culture and Sanpellegrino, but her true passion lies in crafting tantalizing romantic novels that delve into the depths of desire, emotion, and hearty belly laughs.

When she's not penning steamy love stories, you'll find Trilina indulging in Netflix marathons and Korean dramas. To connect with the author and learn more about her work, follow her on Instagram (@authortrilinapucci), Facebook (https://facebook.com/trilinapuccibooks), TikTok (@authortrilinapucci), and BookBub (www.bookbub.com/authors/trilina-pucci).